Other Dover Books by R. T. Campbell

*Bodies in a Bookshop*

*Death for Madame*

*Unholy Dying*

# SWING LOW, SWING DEATH

## R. T. Campbell

Foreword by
**Peter Main**

**DOVER PUBLICATIONS, INC.**
Mineola, New York

*Bibliographical Note*

   This Dover edition, first published in 2018, is an unabridged republication of the work originally published by John Westhouse (Publishers) Ltd., London, July 1946, as part of a double volume along with *The Death Cap*. R. T. Campbell is the pseudonym of Ruthven Todd. A new Foreword by Peter Main has been specially prepared for this volume.

*Library of Congress Cataloging-in-Publication Data*

Names: Campbell, R. T., 1914-1978, author. | Main, Peter, Dr., writer of foreword.
Title: Swing low, swing death / R. T. Campbell ; foreword by Peter Main.
Description: Mineola, New York : Dover Publications, 2018. | Series:Professor Stubbs
Identifiers: LCCN 2017051718| ISBN 9780486822761 (softcover) | ISBN 0486822761
   (softcover)
Subjects: LCSH: Detectives—England—Fiction. | Murder—Investigation—Fiction. |
   London (England)—Fiction. | BISAC:
   FICTION / Mystery & Detective / Traditional British. | GSAFD: Mystery fiction.
Classification: LCC PR6039.O26 S95 2018 | DDC 823/.914—dc23
LC record available at https://lccn.loc.gov/2017051718

Manufactured in the United States by LSC Communications
82276101     2018
www.doverpublications.com

# Contents

# CONTENTS

# Foreword

R. T. CAMPBELL was the pen name of Ruthven Campbell Todd, a man better known under his real name as a poet and leading authority on the printing techniques of William Blake. The true identity of R. T. Campbell was not revealed to the world until the publication of Julian Symons's 1972 history of crime fiction, *Bloody Murder* (published in the United States as *Mortal Consequences*). Symons was a close friend of Todd, who had agreed readily enough to be unmasked. Symons recorded that Todd had written ten detective stories under the name R. T. Campbell, published by John Westhouse, and that the novels were "now distinctly rare." In a revised edition after Todd's death, Symons had to change his tune somewhat: "ten" novels became "twelve."

"A pleasant uncertainty prevails about the publication of four among the twelve books. Did *The Hungry Worms Are Waiting* ever see print, or did Westhouse go broke first? No copy of it is known to have appeared in any specialized bookseller's list."

This uncertainty has since been resolved, and it is now known that only eight novels were published, although Todd probably wrote four more. The missing novels were repeatedly advertised by Westhouse as "forthcoming," but they never forthcame because in 1948 Westhouse went into liquidation.

Todd wrote the novels toward the end of World War II, when he was living in rural Essex, England, having been bombed out of his apartment in central London. He wrote them at speed and claimed he finished one of them in three days. Throughout his life, he remained dismissive of their quality, saying they were "hack work," which he wrote to make money he badly needed to support himself while engaged in what he regarded as his more serious work: poetry and art history. Although the novels are uneven in quality, it is difficult to read them without feeling that he rather enjoyed writing them. Westhouse paid him two hundred pounds for each manuscript—quite a considerable amount at the time!

He was advised by fellow poet Cecil Day Lewis, who wrote detective novels as Nicholas Blake, to try his hand at detective fiction as a means of making money, but to use a pen name in order to avoid "ruining his name." Thus, Todd gave birth to R. T. Campbell by reworking his own full name. These books were his only foray into crime fiction, with the exception of *Mister Death's Blue-Eyed Boy* (set in New York City's Greenwich Village), which was never published and which Todd later said the manuscript was "probably happily, now lost." He also wrote two short stories in crime magazines under his real name, which later found their way into anthologies published by Mystery Writers of America.

Todd's novels are comedic, and all but one of the published works (*Apollo Wore a Wig*, a spy caper in the style of John Buchan's *The Thirty-Nine Steps*) feature a botanist-cum-amateur detective, Professor John Stubbs. The blurb on the dust jacket of his debut appearance in *Unholy Dying* tells us Stubbs is "an explosive and fallible character in the long English tradition of engaging comic figures. Professor Stubbs sets out to unravel the crime with considerable energy and the tact of a herd of elephants."

Stubbs is corpulent, mustachioed, opinionated, smokes a pipe filled with evil-smelling tobacco, and constantly swills beer from a quart mug in order to overcome his susceptibility to "dehydration." He cheerfully accuses innocent people of murder and lumbers on, unabashed, to find the true culprit. His "Watson" for most of the books is Max Boyle, with whom he has an engagingly prickly relationship, as he does with his sparring partner Inspector Reginald Bishop of Scotland Yard.

Here are the seven published Stubbs novels and their publication dates in the order they were presumably written, based on references that appear within them to previously occurring events:

*Unholy Dying* (November 1945)
*Take Thee a Sharp Knife* (February 1946)
*Adventure with a Goat* (April 1946, published as a double volume with *Apollo Wore a Wig*)
*Bodies in a Bookshop* (April 1946)
*The Death Cap* (June 1946)
*Death for Madame* (June 1946)
*Swing Low, Swing Death* (July 1946, published as a double volume with *The Death Cap*)

One of the most attractive features of the novels is they are alive with atmosphere—primarily of London in the 1940s. Todd did not dream up his backgrounds; he drew on his own experiences. Thus, *Unholy Dying* is set in the midst of a congress of geneticists, an environment he had recently experienced firsthand when helping his father-in-law, Francis Crew, himself a distinguished geneticist, to organize the Seventh International Congress of Genetics at Edinburgh University. His first draft of the story (then called *Drugs Fit and Time Agreeing*) was written in 1940, although it did not see publication until 1945. Also in 1940, Todd began writing *When the Bad Bleed*, which he never completed. However, the manuscript survives and leaves no doubt that this was an early version of *Take Thee a Sharp Knife*. This is a sleazy tale of murder in London's Soho and was based on his own all too frequent trips in the company of Dylan Thomas and other hard-drinking cronies around the bars and clubs of Soho and Fitzrovia. *Adventure with a Goat* is the shortest and slightest of the Stubbs novels, whose theme was suggested to him by an incident during childhood when a goat devoured the notes for a local minister's Sunday sermon before it could be delivered. *Bodies in a Bookshop* is a biblio-mystery, and Todd himself was a bibliomaniac who continually trawled the secondhand bookshops of Charing Cross Road to supplement his already groaning bookshelves. From childhood, Todd had been fascinated by the natural world and developed a specialized appreciation of fungi. Drawing on this knowledge, the plot of *The Death Cap* deals with the dastardly poisoning of a young woman using *amanita phalloides*, the deadly "death cap" mushroom. The plot of *Death for Madame* centers around the murder of the owner of a seedy residential hotel, inspired by Todd's dealings with the memorable Rosa Lewis, chef and owner of Cavendish Hotel in St. James's district of London. At the time he wrote the Stubbs novels, Todd was deeply occupied with art historical research, and his understanding of the world of art and artists provided him with the backdrop for *Swing Low, Swing Death*, a book in which a poet called Ruthven Todd makes a cameo appearance! We are lucky that Todd even left a clue in his memoirs about the plot of one of the four missing novels. Its events took place in a "progressive" school, a setting suggested no doubt by his interest in the work of A. S. Neill, founder of Summerhill School, which Todd had visited.

What do we know of Ruthven Campbell Todd himself? He was born in Edinburgh, Scotland, in 1914, the eldest of ten children of Walker Todd, an architect, and his wife, Christian. Ruthven received an elite private school education at Fettes College, which he hated and reacted against, leading to him being "asked to leave." During a short spell at Edinburgh College of Art, he recalled that he spent more time drinking beer and Crabbie's whiskey than attending to his studies. After less than a year, his father became fed up with his son's antics and Ruthven was dispatched to the Isle of Mull in the Scottish Highlands to work as a farm laborer for two years. After a further year as assistant editor to an obscure literary magazine, he left finally for London. Apart from occasional family visits, he never returned to Scotland.

In London, Todd embraced the bohemian world of poets, writers, and artists with rather too much enthusiasm, developing the alcoholism and addiction to strong tobacco that was to undermine his health and, to an extent, his productivity as a writer. Nevertheless, at this time he did publish several volumes of poetry as well as two fantasy novels, *Over the Mountain* and *The Lost Traveller* (the latter became something of a cult classic). His most notable achievement, however, was *Tracks in the Snow*, a book on Blake and his circle, which is still remembered today as a highly original and groundbreaking work.

In 1947, Todd left for the United States to pursue research for a complete catalog of the artworks of Blake. He lived there for the next thirteen years, first in New York City and later in Martha's Vineyard, Massachusetts. Here he became famous among younger readers for his four books about a feline astronaut, Space Cat, and he became a US citizen. In the late 1950s, he was commissioned to write the official life of Dylan Thomas, a project he failed to deliver. In 1960, while visiting Robert Graves in Mallorca, Spain, he became seriously ill with pleurisy and pneumonia and was hospitalized. He recovered, but the treatment costs he incurred meant he was unable to return to the United States. He lived in Mallorca for the rest of his life, first in Palma and then in the mountain village of Galilea, where he died of emphysema in 1978.

Original editions of Todd's detective novels remain elusive and expensive. However, Dover Publications is publishing four of the Stubbs books: *Bodies in a Bookshop; Unholy Dying; Swing Low, Swing Death;* and *Death for Madame.*

Peter Main, author
*A Fervent Mind: The Life of Ruthven Todd*
London, England, 2018

# SWING LOW, SWING DEATH

# *Part 1—Chapter 1

# Autumnal Geometry

MANY MONTHS of intensive work and even more intensive publicity had gone to the making of it. Now it was almost ready. At last London was to have its Museum of Modern Art. Tall and sharply bleak, the new building, inheritor of the traditions of the *Bauhaus,* rose in between the Victorian absurdities and eighteenth century dignities of Iron Street, just behind Bond Street.

The usual letters, from the usual signatories, had been written to the *Times,* protesting against the erection of this "concrete and glass monstrosity" in the confines of Iron Street, where eighteenth century bucks had wined and dined with their bawds and where the fortunes of great houses had been reversed by the turn of a single card. Sir John Squire had interrupted the composition of his autobiography to attempt to save Iron Street. Cameras placed cunningly had stressed the plain and elegant brickwork of the eighteenth century and had omitted the Victorian baroque in all its splendour of encaustic tile and yellow and blue brick and stucco of the *Ely Arms.* The bellied window of Mr. Snodgrass, tailor to half the titled families in England, was well in the forefront, but no one mentioned the Tottenham Court Road modernism of the *Excelsior Beauty Parlours,* where wealthy women had their faces dislocated in the hope that, Phoenix-like, something better might rise from the ruins and ashes of the original.

None of this had availed to protect the street and the slender concrete monolith rose as if unaware of the controversy that beset its being. The façade was carefully finished with its circles and contrasting squares of colour by Ben Nicholson and the slender column by Constantin Brancusi rose on one side of the entrance while the other was guarded by a

---

carving in African wonderstone by Henry Moore. Elderly dilettantes, hurrying from their clubs or mistresses, to inspect the Rembrandt etchings or the lesser Italian paintings at Tooth's or Colnaghi's, averted their scandalised eyes. They shuddered inwardly and wondered why things had changed so much since they were boys. This was indeed the final action which shewed the decadence of a world which had grown beyond them. In some way they felt that the concrete building was a personal attack upon their being, it threatened their security and it bored at the foundations of well-established and unalterable things. It was not that it shouted. No, rather, it whispered subversive phrases in the stillness of the night. It spoke quietly, but insistently, of the breakdown of Civilisation, spelt with a capital, and of the invasion by the new barbarians, nurtured by the harsh winters of the Gothic North.

The outcry did not diminish as the building rose. Instead, as if realising its futility it became the louder, like a dog barking after the wheels of a car. A certain eminent divine, celebrated for his enlightened views upon the modern world and for his stupidity, preached a sermon upon the subject of the tower of Babel, by which his listeners rightly supposed that he referred to the Museum of Modern Art. With a fervour that would have done credit to a Calvinist cursing the Catholic Church he cursed the building and was only prevented by his lack of faith from calling down a thunderbolt from heaven upon it.

In the flighty and inaccurate columns of the *Daily Courier,* Lord Monrose's young men were gaily irreverent. They reproduced a plan of a new public lavatory in Holborn alongside one of the abstract paintings ánd got the titles mixed. The following day's apology was an example of unrepentant absurdity. They published pictures by children and claimed that they were better than those by the well-known artists who were to be hung in the Museum. They asked the granddaughter of a pre-Raphaelite painter for her opinion and displayed it as if it were an opinion of some weight and meaning.

Professor Thomas Bodkin returned to the attack. He proved that Van Gogh and Gauguin suffered from obscene diseases and that, consequently, all modern art was diseased. His logic, having no foundation, was as unassailable as a barrage balloon is to a man with a penknife. D. S. McColl was trenchant and amusing in the columns of the *Times* and Douglas Cooper spent much ink and patience in correcting the factual errors of those who wrote without knowing what they were writing about.

In fact, it might be said, that a very good time was had by all, and that no one really suffered as a result of the sparrow-shot and ill-aimed brickbats. Certainly Miss Emily Wallenstein enjoyed herself.

The daughter of a millionaire meat-importer and shipping magnate, Miss Wallenstein had a penchant for all that was modern. Her sets of magazines such as *Transition* and *Minotaure* had been bound by the French surrealist, Georges Hugnet, in fur and glass, with blobs of mercury running in channels behind the glass. Her house, near Shepherd's Market, was a mixture of the austerity of a Walter Gropius and the fantastic extravagance of a Salvador Dali. Fur-lined teacups and chance-found objects, such as twisted flints and obscene scraps of driftwood, consorted with furniture designed by Marcel Breuer. A stuffed eagle owl looked gravely at the polished whiteness of a carving by Barbara Hepworth, and a tube of coloured sand, from Alum Bay in the Isle of Wight, raised its striped finger to point to a painting by the Dutch constructivist, Piet Mondrian, while a green granite Mexican god inspected an engraving of the Temptation of St. Anthony, after Jacques Callot.

Miss Wallenstein, thin and smart and thirty-fivish, felt that she had at last found her place in this turmoil, and, what made it even better, was that not only was the publicity extremely amusing, but that she really felt that she was being a useful person. Her efforts on behalf of modern art made her feel a second Livingstone in the African wilds of artistic London.

As she said to her stout, henna-haired assistant, Sylvia Rampion: "It isn't, my dear, as though I'd thought there would be all this publicity, but it *will* help, won't it? Can't you just see the crowds flowing in when we open? Some of them will be unconvertible, of course, but we can only hope that there will be some who will come to mock and who will stay to cheer."

The concrete was dry, and the furnishing was going on apace. The library shelves were filling up and the young poet, Douglas Newsome, who had been engaged as librarian, looked gloomily at the shelves of books which he never intended to read. He scowled at the plastic backs of brochures by Moholy-Nagy and Herbert Bayer. He wondered why the hell he had ever accepted the job. The money was all right but he wanted a drink. He wanted a drink more than anything in the world. He wondered if Miss Wallenstein would pull him up if she caught him on the way out to the *Ely Arms*. He decided that he'd make the effort and, anyhow, he might as well start the way he meant to go on. It was too much for anyone to hope that he, Douglas Newsome, could sit all day among a lot of books without wetting his whistle once in a while.

Tactically, he told himself, it would be wiser to go down the stairs than to risk the lift. He would be less likely to encounter Miss Wallenstein that way. He slid his hand along the polished scarlet plastic balustrade and started to descend. As bad luck would have it he ran into his employer in the hall.

"Hullo, Douglas," she said cheerfully, "how are things going in your department? Are all the books all right?"

"Yes, everything's going beautifully," his voice was gloomy, "I just wanted to run out for a minute, if that's all right?"

"Oh, yes, of course," Emily Wallenstein's voice was vague; she was trying to think what she had meant to do next, "Do run out if you want to, Douglas. Once things get going we'll see about getting you an assistant and that'll give you a freer hand."

Douglas did not want an assistant. He had worked in a gallery with an assistant before and the assistant had plainly shewn that she could smell the whisky on his breath. Her dilated nostrils had been a sort of Jiminy Cricket to him. He had even had to take to eating peppermints. He wandered out into the street, sustained only by the thought of the drink at the end of it. He nudged the Henry Moore carving with his elbow and apologised to it mechanically. He wondered gloomily how long it would be before he got used to the thing and stopped saying he was sorry every time he bumped it.

Iron Street is not a very long street. Fifty yards sufficed to bring Douglas to the garish doors of the *Ely*. He hesitated, weighing up the advantages of the saloon bar and the lounge. He decided upon the latter. After all, he was being well paid and it would not ruin him to have to give a tip to the attendant who brought his drink, and he might as well sit in comfort.

He sat down at one of the basket-work tables. He looked in a depressed way at the salted nuts in a plated bowl which was reflected in the glass top. While he waited for his drink he ate the nuts slowly, reflecting that it was a bad thing to do as they would only increase his thirst.

He was roused from his contemplation of the effect of salted peanuts upon his salivary glands by the noise of bickering from the table next to him.

Jeremy Flint was being bullied by his wife, Alison. This was not in the last unusual. Jeremy seemed to be one of nature's bullees.

"But, my dear Jeremy," she was saying in a voice that held more of irritation than of affection, "You really can't expect me to go on wearing that dress any longer. You must give me enough money to buy a new one. A good one. Why, everyone in town must know that old one of mine by now."

Jeremy Flint protested weakly that he was not a rich man and that she had only had that dress for three months. His protest was voiced in a tone that held no hope that it would receive any attention whatsoever. It received none.

Douglas shuddered. There, but for the grace of God, he told himself. He was glad that he had never married if this was what marriage did to a man. He liked Jeremy but he could not stand the sight of Alison. He realised, even more gloomily, that he would need to learn to put up with her. Emily had engaged the couple as sort of secretaries and organisers to the exhibitions. That was their profession. They would organise anything from a bottle-party to a fishing expedition. Fashion was Alison's *forte*. One felt that her soul was stuffed with old numbers of *Vogue* and *Harper's Bazaar*. Jeremy, who looked distinguished in a wizened sort of way, went along with her, or was taken by her in the way that she might have carried a marmoset around with her.

Even the whisky failed to cheer Douglas. He looked gloomily through the contents of his pockets and selected an envelope. He did not open the envelope. He knew that it contained a bill from his dentist. He could have recognised the typewriter a mile off. He made a few notes on the back, despite the spluttering and flooding of his fountain pen:

> Perhaps, said Madame Fashion to her mate,
> You think your sulkiness becoming?
> Perhaps you like to hobnob with the great
> Since I have rescued you, while slumming?
> Her husband stutters, mumbles to his chin,
> Presents a bland, agreeable outside;
> His wife has slobbered out the fires within
> While gobbling up the remnants of his pride.

He read this through carefully and felt slightly better. He folded the envelope up and replaced it in his pocket. He looked across at the Flints speculatively. He wondered whether he should speak to them, and if he did so whether he would have to buy them a drink. He did not want to buy them a drink. If he did it would mean that he could not buy the

Nonesuch *Writings of William Blake,* and he had decided that he wanted the three volumes in marbled boards with a smooth vellum back.

Alison Flint saw him and waved him over. He went reluctantly, holding his glass in his hand to hide the fact that it was almost empty. Jeremy's face lightened. He welcomed the presence of anyone, as a third person meant that his wife gave him some rest.

"Hullo, Douglas," he said, perking up like a sparrow who has just found a wheat-grain in a pile of manure, "What are you drinking? Have another?"

"Whisky, thank you," Douglas was moody. This meant that he would have to buy a round, and would postpone the purchase of the books for a week.

"Have you been working this morning?" Alison was affable. She reserved her venom for her husband. "Is Emily very a-flutter?"

"I wouldn't know. I've being trying to get the books into some order. The trouble is that I know practically no German and so many of the books seem to be written in it. I only saw Emily for a moment when I decided that I'd pop out and have a drink. She seemed full of energy. What are you doing to-day?"

"Oh," it was Jeremy who answered, "we're having lunch with Cornelius Bellamy and Julian Ambleside. Emily wants to buy Julian's large Max Ernst and he seems willing enough to sell, but she thought we should have it vetted by Cornelius. Why on earth she feels that Cornelius needs to see everything she buys is beyond me. Everyone knows Julian's picture and there's no doubt that it's genuine and there's also no doubt that Emily will pay him whatever he wants for it. But still, as dear Cornelius is her adviser, he has to say the word, so we get landed with the job of taking him out to lunch."

Alison Flint frowned. Douglas, percipient, knew exactly why she frowned. Her husband's remarks about Cornelius Bellamy were aimed at destroying the very foundations of her world. Dr. Cornelius Bellamy was the fashionable arbiter of taste. His word on anything from a brassiere to a teacup was sancrosant. A word of praise from him could make the reputation of an interior decorator, or disparagement dictate the destruction of a line of goods meant for the fashionably wealthy. He sat on Committees for the Improvement of Industrial Design, on Committees for the Encouragement of Natural and National Taste, on committees to do this and committees to do that. What he said went.

Douglas thought irritably of the Doctor's various *obiter dicta* on the subject of poetry. "If we," he had said, referring to his friends who had been the *avante garde* of the nineteen-teens, "were the revolution, you," he had included everyone since T. S. Eliot, "are the counter-revolution."

"Oh, but didn't you hear?" Alison turned excitedly to Douglas, "the Doctor has discovered the most marvellous new man? I'm going to have one of the walls of our dining-room done by him. His name is Ben Carr. He's the most amazing find. Positively a moron, but he has invented a perfectly new technique for the decoration of rooms. He just covers one wall with plaster or cement or something and, while it is still wet, he throws things at it and they stick. The effect is stupendous. He throws anything he can find at the walls. I've been out to his own studio. It is an old chapel in the east end and the walls are positively festooned with things that he rescued from bombed buildings. He can give a real significance to a frying-pan without a bottom. There is one on his own walls and he has used it as a frame for a coloured postcard of *The Light of the World*. He can give wit to his significance in a way that no one else can. His work is so penetrating."

Not so penetrating as your voice, Douglas said to himself. He thought that he remembered seeing the same thing done by a Dadaist called Kurt Schwitters, who had made grottoes hung with rubbish, round about 1920. He knew that Schwitters was living at Barnes and that nobody seemed to give him much employment. He wondered gloomily why someone like Dr. Cornelius Bellamy was almost fore-ordained to be taken in by the belated imitator and did not bother to seek out the original man. He decided that he would see that Kurt Schwitters got an invitation to the opening of the Museum. After all, Emily had had to include two of his Merzbild in the historical section. Perhaps something might come of it.

He drained his whisky glass. He was just about to order another round when he saw approaching them, crab-like in his sideways gait, the figure of Julian Ambleside. Curious, he thought, I wonder whether his name had any influence upon him—he does amble sideways.

Julian Ambleside was short and squat. He gave those who met him for the first time the impression that he had been squeezed flat like an opera-hat and was in the process of recovering from the treatment. He always seemed to be on the point of shooting up like the legendary beanstalk, but he never achieved it. His face resembled that of a toad, even down to the warty knobs besprinkled at intervals across the surface. His arms hung down almost to his knees, giving the impression that he might, if he wished, hop across the room. But he moved slowly on enormous flat feet, and a slight inequality in the length of his legs made him appear to walk sideways. When he hurried he scuttled.

Douglas remembered *The Waste Land,* and wondered vaguely whether Julian Ambleside's ample shoes disguised a "pair of ragged claws."

Julian Ambleside was the owner of a gallery. A small gallery, certainly, but one that was haunted by those whose lives were spent being, not only *in* the swim, but slightly ahead of it. He had a genius for picking up cheaply the disregarded trifles of to-day which were destined to become the treasured ornaments of to-morrow. He had bought Victorian glass paper-weights in the days when such objects could be found in every junk-shop and had had several thousands of them when the craze suddenly burst upon him. At the moment he was collecting paintings by unknown English amateur painters, convinced that the American books on *their* primitive and popular painters would bring him a rich dividend when the English started to wonder about their own country. As he always stressed, Ambleside was a dealer, and given a big enough offer he would have parted from his pants in Bond Street. Nothing that he had was permanent. Everything was stock-in-trade.

The Flints watched him approach without enthusiasm. Alison was accustomed to pick his brains, to try and see what he thought would be popular the season after next, but she could not manage to include him among the number of people who she considered it smart to know. Jeremy Flint just quite plainly did not like him.

He came up to the table and reached out a tentacle to grab a chair from a table about four feet away. He placed himself carefully upon the basket-work, as if afraid that he was risking something by sitting down. He looked at the Flints and then at Douglas before he spoke.

"Good morning," he said affably in a high-pitched squeak, "or is it afternoon? What are you drinking?"

Hell, said Douglas to himself, this means a bigger round. I'll never get that book.

"I was just buying a round," he said, "it's my turn. What'll *you* have?"

Julian Ambleside turned his heavy squat face round and looked at Douglas, with the corners of his mouth announcing that he was smiling.

"When I think you're rich enough, young man," he said, "to buy me a drink, I'll ask for it." He turned to the waiter, "Three whiskies and a glass of tonic water."

For some reason, Douglas felt annoyed by this kindness to his pocket. He knew it was unreasonable, but all the same he felt that he could have slapped Julian Ambleside quite cheerfully. He looked unhappily into the amber fluid in his glass. He gestured with it half-heartedly towards Ambleside and poured it down his throat.

"I suppose I should get back to work," he remarked rising, "there are all these blasted German books to catalogue and arrange. I'll be seeing you."

He wandered out into Iron Street. The daylight looked unsympathetic and harsh, but it was not as cruel as the bar "day-light" electricity in the library. He saw no one as he entered the shining monel-metal lift and pressed the plastic button. The lift rose like a fountain and made him feel that he had left part of his digestion behind.

He sat down at his desk and started writing out cards: Klee, Paul, *Pädagogisches Skizzenbuch,* Weimar, 1925, and so on. It was an ideal job as he did not need to devote more than a third of his mind to it. He made up his mind, however, that he would ask Emily if she would let him have a desk-lamp with an ordinary bulb in it. This daylight electricity in an air-conditioned sound-proof room made him feel that he had almost receded into the womb. Ahead of him, so far as he could see, there stretched an endless ribbon of filing cards. He found the thought of them faintly revolting. He wrote on the back of a pale lemon yellow card:

> I wonder if my card is filed
> In God's enormous office scheme,
> And if the notes on me displayed
> Shew me exactly as I seem.

He would have gone on but the door of the library opened and a man came in. He was of medium height, dressed in a black suit and greying sidewhiskers came halfway down his cheeks. He wore a white bow tie with scarlet polka dots.

"Oh Douglas, dear boy," he said, "I thought I would find you here. Can you tell me if you have a copy of Aragon's *Le Peinture au Defi*? If you have, can you lend it to me for a few minutes? I am just checking up on various points in the catalogue."

Douglas slid the card under the blotter on his black bakelite desk. He got up and went to the shelves and pulled out the required volume.

"Here you are, Francis," he said, holding it out. "What do you mean to do with the catalogue? I thought it was finished and printed."

"My dear boy," Francis Varley was shocked, "surely you know our Emily by now. As you say, the catalogue was practically printed. I'd corrected all my proofs and had passed the blocks. However, this morning it suddenly occurred to dear Emily that the catalogue would become out of date very quickly. That is true, considering the rate at which she is buying stuff for the Museum, but I pointed out that we could easily enough prepare a second and a third and so on in the way of editions. But do you think that would satisfy the dear girl? Of course not. Her latest idea is that the catalogue will be a loose-leaf affair and that she will have an extra leaf printed whenever she buys a new picture. And, having thought up this idea, she then decides that the catalogue does not give enough information about the pictures. So, alas, your humble servant has to sit down and try and prepare a bibliography for each picture in the Museum, saying where it is mentioned and where it has been reproduced."

He sighed affectedly, and wiped his face with a white, silk handkerchief.

"I may say, confidentially, of course," he went on, "that our Emily is just a little bit peeved with me. I had the nerve to suggest that, perhaps, one of the Chiricos was not as genuine as it might seem, and that, as a matter of fact, it was one of the forgeries of his early work which he did during the twenties. She could not have been more insulted if I had told her that one of her cheques had bounced. She pointed out stiffly that the picture had been passed by the Great Bellamy himself, and asked me who I thought I was to presume to know better than the Doctor. I made a feeble effort to justify my opinion, but I sadly fear that I was not impressive. Ah well," he sighed theatrically, "I suppose I will have to go and apologise, pretending I had a brainstorm. These reconciliations with Emily are so touching. Last time she gave me a watch. I wonder what it will be this time? I think I would like that large etching by Miró. You know, Douglas my dear boy, you should try bickering with dear Emily occasionally. You'd find it very profitable." Francis Varley tucked the green wrapped book under his arm and went out. Douglas returned to his cards. Francis really *was* a scrounger, he told himself, but he did it so charmingly that no one minded it. By the time he had filled half-a-dozen cards Douglas knew that Francis Varley would own the etching he had coveted. He wondered vaguely if the Chirico really was a wrong one, or whether it was just part of Francis's game. Anyhow, it was none of his business. He was only the librarian.

# Chapter 2

# Small Metaphysical Interior

BEN CARR was engaged in decorating the ladies' lavatory. He took a miscellaneous collection from his pockets and squeezed it against the walls. A tired stub of *Woodbine* peered coyly round a bus ticket and a farthing rubbed up against a coloured glass marble. Mr. Carr retired to the other end of the room and looked at his handiwork with distaste.

"Haven't you got anything in your pockets?" he demanded of the melancholy Douglas who leaned against a hand-basin watching him. Douglas looked through all his pockets but could find nothing that he wanted to discard. At last, in desperation, he looked at the wall and saw the farthing, and assumed that a coin of the realm might be acceptable. He disengaged half-a-crown from the coppers in his trouser-pockets. He handed it to Ben Carr who looked at it suspiciously and bit it. It did not disintegrate beneath this treatment. Mr. Carr looked at the wall and then at the half-crown. He shook his head sadly and slid the coin into his pocket.

"Thanks, chum," he said. "As I was saying this modern business of trying to see that everyone leads a hygienic life is really getting me down. My trouble is that I've got five children and two wives. The mother of the children has left me, but I was managing beautifully with the other and with the children. I couldn't get a house so I just hired a marquee from Harridges and put it up in a field in the country. I had almost all the family under one roof and it was certainly healthy. Well, there I was, feeling as pleased as can be. But do you think they'd leave me alone? Not likely. Along comes an old josser from the Council and he looks round the place. 'Oh,' he says, 'You can't bring up five children in a marquee.' 'Oh,' I say, 'what do you think I'm doing? I seem to be bringing them up all right.' 'I don't mean that,' he says, 'I mean you've got to have a house.' 'All right,' I say, 'give me the house.' So I'm damned if they don't give me a council house. It's certainly less draughty than the marquee was but all the same it's no great shakes. Now they come along and have the blinking cheek to ask why I've never paid any rent. 'Who put me here?' I ask and that stumps them, so I go on and I point out that I haven't paid the rent of much better houses than their little hen-roost. I'd clear out to-morrow, but the trouble is that Harley, that's my second son, made a bonfire out of the marquee and Harridges are threatening to sue me for it. So far as I'm concerned they can sue away. They won't get much out of me."

He looked disconsolately at the hand-basins. A nailbrush caught his fancy and he picked it up and struck it into the wall, above an enamelled notice requesting gentlemen to adjust their clothing.

For a moment Douglas thought of drawing his attention to the fact that the apartment he was decorating was intended for ladies only, but he held his peace, imagining that perhaps there was some deep and disturbing significance in the appearance of that notice there. He left Ben Carr fixing the head of a horse, broken from some child's toy, so that it appeared to be about to take a bite from the plump rump of a Victorian ballerina, lithographed on the cover of a song.

Inside the principal gallery there was a certain amount of activity. Dr. Cornelius Bellamy, his pince-nez fixed firmly on the saddle of his Roman nose, was engaged in examining a large painting by Paul Delvaux in which a forest suddenly changed its mind and became young nude females from the waist up. The Doctor tilted his head this way and that. He stepped back and he stepped forward. He held up one hand as if measuring with it and then he nodded.

"Yes, my dear Emily, yes," he spoke with the decisiveness of one who is accustomed to have his words treated seriously, "I certainly do think it is an acquisition, a very distinct acquisition. A very remarkable painting, if I may say so."

In front of the Chirico which he had disparaged in the morning, Francis Varley stood with Julian Ambleside.

"But, my dear Ambleside," he was saying irritably, "can't you see the difference in the handling of the paint between this picture and that out there?"

Julian Ambleside scuttled sideways between the two pictures. His broad ugly face was intent upon details of technique.

"I think I see what you mean, Varley," he replied, "but I can't say that I agree with your deductions from the difference in handling. After all there *is* five years difference between the dates of the paintings and that, surely, is sufficient to explain the increase in looseness. I may tell you, privately, that this picture came to me from an absolutely unimpeachable source. On documentary grounds alone I would have no hesitation in saying that it is exactly what it purports to be, a picture painted by Chirico in 1917."

Francis Varley shook his head sadly. Douglas could see that he was not convinced. He wondered what luck Francis had had in his apologies to Emily.

"How did you get on, Francis?" he asked, "did you get your Miró etching? Have you changed your mind about the picture?"

"Hush, my dear boy," Francis looked grave, "the very walls have ears." He looked towards Emily and Dr. Bellamy who were strolling slowly round the room. "As a matter of fact, my boy, I got my Miró *and* a Klee lithograph. But the picture still worries me. However, that's not my pigeon. Mine but to catalogue and arrange. I shed my expertise with my coat and hat when I enter these portals. I become the instrument of the almighty dollar."

Douglas turned his head in time to see Mr. Carr slink into the room, pick up a fur-glove lying on the floor and disappear again. He shook his head sadly. He noticed that Emily had the companion glove under her arm.

"If you want your glove, Emily," he said gloomily, "before it becomes a part of the decoration of the ladies' lavatory you'd better hurry. Carr has just walked off with it."

Emily seemed to be about to go to the rescue of her glove. It looked, Douglas thought, one of a most expensive pair. However, as she was about to go, she was restrained by Dr. Cornelius Bellamy's hand on her arm.

"My dear lady," he said earnestly, "consider for a moment. What does your glove mean to you? Is your glove more valuable than the creative instincts of an artist? Would you be responsible for a trauma in the creative process? Think, my dear Emily, and you will see that I am right. Carr is a sensitive man and the thought that you resented some small activity on his part, such as taking your glove, merely because he *felt* that his decoration required it, might be quite enough to interrupt the whole process and destroy the masterpiece which he is creating for you. You, my dear Emily, have enough of the imagination of an artist to know how a seemingly trivial setback can ruin a major work, and I think I can safely say that, at this very moment, Ben Carr is engaged in the toils of creating his masterpiece, creating it for you, my dear Emily."

Emily Wallenstein flushed. To think that she had been sufficiently insensitive as to consider, even for a moment, disturbing the creative work of an artist.

She need not have concerned herself. Having placed her glove so that it pointed to a miniature water-closet labelled "Gentlemen," Mr. Carr had retired round several corners to a comfortable café, much frequented by the chauffeurs of those who were eating worse and at much greater expense in the larger and gaudier parts of the district. He was engaged, figuratively, in casting his bread upon the waters. In other words, he was playing poker with Emily's chauffeur and another gentleman of indeterminate profession. With Douglas's half-crown as capital he was, as he said to himself, making a killing. It really was fortunate that he was so friendly with the man who prepared these cards. A tiny spot here or the absence of one there made all the difference and, after the cards had been "finished" in all senses of the word, they were so perfectly repacked that no one could tell the difference between them and a pack just purchased at random in a shop.

As he dealt himself a straight flush, Mr. Carr whistled softly between his teeth. He decided that he would call it a day when he had won fifteen pounds, and he hoped to God that Maggie, who was his wife in everything but fact, wouldn't take it all off him later in the evening at dice. He kept on meaning to do something about those dice of hers; he knew that they were loaded, but he was too lazy and the result was that she always cleaned him out of every penny he had. She was a bitch, she was, he told himself bitterly, it was no use trying to fob *her* off with I.O.U.s. One of these days, perhaps, if his luck held and Emily was as rich as she seemed to be, he might have a bank account and then he'd pay Maggie back. He'd give her a dud cheque—he was damned if he wouldn't.

He still could not quite understand how he had become an interior decorator. It was all an accident. One of his children, the one called Dorinda about whom he was not certain of his side of the paternity, had run off to find her undoubted mother. He had received an urgent postcard, from an address in the east of London, asking him for God's sake to come and take the child away. A man of patriarchal instincts, he had not hesitated but had departed forthwith on the back of a vegetable van to collect the cuckoo missing from his nest. He had failed to locate his rightful wife but had heard Dorinda's cheerful voice issuing from the inside of the deserted bomb-damaged chapel.

She had been speaking to herself. "Well," she said, putting a piece of encaustic tile next to a worn-out shoe in the wall which she had coated with cement, pilfered from a nearby builder's lot, "suppose we put this here. Yes."

She had stepped back to admire her handiwork and had caught sight of her father. "I'm having such fun," she said, "come on and give me a hand."

Mr. Carr, a man of simple imagination, had entered into the spirit of the game. He had actually collected more cement behind the builders' backs and had let his fancy run riot among the remains of bombed houses. After two hours' work the deserted chapel had become transformed.

Dr. Cornelius Bellamy, walking in search of a taxi after giving a lecture on the subject of children's paintings, had heard the noise of joyous creation issuing from the chapel and had allowed his curiosity to direct his steps. He was, as he afterwards said, frankly astounded by what he saw. From that moment Mr. Carr had not looked back. He did not look ahead either. He swept up his winnings and, apologising to the disappointed players and promising them their revenge upon a later date, he departed.

The feeling of money in his pockets was pleasing, although he knew that the pleasure was bound to be transitory. He walked back to the Museum, pausing only to buy three shillings' worth of the most violently coloured sweets he could find.

When he had cemented the sweets to the walls of the ladies' lavatory he decided that the effect was all that could be desired. He looked in at the gallery again. The Doctor was still lecturing Emily Wallenstein upon the subject of art.

"Oy, Doc," cried Mr. Carr, "come and give us a bit of criticism. I think it's going fine."

Emily and Dr. Bellamy entered the lavatory together. They looked in awestruck wonder at the walls. Emily was just about to make a remark about the behaviour of sweets in a steamy atmosphere, when the Doctor spoke first.

"What a touch, my dear Carr," he exclaimed in admiration, "these sweets will gradually perish and remind the spectator of the transitoriness of all human endeavours. To no one but yourself, my dear Carr, could such a stroke of genius have occurred. Now take myself, or Miss Wallenstein here, if we had had the idea of doing what you have done, we would have been certain to use coloured glass, but how apt, how very much more apt, are the melting sweets of childhood. 'Shades of the prison house,' my dear Carr, close around all of us, leaving you as the only free man in a servile world. Magnificent, my dear fellow. This is your supreme creation. It now lies with you to decide whether you will rest upon your laurels, these laurels which you have so royally earned, or whether you will go on to scale fresh heights. Which is it to be?"

Ben Carr looked at the Doctor in a slightly puzzled kind of way. He did not know what the man was talking about. If people did want to have the walls of their houses covered with rubbish—well, he saw no reason why he should not humour them in their fancy, particularly as it paid well. But, for himself, if they wanted modern walls, he did not see why they should not cover them with a decent wallpaper. Now, only the other day, he had seen a very fine bit of jazz wallpaper, orange and muddy green and brown, in a shop in the Tottenham Court Road, and it had only cost eightpence a roll. It was a damn sight cheaper and a damn sight cleaner. But, he shrugged his shoulders, if people wanted to be mad, why let them.

Douglas Newsome sat upstairs in the library. He looked at the cards he had already completed. There seemed to be no end to them. He was glad that they were not envelopes requiring to be stamped. His mouth felt dry at the very thought. He unlocked one side of his desk and took out a quart bottle of Tolly. Ah, that was better.

The scarlet telephone beside him shrilled. He jumped nervously. It really was ridiculous the way his nerves seemed to have betrayed him of late. He reached out for the instrument. It was Emily. She had just received two parcels of books and she thought he ought to have them at once, so that he could fit them into their proper places in the shelves and on the cards. Douglas rang off and laughed a little bitterly to himself. He knew that, somehow or other, he would succeed in messing up the job. Perhaps it would be as well if Emily was to provide him with an assistant. He would, at least, be able to put the blame on the assistant. He felt rather ashamed of himself for the thought and went out into the lift.

In Emily's smart office Francis Varley was busily engaged in making notes on sheets of printed paper. Douglas recognised them as the proofs of the catalogue.

Emily indicated two enormous parcels. Douglas's heart went down with a thud. He had been hoping for two little parcels with one or two books in them, while it seemed that he would need to alter the arrangement of the whole library to engulf these.

Just as he was about to leave the office, Francis looked up and spoke to him.

"I say, Douglas, old dear," his voice was ingratiating, "when you've pushed these books into the shelves I wonder if you'd be an angel and check over these proofs for me? I only want you to add any extra facts you know about reproductions and so on. It won't take you a minute."

"Yes, Douglas," Emily chipped in, "it would be good of you if you could do that. You might be able to remember something that occurred to neither Francis or myself. I would have asked the Doctor to do it, but he had to rush away to give a lecture on The Curative Powers of Art."

"All right," Douglas was as ungraceful as he could manage without being positively offensive. It's all very well for him, he thought of Francis Varley, he gets presents of drawings and prints. I get nothing but the thick and mucky end of the stick.

He hauled the parcels out and placed them in the lift, and then he returned and collected the papers from Francis. When he got back into the lift he found that Julian Ambleside had crawled into it.

"Are you going up to the library?" he squeaked. "Do you mind if I come with you? There are one or two things I want to look up."

Douglas indicated that he did not mind if the whole world tried to get into the lift. He shrugged his shoulders. He didn't care if the whole of the Museum came up to the library.

At the top Ambleside got out and scuttled into the library without paying the least attention to Douglas's load of books. The latter looked after him in a way that was half mild reproach and half speechless fury. When Douglas had hauled the two parcels in and placed them on one of the tables, he turned to Julian Ambleside and asked him what he wanted to look at.

"I would like to see Soby's *The Early Chirico*," the high thin voice replied, "and I would also like the files of *Le Revolution Surréaliste*. You have them both?"

"Yes," Douglas wasted no breath and collected the volumes. Oh ho, he said to himself, I know what is worrying you, my friend; Francis has started to make you doubt whether after all that picture isn't one of the copies Chirico made during the nineteen-twenties.

He left Ambleside to his researches and started to unpack the two bulky parcels. It was worse than he had feared. The contents were largely made up of pamphlets and odd copies of rare magazines such as *Orbes* and *Proverbe*. The trouble about most of these things was that they needed binding. The paper was frail as a dried bay-leaf. Douglas put them each in an envelope, writing the date and place of publication under the title and the editor's or author's name. As he thought, this was a slow and tiring job.

Half-way through he was interrupted by Julian Ambleside who looked up from the books which were spread before him on a steel and plywood table made by Marcel Breuer in 1928 (most of the Museum furniture had some historical significance).

The high thin voice piped at him querulously. "Douglas," it asked, "can I see any photographs of Chirico's paintings or drawings which you have in the files?"

Well, Douglas said to himself, at least I've managed to file all the photographs, so I can do that. He went across to the battery of desk-drawer units, also of historical importance having been made in the carpentry workshop of the Bahaus at Dessau in the nineteen-twenties.

He ran his finger through the "C's." Cézanne, Corot, Courbet, Chagall, Calder, Cornell, Chevall. He had not yet had time to arrange them in their proper order within the initial letters. He pawed through the folders again. Chirico was not there. He was sure that he had filed him under C. He remembered writing the name at the top of the folder:

CHIRICO, Giorgio de.

It was impossible that he should have filed it under D. All the same he took a look. No. The file of photographs had vanished.

"I'm terribly sorry, Mr. Ambleside," his tone was worried, "some-one seems to have borrowed the folder of Chirico's paintings. I know it was there because I filed it only yesterday. I wonder if Francis bor-rowed it?"

"I wouldn't know," Julian Ambleside sounded irritated. "Will you give him a ring and find out? It is rather important that I should see them. In fact, I may say that I want to see them very badly indeed. In the meantime can you give me all the reproductions of Chirico which you have. They may help me a little."

Douglas went round the shelves, pulling down back numbers of the *London Bulletin,* the American periodical *View* and so on. He laid the pile on the table beside Julian.

Then he sat down at his desk and picked up the scarlet telephone. Francis Varley was still in Emily's office. Douglas could hear the bright tinkle of glass and guessed that he was having a glass of sherry. The thought parched his tongue and he could barely speak.

"I say, Francis," he said through dry lips, "did you by any chance come up here and borrow the folder of Chirico photographs?"

"No," Francis was positive, "I'd have asked you if I was going to do that. Why? What's the matter? Can't you find them?"

"They seem to have vanished," Douglas said sadly, reflecting that with his personal genius for losing things no one would believe that he had not lost them. It was a damned nuisance that a thing like this should happen so early on in his new job. He rang off gloomily and went and looked through the C's again. It had occurred to him that perhaps one folder might have slipped inside another. He took all the folders out and looked through the contents. He had made no mistake. The Chirico folder had completely vanished.

Julian Ambleside seemed rather put out by the information. He clucked like a broody soprano hen. "Most annoying," he said, "there were one or two points which I might have solved by looking at photographs which I cannot decide upon from these wretched half-tones. When they turn up, Douglas, I hope you will let me know immediately?"

"Yes, I'll let you know," Douglas was melancholy, "I didn't lose them, you know. I filed them yesterday and they should have been there. There were about sixty to seventy photos in the folder. Of course I hadn't yet got round to the job of cataloguing them by making a list on the front of the folder. But then," his voice was sepulchral, "as the folder has gone it would not make much difference, would it, if I had listed them?"

He was not cheered. He returned to his desk and went on with his card-index.

> Crab-like Julian lost his way
> In Chirico's melancholy squares;
> He wandered there for half-a-day
> And quite forgot to say his prayers.

He wrote the above and considered it carefully. Then he looked across at Julian Ambleside. That person was filling scraps of paper with notes. His broad knobby face was twisted in grim determination as if he loathed the job of writing. Douglas wondered if he moved his tongue along his lips as the pencil ran along the lines. He tried to see but Julian's face was slightly turned from him.

Downstairs, in their office, the Flints were drawing out lists of people who were to be invited to the opening of the Museum of Modern Art.

The balance had to be well preserved. Not more than a certain proportion of the arts could be invited to mix with money and with fashion.

"I suppose," said Jeremy, "that we had better invite the Press too. The art critics, of course, will come to the Press show, but we'd better have the social editors and so on at the opening?"

"Of course," Alison was acid, "surely you don't need to ask me questions like that? Of course you invite the Press. Which reminds me that it might be as well to put aside one of the offices for them. If we leave plenty of drink around they will take it as a favour, and their reports will be correspondingly good."

Sylvia Rampion, Emily and Francis were sitting in Emily's office, drinking sherry. Douglas had been right. Emily was looking very pleased.

"Only three more days," she said to Sylvia, "and I think everything will be ready in time. Don't you?"

"Of course, it will," Sylvia was positive. Her hennaed hair shone like copper. "When is the Ernst from Ambleside due to arrive?"

"To-morrow morning," Emily said. "The dear Doctor had a brilliant idea about it. He suggested that we keep it veiled until the opening night and then unveil it, by releasing a large clockwork rat attached to the cloth by a cord. He suggests, and rightly, that the sight of the large rat will act as a reminder to people of their insecurity. It will make them look upon the pictures as things which are liable to explode in their minds. Too often, he said, people accept pictures as merely holes in their walls. We want to remind them that pictures are dangerous, that they bite. People forget, he said, that pictures are magic, often dangerous magic, and that they can be powers for good or evil. Emily, he told me, you have undertaken a great responsibility in founding this Museum, see that you do not weaken. I don't know what I would do without the dear, dear Doctor. He has been a pillar of strength during these last weeks. But for him I sometimes wonder if the Museum would ever have got started."

"Yes, he has been most helpful," said Sylvia dutifully. She wondered how much the Doctor got in the way of rake-off on the various pictures he had persuaded Emily to buy. Sylvia Rampion's life had not been easy, and she had learned a habit of suspecting the motives of others. She took a good sip of sherry, reflecting that even if much about the Museum was intolerably bogus, at least the sherry was more than tolerably good.

Emily smiled happily as she thought of her loyal band of helpers.

# Chapter 3

# Melancholy of a Day

AS DOUGLAS walked slowly along Oxford Street he screwed his face up against the driving drizzling rain and reflected that he had never liked, and never would like, a job which required his presence at a set hour of each day. He was due at the Museum at ten in the morning, which meant that he had to get there about a quarter of an hour before that to open letters and do the general odds and ends. It would not have made the least difference, he thought, if he had been due at five in the afternoon. He would still have disapproved of the set hours. He looked at his Ingersoll. As he had suspected, he was late.

He did not increase his pace. If he was late, well, he might as well be later. His mind formulated a verse about himself:

> Perpetually late he strode
> Through Oxford Street beneath the rain,
> The heavy minutes were his load,
> The loss of them he counted gain.

One of Bourlet's enormous vans stood outside the Museum in Iron Street. Men in green baize aprons were carrying in pictures of all sorts and sizes. Douglas stood aside to allow a weeping tormented face by Picasso to pass him.

The lift shot him upwards and he got out, letting the spring gates close behind him. He entered the library. Dr. Cornelius Bellamy was standing talking to Julian Ambleside. Douglas looked at them without pleasure in his expression. He was convinced that they had arrived to torment him. They advanced towards him together, Dr. Bellamy slowing his determined pace to the crab-like scuttle of Julian.

Douglas looked at the papers on his desk. The sight of them did nothing to cheer him. He realised that the announcement in *World's*

22

*Press News* that he had been appointed librarian to the new Museum of Modern Art had put all his creditors on his track. He recognised the handwriting of Mr. Dobell the bookseller of Tunbridge Wells. Hell, he said to himself, I thought I had paid that.

"My dear Douglas," the Doctor was affability itself, "Julian tells me that you have mislaid the folders of Chirico photographs. Is this so?"

"No," Douglas was short, "*I* haven't mislaid it. I filed it in its proper place the day before yesterday and when Julian asked me for it, it was gone. I thought that Francis had borrowed it but he says he didn't. Anyhow, I think he would have asked me if he had wanted it. He has enough sense to realise that I can't keep things in order if I don't know where they are. I expect someone took them to look at, and has forgotten to put them back. Oh, I know," an idea occurred to him, "Francis had some idea yesterday morning that one of the Chirico's might be one of his nineteen-twenties' copies of his earlier work and not so early as the date on it implied. He told me he had mentioned it to Emily. Perhaps she came and took the folder, just to satisfy herself that he was wrong. After all, it's her Museum and she'd feel no need to tell me what she was doing. I'll ring her up and see."

Before Douglas had time to pick up the phone, however, the Doctor had taken a couple of enormous paces and pulled up in front of the desk-drawer units. He pulled one of the drawers open. He ruffled the tops of the folders, and took out one of them.

"My dear Douglas," his face was adorned with a frosty smile, "it just occurred to me that you, working under pressure, might quite easily have filed de Chirico under D, and not under C. I take a look and what do I find. I find the Chirico folder has slipped into that belonging to Salvador Dali. Here you are."

He placed the folder on the desk. His face held the satisfied expression of a man who has just solved a difficult problem in Euclid successfully.

Douglas opened his mouth to protest that he had looked through the "D's" the evening before, and that the idea that he might have made a slip had already occurred to him and been proved wrong. He shut his mouth again. What the hell, he thought, if they want to play the fool with folders why should I care?

"Thank you," he said politely and passed the folder to Julian Ambleside, who moved sideways towards the table where his books were still piled. He sat down heavily in the steel and fabric chair, another early piece by Marcel Breuer, dating from 1925.

Dr. Cornelius Bellamy smiled. His benevolence shone on both Julian and Douglas. The latter did not feel gratified by it, but he could see no reason for expressing his disapproval.

"Ah well, my dear Douglas," the learned Doctor sighed, "we are all of us bound to make mistakes at one time or another. It is quite obvious to me that for some reason your subconscious desire was that the Chirico folder should be lost. Perhaps, my dear boy, your natural melancholy is in conflict with the melancholy expressed by Chirico in these early paintings? You required the assistance of an uninhibited character, such as I may say I am, to guide you to the photographs which your unconscious desire had buried out of your sight."

Hell, Douglas was not only gloomy but cross as he thought of answers, the damned things were not there, whatever my unconscious desire wanted to do to them. But he kept his peace. There was no point in starting an argument about the validity of Freud's *Psychopathology of Everyday Things* at that hour in the morning.

Dr. Cornelius Bellamy raised a hand in greeting. There was something of an episcopal blessing in his gesture.

"I will leave you now, my dear boy," he addressed Douglas, "having, let us say, solved one of the minor problems of your Psyche. I have, I regret to acknowledge it, work to do. Julian," he turned towards Ambleside, "I will be interested to hear what you decided. Come round and have a drink this evening. About six?"

"Thank you," Julian Ambleside did not look up from the photographs, "I'll be there at six."

Dr. Bellamy again raised his hand in salutation and departed. Douglas set to work to file the cards he had prepared the previous day. He was half-way through the job when he remembered that he had not yet filled in all the necessary details on the proofs which he had undertaken, or had had thrust upon him, to correct. He retired to his desk and looked at them with disgust.

"Douglas," the high voice interrupted him like the squeaking of a particularly obtrusive mouse, "Douglas, are you sure that these are all the photographs of Chirico that you have?"

"Yes," Douglas replied without looking up. "I sorted them out from the immense bundle of photos that Bellamy and Emily gave me. There should be about sixty or seventy of them."

Julian Ambleside wheezed on a high note. He started rustling the photographs noisily. The sound irritated Douglas.

"But, Douglas," the sharp voice was insistent, "there are nothing like that number here. There are only about forty odd, and none of them are of pictures of the date I particularly wanted."

"Oh, all right," Douglas rose with an ungracious sigh and walked over to the table. He picked up the folder and looked quickly through the photographs. He ran through them again.

There was no doubt that Julian Ambleside was right. About a third of the photographs were missing. He could remember that there had been photographs which he could not now find.

"I'm sorry," he said, "someone must have been fiddling with them. I thought they weren't in that drawer last night—in spite of old Bellamy and my psyche."

Rather surprisingly Julian Ambleside gave a high-pitched giggle. He stopped it half-way as if ashamed of himself. "The uninhibited character," he said, "has been proved wrong."

"All the same," Douglas went on, "I'm in charge of these photos, and it's my job to see that they don't get lost. I think I'd better go and see Emily about them."

"I wouldn't bother her," Julian Ambleside said, "it isn't really of any importance. I can manage without them. Don't bother."

Douglas was stubborn. "Damn it," he said, "I've just said that I'm in charge of this library and I don't like to find things getting lost so soon. If they start getting lost before the Museum opens what the hell will it be like after the place is open to the public. I must see Emily about it and report the loss to her."

"Very well," Julian did not seem to be much interested in the loss of the photographs and had returned to James Thrall Soby's *The Early Chirico*.

Douglas decided that he would descend by the stairs. The lift moved so fast that it upset his digestion. He found Emily with Dr. Cornelius Bellamy in the main gallery. They were organising the erection of a vast mobile by Alexander Calder, driven by a small electric motor. The red and blue and black knobs whirled gaily or shimmered like aspen leaves when the Doctor turned the switch that made it go.

"Emily," Douglas was tentative, "I wonder if I can see you for a minute? I want to ask you about something."

Emily Wallenstein turned a vague smiling face. "Good morning, Douglas," she said, "How are you and how is the library?"

"I'm alive," Douglas was mournful and his tone suggested that it was only by the use of terrific will-power that he was avoiding the grave which yawned open at his feet, "but it's about the library that I wanted to see you."

"Oh, I'm sure the library's all right in your hands, Douglas," Emily was still vague. It was quite obvious that her mind was occupied by other things. The Doctor smiled at Douglas encouragingly. He made another start.

"It's just," he said hurriedly, "that some twenty or more of the photos of paintings by Chirico are missing. I've looked for them and can't find them."

"Oh, they'll turn up, Douglas, don't you worry," Emily did not seem to be concerned about the loss. Douglas, who realised that some of the photographs were irreplaceable, being photos taken of the pictures at the time when they were painted, thought that she took the loss very lightly, but he shrugged his shoulders. It was none of his concern if Emily did not mind. He went back towards the door of the gallery.

Ben Carr was just coming in. Under one arm he carried a loosely wrapped brown-paper parcel. The brown paper was stained with blood. Douglas assumed that he was carrying the joint which was to feed his brood of children.

"Good morning, cock," Mr. Carr spoke in a whisper, "can you lend me another half-dollar? I'd fifteen pounds last night, but Maggie took it off me at dice. Trouble is," he became confidential, "that her dice are not straight. She always wins. She's a bitch, she is. She'd only give me five bob this morning and I had to get this out of it." He waved the meaty parcel. "It's left me absolutely flat."

Douglas disinterred the required coin from his trouser pocket and went on, wrapped in the cloak of melancholy.

Mr. Carr advanced into the room until he came up with Emily and the Doctor who were standing spellbound in front of a picture by Yves Tanguy of lonely little shapes in an immense desert beneath a volcanic sky.

"Hullo, hullo, hullo," he said cheerfully, and they turned to greet him. He fixed the Doctor with a determined eye and waved the meat at him. A large part of the paper flapped open, displaying the juicy red of uncooked rump-steak.

"What you said last night, Doc," Mr. Carr was unabashed by the strip-tease antics of his parcel, "put an idea into my head. I thought that even better than sweets on the wall would be chunks of meat. They'd give a proper putrifying atmosphere to the place as they went off. There's nothing pongs like a piece of good meat going bad, and then there'd be the flies and the maggots. I reckon the whole setup would be pretty tasty after a few weeks, don't you?"

Emily did not seem to be entranced by the idea that her hygienic twentieth-century ladies' lavatory should be made to pong like an old-fashioned charnel house. Even Dr. Cornelius Bellamy seemed to be somewhat startled by the fertility of Mr. Carr's imagination. His face shewed that he had not given thought to the possible fruit that his carelessly broadcast seed of the previous afternoon might bear. He was obviously thinking of some excuse which would not hurt the feelings of the artist.

"My dear Carr," he began tentatively, "I must applaud the magnificent freedom of your conception. In fact I must say that I have never encountered a genius like yours for the unexpected and the appropriate. I may say that this gesture brings my opinion of your genius even higher, if that is possible, than it stood before. Your supreme gift, my dear Carr, is your complete disregard of inessentials and your remarkable grasp of the subject as a whole. But, my dear Carr, we have to consider not only the immediate or eventual intention of a work of art, but also its social significance. We have to consider whether decaying meat, ah, suspended in the, ah, ladies' lavatory would not, let us say, create an immediate prejudice against the gifts which you display, my dear Carr, to such a remarkable extent. We have to consider whether the, ah, pong might not serve as a deterrent to those of whom we might in other circumstances make disciples."

"I get you, Doc," Mr. Carr was unabashed. He swung the meat gently to and fro spattering blood on the polished floor. "The answer is no. That's O.K. by me, cock." He turned to Emily, "You got a frying pan around?" he asked in a friendly voice, "if you have I might as well cook this bit of meat up for my lunch. Waste not, want not. That's the motto of Ben Carr."

Rather tremulously, Emily explained that she regretted that the Museum did not include frying-pans among its equipment, except in the small department that was devoted to the improvement in taste in Industrial Design.

Mr. Carr did not appear to be satisfied by this explanation. "I won't spoil the pan," he urged, "I've cooked for years and I've never spoiled a pan. But if you won't, you won't and that's all there is to it. I *did* think the meat would look kind of tasty stuck on the walls, but if you'd rather it wasn't stuck on the walls, I guess the kids will eat it up this evening."

He walked out of the gallery, followed by a trail of drips of blood.

Emily looked at the Doctor rather doubtfully. The Doctor had recovered his composure.

"What a man, my dear Emily," he said loftily. "One does not often meet a genius with such a magnificent and complete disregard for the usual social taboos. How magnificent was his conception! How supremely appropriate and satisfying! Those who retire from the disturbing presence of the pictures and the sculpture, in search of a momentary tower of escapism, are followed even there by the smell of rotting meat and the sight of maggots crawling across the walls. Their upset is not dispersed but increased a thousandfold and they fly back to the pictures, to find that there is no rest for them anywhere."

The Doctor gestured magnificently himself and knocked over a construction made of perspex by Gabo. He was not perturbed by the accident but stooped and set the construction upright once more. He turned his delighted face towards Emily.

"Of course, my dear Emily," he continued, "a man of the violent genius of our friend needs someone to act as his mentor and controller. The whole problem of the artist and his guide or friend is implicit in the case. Now, for instance, if I had brusquely refused to permit Carr to place that meat in the ladies' lavatory I might have done incalculable harm to his creative ego. As it is, by praising the freedom of his imagination, I have managed to avoid the disaster, for I think it might have been nothing less—imagine the face of dear, dear Lady Swivelton— while at the same time I have left Carr feeling more certain than ever of the essential *rightness* of his ideas. You see, my dear Emily, how important some understanding of the major psychological discoveries of our day becomes. But for my intensive, and I may say exhaustive, study of the works of Freud and Jung, I might permanently have injured Ben Carr as a *creator*. As things are he will go on from strength to greater strength, producing walls that vie with one another in their startling modernity and audacity. Who knows but that, some day, he may build a house to vie in fantasy with the Dream Palace at Hauterives erected by the postman Cheval between the years eighteen seventy-nine and nineteen-twelve. Who knows what height he may not scale. Ah, me."

The Doctor fell silent. Emily did not speak. She knew that Dr. Cornelius Bellamy was contemplating the wonders that Ben Carr was destined to perform. As a matter of fact she was wrong. The Doctor was thinking that he must instruct his cook to omit onion from his omelettes. Onion, he told himself irritably, always repeated on him in the most annoying and sometimes embarrassing way.

Douglas felt that he was building a bulwark of books between himself and the world. It seemed to him that Francis Varley had failed to give more than one reproduction to each picture. Vast bundles of bound volumes of *Cahiers d'Art* rose before him on his desk. *Abstraction-Creation* and *Axis* lay beside his feet. The catalogues of the Museum of Modern Art and the Museum of Living Art in New York lay up against his elbows. He made a few entries dutifully. He was beginning to feel most damnably thirsty. He supposed, vaguely, it was something to do with paper. The sight of a great deal of paper always made him want a drink.

Julian Ambleside had finally finished with his research into the matter of Chirico and Douglas had replaced the books and periodicals in their proper places.

In a few minutes, Douglas knew, he would need to go and have a drink. The quart bottle of Tolly was as empty as it could be. He knew that once he let his mind start wandering it was a sign that he needed a drink. He started to scribble an elegy on the subject of the learned Doctor:

> When Dr. Bellamy went to hell
> The devil asked him his advice on art,
> He spoke so gentlemanly and so well
> They allowed him to open a picture mart.

He was interrupted in the composition of this by the appearance of Francis Varley who pushed his well-groomed graying head shortsightedly round the door.

"Ah, there you are, my dear Douglas," he spoke with the air of a Stanley who had suddenly, and most unexpectedly, come upon the Martin Johnson's photographing big game, "How are you this morning, my dear fellow?"

He asked as if he really cared how Douglas's health was treating him, and Douglas answered, "Oh, I'm all right, but I'm hellish dry. How about going out for a drink? The *Ely* will be open by now."

"That, my dear Douglas," said Francis, "is a most excellent idea. How are you getting on with my proofs?"

He sauntered slowly across the room and Douglas, who was aware of the oddness of his own clothes only occasionally, was impressed by the languid grace of the expensive tailor's cutting. He really would need to buy himself a new suit one of these days instead of going around dressed in the oddments discarded by his friends. He wondered absently whether, if he gave his position and the Museum as his address, Mr. Snodgrass would allow him credit. He doubted it, but it might be worth trying. The most unexpected people sometimes allowed him to have credit. He really felt very sorry for them every time he failed to pay his bill. He wished he was like Ben Carr who apparently had no conscience about the feelings or requirements of those to whom he owed money.

Francis leaned languidly against the desk and looked down at the sheets of proofs, besprinkled with additions and corrections in the smallest, neatest hand Douglas could manage. He reached out a pale and well manicured hand and picked the papers up. He ruffled through them.

"My dear Douglas," he sounded gratified. "You are surprising. I did not know that you knew as much as this."

"I don't," Douglas was honest, "I just sat down and wondered where I would find certain paintings illustrated. You see I'm like the idiot boy who found the horse—he just wondered where he would have gone if he had been a horse. Well, I applied the same system to the pictures."

Francis laughed. "All right, my charming idiot boy," he said, "I must say that you have made a very good job of your horse-hunting. I'll send these straight off to the printers. Emily, my dear, is quite devastated to discover that it will take a week or two to make the loose-leaf covers for the catalogue and that, willy-nilly, she'll have to have a small number of catalogues printed off in the ordinary way and bound up in paper wrappers. She takes it hard, as her money has enabled her to get everything else finished in time. The non-appearance of the covers is her only set-back. I have pointed out to her that she only thought of the idea yesterday, so she can hardly blame the binders for the failure, but she seems convinced that money should be able to hurry them up. Money, my dear Douglas, should according to her be able to alter the physical properties of glue."

Douglas looked at the wad of proofs in Francis's hand. He knew how incomplete they were, but he felt that he had had enough to do with them for the time being. He hesitated.

"As a matter of fact, Francis," he said honestly, "I haven't nearly done with the proofs. I've only put in the more obvious reproductions. I wonder if you could get the printer to use these for the make-shift catalogue and get him to give me a copy of it interleaved? Then, you see, I could fill in the gaps and they could print the revised version to fit the loose-leaf covers. Do you think that a good idea?"

"My dear," Francis was enthusiastic, "I think that is an excellent idea, but we'll have to try it out on the dog. In other words, we'll have to ask dear Emily whether she agrees."

Douglas started putting the books and magazines back on their shelves. He had realised as soon as he had taken the job that he would need to make a practice of this, as otherwise the books would soon become a conglomerate mass upon his desk.

He followed Francis into the lift, wondering gloomily whether he would get his drink or whether Emily would think of something that just *had* to be done before he went out. Being pessimistic by nature, Douglas was already preparing himself for her refusal to let him go.

The door of Emily's office was ajar. Through it they could hear the mellow and experienced accents of Dr. Cornelius Bellamy laying down the law.

"But, dear Mrs. Rampion," he was saying, "you fail to appreciate the plastic qualities of his work."

Francis did not hesitate to discover whose work was calling up the learned Doctor's plastic batteries. He pushed open the door. Emily was seated in an early *Bauhaus* wooden chair which belied its angularity by being very comfortable. She was listening to the words dripping from the Doctor's thin lips with the intensity and pleasure of a music lover hearing a Bach *Prelude*.

"Hullo, Emily dear," Francis was gay, "I've just got hold of the proofs from Douglas here. He has a bright suggestion to make. He thinks it would be a good idea if we let these be printed with the corrections he has made so far, and let him go on making corrections for the proper, loose-leaf catalogue. I think that is very sound. He would not need to hurry so much with these and they would be very complete. He really has done a lot of work on them already."

Dr. Bellamy held out an imperious hand and took the proofs from Francis. He looked at them carefully and then he looked at Douglas.

"My dear boy," he said, disguising his annoyance, "as you say, these proofs are by no means complete. For instance I reproduced this Klee in my book on *Man and Art To-day,* and you have made no reference to it. In fact," he ruffled the pages quickly, "I do not see that you make any reference to any of my books at all, and, it may interest you to know, I have reproduced and discussed many of the paintings which have now, thanks to the generosity of our benefactor," he bowed stiffly to Emily, "found their permanent home in this Museum. I will myself enter them upon the proofs."

He took out a slender streamlined fountain pen. Douglas wondered why the designers of the pen had thought it necessary to streamline it. It was not as though anyone was in the habit of using fountain pens as darts, and he had to confess that the resistance of the air had never interfered with his speed of writing.

"I'm terribly sorry, Dr. Bellamy," he said quickly, "I told Francis I had not finished with the proofs, but he thought they would do until I had time to prepare the final edition of them. I meant to go through your books this afternoon, filling in the gaps."

"I accept your word for it," the Doctor was stiff, "that you did not mean to slight me intentionally. My dear boy, I merely hope that this will be a lesson to you to be more careful in future."

"Of course, Douglas meant no harm, Bellamy," Francis was cheerful. "He's been busier than the whole lot of us put together, and he was bound to slip up somewhere. We should be thankful that it wasn't anywhere really serious."

Dr. Bellamy looked up sharply, as if to see whether Francis was intentionally insulting him. Francis, however, had turned to Emily.

"I'm taking Douglas out for a drink, my dear," he announced, "I feel that he has done a very good morning's work and when I arrived I found him sitting in the library with his tongue dangling round about his boots. You don't mind if I take him out for a few minutes, do you?"

Emily had been listening to this affair with her beloved Doctor. She smiled at Francis.

"You are a terror," she said fondly, and Francis straightened his bow tie. Douglas noticed that the polka dots for the day were dark olive green. "Of course you can take Douglas out for a drink, if you would rather do that than have one here. Perhaps it's just as well that the Doctor is filling in his own entries on the proofs. They are bound to be accurate now. Are you sure you wouldn't like a drink here?"

"Yes, my dear," replied Francis, "I'm sure that what Douglas needs is a change of atmosphere as much as the drink. Once that Bellamy has finished with the proofs I think they should go back to the printers. It will take them all their time to get enough copies of the interim catalogue ready."

Emily nodded her head wisely. Douglas had been looking on very gloomily. For some minutes he felt his drink had been a feather in the balance against the weight of Dr. Cornelius Bellamy. Thank God, he thought, that I am not the elder Pitt—I would loathe one of Bellamy's pies.

# Chapter 4

# Delights of the Poet

THE LOUNGE of the *Ely* was not crowded. Douglas and Francis found a table in a corner, bowed over by nodding palm-branches. Douglas sat eating salted peanuts mechanically until the drinks arrived. The sight of the mellow amber of the whisky brought some signs of animation back into his face.

"I've just remembered something, Francis," he said. "Do you remember me ringing you up last night to ask if you had seen the folder with the Chirico photographs? Well, this morning when I got in—I was, I'm afraid, a minute or two late—I found Dr. Bellamy and Julian Ambleside already in the library. Julian had apparently told Bellamy that the photos were missing for the old beast went across to look for them himself. He found them squeezed into the Dali folder and then he had the nerve to tell me that I hadn't found them myself because, subconsciously, I had wished not to find them. He had some line about Chirico's melancholy being oppressive to one of my temperament. Now the fact is that I looked all through the D's last night when I failed to find the folder myself—I too had thought that in the bustle I might have filed Chirico under de Chirico. But then the funny thing is that I gave the photos to Julian who was looking at Chiricos. After a few minutes he asked me if that was all there were. I said it was and he then told me that all the 1916 and 1917 photos were missing. I went and took a look and realised that he was right, for, although I had not yet got round to listing all the photographs in each folder, I had sorted them out myself and I remembered that there were photographs of the *Grand metaphysical interior,* the *Toys of a Philosopher* and the *Troubadour* among them. You see, in spite of the learned Doctor, I really do like Chirico rather a lot, and his pictures stick in my mind. Now if it had been the Mondrian folder I might easily have failed to know if any were missing, but as it was the Chiricos I am sure they are missing. You didn't, by any chance Francis, borrow them and forget to put them back, did you?"

"No, my dear Douglas," Francis was positive, "as I told you last night I'd have asked you for anything I wanted from the library. I know what it is to try and keep order among my own books and drawings, when I am the only person to disturb them, so I can just imagine the chaos you would get into if everyone went into the library and started helping themselves without telling you."

He took a sip of his whisky and then felt in his pockets for a tin of Balkan Sobranie. He offered one of the fat cigarettes to Douglas. Then, in an undertone, as if talking to himself, he said, "I wonder what he wanted with the photographs. It isn't as if photographs were not repeatable."

"You wonder," said Douglas, "what, who wanted the photographs?"

"Oh, nobody, my dear fellow," Francis replied. "I'm just wondering who could have wanted them."

"You are wrong anyhow," Douglas went on, "in thinking that the photos can be replaced. Most of them are photographs taken before nineteen-twenty in Paris and elsewhere, and it's damned unlikely that the plates will have survived slumps and wars. Anyhow, if they have, and can still be printed from, you will need to know the name of the photographer and his serial number on the print to get a repeat. No, Francis, if they are lost I'm afraid they've gone for good. Even Emily with all her money will not be able to repeat them. Apart from that, some of the photographs were of pictures which have been destroyed, so even though some photos could be taken again, if you can trace the pictures, these can't."

He drained the last precious drops of pungent fluid out of his glass and beckoned to the waiter to repeat the dose.

"I say, Francis," he spoke as the new drinks arrived, "I really did drop a whacking great brick by forgetting to include Bellamy's books in that damned catalogue, didn't I?"

Francis seemed relieved that the subject had moved on from the question of the missing photographs. He laughed. "I don't think, my dear Douglas," he said cheerfully, "that you could have insulted the learned Doctor more deeply if you had sat down and tried to think of some way of doing it. He is most extremely jealous of his position as the major apostle of modernism in this country. What was it he was once called—oh, yes—'the old hack of modernism.' He does not believe that anyone knows how to look at a picture who has not made a careful study of his books. He believes that his books are the absolute essentials to anything in the way of an understanding of, say, a Miró, a Klee, or a Picasso. Of course you realise, my dear, what the Doctor suffers from as an art-critic? No? Oh, well, he suffers from the fact that he does not really like art. He really loathes painting. He agrees with Plato that there is no place for art in the ideal republic. But, as he has lived so fatly as a handmaiden of the arts for so many years, he feels that, raddled though she may be, he owes his old mistress something. Hence the long quotations from Plato in his books and the excursions into psycho-analysis. He is trying to find out something that will make him like art. His latest idea is that Art, with a capital A, is probably a curative agent. No matter if you break your leg or suffer from appendicitis—Dr. Bellamy will give you a pencil and some coloured chalks and you can work the illness out of your system by doodling till you are tired of it."

Douglas thought of a scrap more of his elegy on the learned Doctor. He fished out a pencil and jotted it down on the back of a cardboard beer-mat:

> To Bellamy it was a shock
> To find that in the depths of hell
> The kind of pictures that he'd stock.
> Were bought by devils very well.

He slipped the beer-mat into his pocket. "I see," he said, "Bellamy's just playing some kind of variation on Homer Lane's ideas, is he? You can cure the liar's quinsy by drawing the truth—is that it?"

"That's more or less it," Francis replied. "He is trying to justify his distaste for art, by making it appear useful. Once he has made art into a public utility it will cease to worry him. He will be able to dismiss the subject from his mind."

> He thought that art should really be
> A kind of universal pill,
> Old Nick himself refused, saying, We
> Take pride in always being ill.

It seemed to Douglas that before he had finished he would have made a kind of *Vision of Judgment* on the subject of Dr. Cornelius Bellamy. He was beginning to be slightly surfeited with the subject.

"I wonder what Mr. Ben Carr, the Doctor's protegé, is up to now?" he said, and Francis ordered another round of drinks.

Mr. Carr, unused as he was to the purlieus of Bond Street, was doing very well. He had found a pub in a mews, the *Groom and Horses,* and had got into conversation with the inhabitants. The conversation was instructive and edifying. It dealt practically entirely with the prospects to be enjoyed by certain horses during the course of the afternoon. Mr. Carr made mental notes of the names of some of them. Although he never risked a gamble at cards, and indeed would have looked shocked had anyone except himself produced a pack of them, he was not averse to risking a little money on the turf.

As he argued it out to himself; since I am unlucky at cards or would be if I did not make certain that I did not lose (he shuddered as he remembered sundry occasions upon which he had had to play with simple unmarked cards), I should make a great deal of money on horses. As a matter of fact, he was in the habit of being fortunate in his bets, but Maggie's skilful dice had robbed him of his lawful winnings.

Mr. Carr looked up at the clock. "Whose turn is it?" he enquired. "I'll have to be going after this one."

"It's mine," the speaker had been the source of most of Mr. Carr's most favoured horses for the afternoon.

"Tell you what," said Mr. Carr, "I'll toss you for it. Heads. Heads it is." He slid the two-headed penny back into his waistcoat pocket having made his gesture of sportsmanship. "Well, down the hatch with it. It's my turn next time."

When Douglas returned to the library after lunch, and as usual a little late, he found that he had been forestalled at his desk. Mr. Carr was sitting there. He was smoking a small but pungent cigar which still had its band of scarlet and gold. He was engrossed in the study of the *Sporting Times.* On the desk beside him there stood an open bottle of whisky and a couple of glasses, obviously borrowed from the Industrial Design section.

He looked up when Douglas entered the room and blew a ring of malodorous smoke. He turned over a page of the *Sporting Times.*

"Hullo, Douglas cock," he said cheerfully, "have a drink? It's worth having. It's Crabbie's. That's me. I don't like anything but the best. Take this cigar now," he looked at it affectionately, "you mightn't believe it, but it set me back one-and-six. It's a fact."

There was no doubt that Douglas was astonished. Judging from the smell of the cigar he would have guessed that it had been given to Mr. Carr by a garbage factory as a sample of its wares.

"Yes," he said mechanically, "I'd love a drink."

Mr. Carr poured a generous measure into the glass. "Sorry," he said, "I haven't got any soda or any fancy stuff. You'll just need to take it the way it came from the cow, or," he added darkly, "the haggis. I don't know which. I never was great on natural history. I know how to make babies, but that is all."

Douglas helped himself to the Marcel Breuer steel chair and sank into it, sipping thankfully at his drink.

"The trouble with biology," Mr. Carr continued, "is that it makes you think and puts you off your stroke. The great thing to remember, old cock, is never think. Look at my old mother. She must be a hundred-and-two if she's a day. To what does she attribute her great age? To someone's patent medicine? No! To fresh air and plenty of it? No, the old girl likes a fug as much as I do and that's saying something. To leading a sober life? No, most assuredly no! Saying that she is a hundred-and-two at the moment and that she started to booze at the age of twelve, that will mean, let me think," Mr. Carr screwed up his face under the strain of mathematical calculation, "that means she hasn't gone sober to bed for ninety years, and it looks to me as though she was good for another ninety." He said this rather regretfully. "To what then does she attribute her great age? I ask you. You can't guess? Why it is simple, Douglas old cock; she has lived to this great age solely by virtue of the fact that she never thinks. She has never been known to express an opinion on anything. A statement of fact, such as that she'd like another drink—yes—but an opinion—no! Take it from me, Douglas, as a man who has seen a good deal of the world and learned nothing by it, that thinking is the start of all trouble. Once you start thinking there is no telling where you will end. It might be Dartmoor," he said this cheerfully, but his voice fell with apprehension as he nodded, "or it might be Ten Downing Street."

He shuddered as he thought of the awful fate that might befall those who used their brains. He took up the bottle of whisky and politely emptied about another gill into Douglas's glass before replenishing his own. Douglas felt rather as though he had been beaten about the head with thin steel rods. He was not quite sure what he had done to deserve this visitation. He surely had not had all that much to drink at lunch.

The telephone rang briskly. Douglas started to hoist himself out of the chair, but Mr. Carr stayed him with an imperious gesture. "It'll be for me," he announced, taking off the microphone, "Hullo, this is the Museum of Modern Art, Iron Street, and this *is* Mr. Carr." He sounded as though he was slightly astonished. "What, you say they both won? How very pleasing of them."

He rang off and looked at Douglas sternly. "Never back a horse," he said, "unless you are a hundred per cent. certain it will win. I have just backed two that I felt that way about. I had a double on them. I am now the owner of three hundred and seventy-six pounds, eleven shillings and some pennies. Here," he dug in his pocket, "is the half-crown you lent me this morning."

He looked gloomily at the change he took out. "You might as well have the half-crown you gave me yesterday as well," he said, "if you don't Maggie will. God alone knows what she does with all the money she wins off me with her crooked dice. I'll either have to get a new wife or some new dice. I can't afford both. The trouble with her is that she is very mean. Take, take, take, that's her motto. Why, I discovered that she had shewn the children a big money-box and I became suspicious. I was quite right. She had shewn them the gas-meter, and there the little bastards were, shovelling in pennies as quickly as they could steal them."

He looked moodily at his glass and then at the bottle of whisky. It had certainly suffered. He tilted it against the light and shook his head sadly.

"Nothing's the same as it was when I was a boy," he remarked. "Even whisky hasn't got the staying power it used to have. Why I remember the times when one bottle of whisky would last me a whole day. You mayn't believe it, but it's a fact. Now I just look at a bottle and, hey presto, it's gone. When I was at Eton," he looked at Douglas to see how he took this and was satisfied that, as Douglas's expression did not change, he had accepted the statement, "I believe a bottle used to last me *two* days. That, of course, is a long time ago, and I may be exaggerating. I cannot say that I remember those days clearly."

He looked at the bottle again and decided to be generous. He poured half into Douglas's glass and the rest into his own. He then placed the glasses side by side.

"Not bad," his expression was happy, "not a hair's breadth between 'em. I thought the old eye was still holding out. Well," he poured the drink back, "I must be going now. Dear Emily," he said this in a voice that very closely mimicked Dr. Bellamy, "has a bit of decorating for me to do."

He got up and put the *Sporting Times* in his pocket. He deposited the empty whisky bottle in the perspex wastepaper basket where it looked extremely odd. He left the room and then he looked back round the door.

"Have *you* ever thought of trying *your* hand as an interior decorator?" he enquired. "It's easy and it's well paid. You just stick things all over the wall, arranging them as it takes your fancy. Along comes the Doc and before you know where you are you find you've created a blinking masterpiece. Not bloody likely!"

He shut the door softly and Douglas heard the muted whine of the lift. Douglas got up and took the two glasses. He took them into the little lavatory off the library and washed and polished them. Then he took them downstairs to the Industrial Gallery. He placed them on a table beside the door. The gallery shone with chromium and glass. Working in it, Douglas thought, would be rather like working in Fortnum and Mason's. He admitted to himself that he liked his living to be a little less obviously hygienic.

He was about to climb again to his own department when he met the Flints. They seemed to be suppressing some hidden excitement. Douglas had sufficient drink in him to allow him to forget all he had ever known of tact.

"What's up?" he asked, "you both look as though you'd taken Seidlitz powders and they were fizzing inside you."

"It really is most extraordinary, most extraordinary," Jeremy replied while Douglas bottled his curiosity, "you know that large painting by the Italian chappie? Chirico? Yes? Well, while most of the people were out at lunch, someone has come in and cut it to pieces with a razor. It's hanging in shreds over the floor. There is absolutely nothing that can be done for it. Dr. Bellamy says that it is ruined beyond repair."

Douglas pushed past the Flints and went into the gallery. Emily, Dr. Cornelius Bellamy, Julian Ambleside and Francis Varley were gathered in a small circle in front of the destroyed picture. As usual, the Doctor was holding the floor.

"While nothing, my dearest Emily," he said, "can ever replace a work of art that has been destroyed wantonly, yet we must confess that this affair has its compensations. The fact that some stranger was urged to enter the Museum and destroy a work of art shews how disturbing such works must be to the neurotic personality. No doubt the destroyer of this work had in some way identified himself with it. We might almost call it a Dorian Gray complex. By destroying the painting no doubt he hoped to free himself from its clutches. It must have required considerable desperation to take the first cut at the canvas, for doubtless the possessor of a complex like that would be convinced that, in destroying the picture, he was running considerable risk of destroying himself. Once, however, he had discovered that he had taken the first stroke with impunity, he would doubtless go on cutting until the spasm passed."

"Then," said Emily, hollowly, "you don't think that I should inform the police about the outrage?"

"Think, my dear Emily," the Doctor said, "what prospect have the police of catching a man who was probably, to all intents and purposes, as ordinary a person as you'll meet in the streets? And, if by one chance in eight million, they should catch him, what could be done with him. It would not be fitting to send the man to jail for a psychopathic disease, and yet any alienist would tell you that having destroyed the object of his obsession he was now as sane as I am, so that he could not be confined in any asylum, even if you wished to have the fact of such a confinement on your conscience, my dear Emily."

"It was fortunate," Francis Varley said, "that it was this one and not any of the others that suffered."

Julian Ambleside looked at him sharply. He seemed about to say something, but he closed his large mouth with a snap, like a frog that had just eaten a gnat.

"Oh I know, Francis, that you weren't satisfied with the painting," Emily was impatient, "you had some theory that it was one of those that Chirico painted ten years later and signed as if they had been done when he was young. You mayn't have been satisfied with the picture, but I was. I thought it was one of the finest Chiricos in the collection. One of the finest I have ever seen. And now, look at it, ruined. It is a beastly shame."

Douglas thought that she was about to burst into tears, but she recovered herself as Dr. Cornelius Bellamy bore up on her flank like one of Nelson's ships.

"I may say, my dear Emily," he was ponderous, "that I agree with everything you say about the painting. It was undoubtedly a major work and we will not see its like again. While I have heard that absurd story of Chirico's painting copies of his earlier works and dating them wrongly, I do not for a minute believe that one of these copies, if indeed they existed beyond the imaginations of the surrealists who were, as even Francis must admit, grossly prejudiced on the subject of Chirico, I do not for one minute believe that I would be deceived by such a copy. It would be bound to be a travesty, a mere shadow of the real thing. Anyone with the slightest aesthetic feeling would be certain to distinguish it at once. I remember having a discussion with you, Ambleside," he turned to Julian who had been watching him closely, "on this very subject, after you had asked my opinion upon the four large paintings by Chirico which you own. You will remember that I was able to put your mind completely at rest. I do not believe that, if such copies existed, a point upon which I must admit I am doubtful, that they ever left the artist's studio. You may take it from me, my dear Emily, that that painting which has just been destroyed was indeed a masterpiece, and that we are fortunate in possessing such excellent photographs of it, not to mention the colour-plate in my *Man Art in a Machine Age,* to transmit even a shadow of its glories to posterity."

"The trouble with the Doctor, my dear boy," Francis whispered to Douglas, "is that he's always flirting with posterity, and he doesn't know what kind of a girl she is. He should remember Christopher Smart's warning about the Muses in *The Hilliad,* where he says, 'The Muses are all whores, and they frequently give an intellectual gonorrhoea!'"

Julian Ambleside moved sideways towards the tattered shreds of canvas. He fingered them gently, rubbing the painted surface with a smooth finger. He tried placing fragments alongside one another, but shook his head sadly.

"I'm afraid," he remarked in his piping voice, "that absolutely nothing can be done with it. The vandal has not been content with the comparatively clean cut of the razor-blade, but has actually torn and twisted at the canvas with brutal strength so that the paint has cracked and flaked and vanished from large stretches. I doubt if the best picture restorer in England, even with the photographs and the coloured plate in Bellamy's book, could do anything with it. But if you like," he turned to Emily, "I'll see what can be done?"

"I think," the Doctor spoke heavily, "that Emily would prefer to have no picture to one which had been botched about by a picture restorer. No picture restorer, however skilful, could restore the original spirit of the work. It would be worse than a good photograph. All the essential falsities of the restorer's handiwork would become more and more important as time passed and succeeding generations would be deceived. We owe a duty to posterity which we cannot avoid. I say discard the damaged masterpiece. Do you agree with me, my dear Emily?"

Francis Varley nudged Douglas. "What did I say about posterity?" he said with a grin. "My dear boy, he just can't avoid his little pomposities about the future. He is convinced that his works will last as long as Vasari."

Emily was thinking. She flicked one polished finger-nail against another. She looked at the tattered mess of canvas sadly, and then she turned. Her mind was made up.

"Cornelius," she said, "I am in complete agreement with you. After all this is a Museum of *living* art and not of copies or poor botched things. From now on this painting has ceased to exist. Francis," she looked at him, "will you be a dear and ring the printers and get them to exclude it from the catalogue? If it is too late to cut it out of the proofs they must print a black block over the page where it is reproduced and described."

"How right you are, my dear Emily," the Doctor was flattered by her complete agreement with him. "Let the dead bury their dead and let us, all of us, look to the future."

Douglas, who was suffering slightly from the amount of whisky he had taken during lunch and after, suddenly said, plainly and clearly, "Tally ho. The future has gone to covert!"

Everyone looked at him severely. He held his breath slightly as if afraid that it was explosive and might catch fire. "Sorry," he said, "it was just something that occurred to me."

Dr. Cornelius Bellamy looked at him more severely than the others. Douglas felt that he would not retain his job as librarian for long if the Doctor had any say in the matter and he was afraid that the Doctor had.

Fortunately there was a diversion. Mr. Ben Carr came in through the door. He was smoking a slightly larger but no less vile cigar. He looked very pleased with himself. He had just heard that the third horse of his treble had won. Until he saw Maggie he was a rich man.

Sticking from his pocket was the neck of a bottle of *Johnny Walker's Black Label*. Judging from the slightly glazed look in his eyes and the maritime lilt of his steps he had been sampling the fluid this contained.

"Hullo, hullo, hullo," he said and gave one more in case no one had heard him, "Hullo. What's going on here?" He caught sight of the ripped tatters of the Chirico, "Someone been cutting up rough, eh?" He laughed at his own wit. "Now I come to think of it I could do with some of that. It will look fine on my new wall. Can I have it?"

"Certainly, my dear Carr," the Doctor spoke for Emily, "take it away. Do what you like with it."

Mr. Carr advanced unsteadily to the picture. He took hold of the canvas tentatively and gave a tug. Nothing happened. He laid his bottle carefully on the ground and spat on his hands. He took a firmer grip and still nothing happened. He jerked suddenly and the frame fell over on top of him. He sat down and looked indignantly at those around him, a babe in the wood covered with leaves of jute. No one laughed and he realised that no one had been near enough to play a practical joke on him. He rose with a sudden access of dignity, gathering his bottle, and departed, holding the frame round him like a gargantuan lifebelt.

"Dear man," Dr. Cornelius Bellamy was mildly amused, "the true genius to whom nothing comes amiss. It would have been all the same to him had it been a Leonardo. My dear Emily, you should be grateful to him. From your loss there will arise another masterpiece. Nothing perishes. There is a biological continuity in all things."

Quietly, so that no one except Francis could hear him, Douglas began to sing "On Ilkla Moor." Francis looked at him reprovingly. The door of the gallery was opened again and Mr. Carr popped his head in.

"Did I hear you speaking about biology, Doc?" he asked, and there was a wild gleam in his eye.

"Why, yes," the Doctor replied, "I merely remarked that there is a biological continuity about all things and that nothing dies."

"Don't you believe it, Doc," Mr. Carr was earnest, "I am not part of a biological chain. You ask my old mother. She'll tell you." He looked threateningly at the gathering and made another exit.

Dr. Cornelius Bellamy smiled wanly. He could think of no comment upon Mr. Carr's startling statement. "Well, my dear Emily," he said, "there is work to be done. Let us put our shoulders to the wheel." He turned towards the door, encountering Julian Ambleside.

"I think, Bellamy," the high voice announced, "that my problem has solved itself and that there is no reason why I should trouble you to-night. Do you agree?"

"Why, certainly, my dear fellow," the Doctor looked surprised, "but come round for a drink anyhow if you feel like it. I'll be there."

Douglas wondered vaguely what everyone was talking about. He came to the conclusion that it was none of his business, even if he had been able to understand it.

# Chapter 5

# The Disquieting Muses

AS HE had sadly feared would be the case, Douglas was rooted out of his quiet retreat in the library, where he was beginning to get the books under control, and asked to help with the final hanging and placing of the pictures and objects.

When he had looked at the gallery during the previous afternoon he had hoped that all the pictures would remain where they were hanging at that moment, but he might as well have hoped that the sun would stand still.

Dr. Cornelius Bellamy, looking like a lankier version of Benjamin Robert Haydon's Napoleon brooding on the island of St. Helena, stood in the middle of the room, apparently oblivious to the rustle and bustle about him. He was sunk in aesthetic contemplation. Emily stood beside him, not daring to speak in case she broke the golden cord that was destined to lead the learned Doctor in through the hole in Jerusalem's wall.

The Doctor nodded his head heavily and then readjusted his pincenez which became dislodged in the process. "My dear Emily," he said, slowly, weighing out each word as though it was an ounce of platinum, "what we have to do is to consider the effect of the gallery as a whole. And, it is most important that we should not fall into the usual error of gallery arrangers, the error of tastefulness. For God's sake, I say, let us be brutal and forthright. Let us shock. Let the pictures clash with one another. We do not wish our public to be comfortable. We do not wish them to go away remembering that they have seen some pictures. We want them to go away feeling that they have been insulted and outraged. If I may coin a phrase, we wish the pictures to commit a mental rape upon their virgin security. I would suggest that that painting by Mondrian be placed above the public urinal, the Fountain by Marcel Duchamp. By arranging things in this manner we will bring them into a new perspective. The perspective of to-day is the new perspective of new man in a machine-age." Douglas thought gloomily that the Doctor had stuck fast with the Italian Futurists of 1914 who had seen a machine, any machine, as a terrifically romantic object. To himself a machine was just something that was useful, no more wonderful than a cow and no less useful. But then, he thought, I may be wrong, I usually am.

Francis Varley was standing by, in the attitude of one who collects pearls of wisdom to feed them to the swine.

"Good morning, my dear Douglas," he said, "you see that we have got down to work already? That Picasso has already changed its location seven times and judging from the determination on Bellamy's face it will change seventy times more. Poor dear Emily would have been content to hang the pictures on the walls and leave them there, thus obtaining the Doctor's *sine qua non* of tastelessness, but it was not to be. By the time the pictures have been rehung, according to the tenets of violence, their surprise value will have vanished. Oh, by the way, here are a revised set of proofs for you to work on."

He handed Douglas the sheaf of papers. Douglas groaned mentally. It seemed as though he was already condemned to work for his money. He looked through them quickly and realised that the printers had managed to cut out the vanished Chirico. Personally, he thought, it was very absurd of Emily to remove the picture from the catalogue. She should have relegated it to a sort of appendix.

"My dear Douglas," it was the Doctor speaking in a lofty tone, "I wonder whether you would hold up that Miró next to the large Magritte. I have a feeling," he turned to Emily, "that they will offset each other very well. The fantasy of Miró's Catalan conception of a Dutch interior will compare excellently with the painting of the Flemish Magritte."

Douglas wandered across the room and picked up the gaily painted and charming painting which the Doctor had indicated. He held it up in the position required. It was not heavy, but after a minute or two, while Dr. Bellamy cocked his head this way and that, Douglas's arms started to ache. The Doctor seemed to have forgotten that the picture was not hung upon the wall, his mental eye seemed to have cut out the figure of Douglas supporting it. The picture started to waver. The Doctor was recalled to reality by this. He eyed Douglas severely.

"My dear Douglas," his voice was petulant, "would you mind holding the picture steady? It is not a heavy picture and you surely are capable of supporting it for a moment."

The trouble, Douglas found, was that once he had become aware of the slight shivering of the canvas, it became quite impossible to still it.

"I'm most terribly sorry," he said, employing a form of words which he did not mean, "but the thing is that I'm holding it in an awkward position and can't keep it any steadier."

Francis came to his rescue by bringing forward a chair. By resting his elbows on the back of it he found that he could hold the picture easily. He glared at the Doctor. The Doctor was unabashed.

"That's much better, my dear fellow," he said portentously, the tone shewing that the endearment was automatic and unmeant.

The morning went slowly. By eleven-thirty Douglas would have given all the contents of the Museum of Modern Art for one glass of beer. He was finally rescued by the Doctor himself who turned to Emily.

"I think, my dear Emily," he announced, "that that is enough for the moment. We mustn't let our eyes get stale, the freshness of vision perishes too easily. *Ah, tempora, ah, mores.*"

He took on the look of a man who felt age creeping up on him. Emily looked at him in concern.

"My dear Cornelius," she said soberly, "you *are* tired. Of course we'll stop now. Come and have a glass of sherry."

The vision of Bristol Cream floated before Douglas's eyes. He rejected it and fastened his mind firmly on a pint of bitter. It seemed to him that the room cleared very slowly. Francis was hauled in on the party that was retiring to Emily's office. No one thought of inviting Douglas. Indeed he himself felt that he had become a fixture in the gallery, and did not blame them. After all who would have invited an easel to have a drink.

He waited until he thought that they were all safely ensconced in the holy of holies and then he made for the stairs as fast as he could. Outside on the edge of the pavement he encountered Mr. Carr. Mr. Carr was deep in the midday edition of the *Star.*

"Hullo, hullo, hullo," he said, "how are you this morning, Douglas old cock? Feel like a drink? I wish you were. Ha, ha," he grunted at the chestnut, "well, we will go and see what we can find."

He folded the paper carefully and put it in his pocket. He made off down the street as if he had been an electric hare chased by a persistent and unusually fast greyhound. Douglas trotted after him. They passed the *Ely* at a brisk canter. Mr. Carr turned down several side streets and they finished up at a small beer-only house.

"What are you having?" he enquired, "there's only beer. Two pints of bitter, please, Miss." The whole of this came out so quickly that even had Douglas desired mild he would not have had time to express his wishes.

"I got a horse," his voice was slightly reminiscent of Prince Monolulu on Derby Day, "in fact," he was confidential, "I've got three horses which are bound to win. They are one hundred per cent. certs. Would you like to risk something on them?"

Douglas, whose knowledge of horses was confined to the fact that they were mammals and quadrupeds and performed useful services on behalf of mankind, did not know anything about betting, but he took five shillings from his pocket. He handed it over.

"I'll probably forget to place the bet," Mr. Carr was frank, "and if it should be a case that you should win anything I might tell you you had lost. Trouble is, you see, I'm not honest. I was expelled from Harrow for stealing."

"I thought," Douglas was tentative, "that you said you were at Eton?"

"I was at both," Mr. Carr was firmly unblushing, "I went to Eton after I was expelled from Harrow. But that is a matter of little importance. How is the worthy Doc this morning? Full of genius and Bile Beans?"

"I wish I could forget the Doctor," said Douglas gloomily, "I don't think he likes me and the feeling is mutual. I think he'll get me sacked. Not that I care. I've not had jobs for long enough not to worry about the situation."

"Have you ever thought of being a genius?" Mr. Carr leaned forward and placed his hand on Douglas's knee. "If you were a genius he'd treat you proper. He's got a great respect for genius, the Doctor has. You write him a poem which he can't understand. All nonsense like, you understand? He'll start saying you are the best poet in the country. Put in lots of dirty words so's they don't seem dirty, you know? He'll think you've got genius. Then you'll find he can't do enough for you. I'm a genius, you see. Look at the way he treats me. 'My dear Carr this,' and 'My dear Carr that.' You should try your hand at being a genius, cock. It pays. Just you do as you want and persuade 'em that that's the way to behave and they'll be eating out of your hand before you know where you are. Now I've been a genius all my life. When I was at Winchester," he caught Douglas's look of incredulity and hurried on, "I didn't tell you I was there too, did I? Well I was. I went there after they sacked me from Eton. As I was saying, when I was at Winchester, they thought I would be a genius. It only shews that sometimes schoolmasters *do* know, don't they. Now you, Douglas, are a poet. You are a genius. You must behave like a genius. Let me see something you've written."

Douglas dug through his pockets but the only thing he could find was a hastily scribbled attack on the learned Doctor. He handed it to Mr. Carr who took it as if he had been receiving the Crown Jewels.

> Bellamy died in the middle of the night
> And went at once to the judgment seat.
> "My dear friend God," said he with delight,
> "I did not dream we two would meet
> In surroundings as cheap as these are here."
> He waved in disgust at the marble towers,
> Said, "Don't you think that ornament drear?
> And my friend, just look at those bowers!"
> The Almighty scowled and took up his pen,
> Waggled his beard and let out a roar;
> "Bah," he yelled, "you're a wart and a wen,
> I made you clever, you became a bore,
> Through eternal Academies you shall ride
> With Sir A. J. Munnings as your only guide!"

Mr. Carr read this through carefully. He shook his head solemnly.

"Munnings now," he asked, "he paints horses, doesn't he? I thought so. No, Douglas old cock, speaking as one friend to another, I don't think you'd get very far with the Doc on the strength of that. Not that I don't think it good, for it is good; goes, as you might say, right to the point. I don't think," his air was that of a man announcing a profound discovery, "that you like the Doc much, do you? No, I thought not."

He shook his head solemnly and absent-mindedly finished off the reminder of Douglas's pint. Douglas had the glasses recharged.

"Now take me," Mr. Carr began again, "or you needn't if you don't want to. I'm going to tell you anyhow. Now, I had no ideas myself that I was as high a quality of genius as it seems I am. I always assumed that I was somewhere at the bottom of the class. Not a bit of it. Old Bellamy finds me and I'm up along with Michelangelo and Leonardo da Vinci and, believe me, living a good deal fatter than ever they did. You think it over. Just you become a copper-bottomed genius and you'll be set for life—or until they find you out."

The thought of himself as genius-in-chief to Dr. Cornelius Bellamy did nothing to cheer Douglas. He glowered hopelessly into his beer glass.

"How did you get on last night night with the dice?" he asked, thinking it as good a way of changing the subject as any he could think of.

"Cock," Mr. Carr was excessively solemn, "let me give you a word of advice. Never play cards with a woman. I told her that I couldn't put up with her crooked dice and she said she'd play me at cards. How the hell," he sounded aggrieved, "was I to know that she changed me cards for a set of her own, I ask you? Was that fair?"

"Does that mean that you're broke again?" Douglas asked sympathetically. Being broke was a condition which, having experienced himself, he could well understand.

"Not broke," said Mr. Carr rather more cheerfully, "only a bit bent, if you take my meaning. Sometimes I think I've got sense as well as genius. I left half my winnings with the bookie to put on for me again to-day. I only took a little home with me. That I lost. I expected that. I've got no grumble, no grumble at all. What's happening in the jolly old Museum this afternoon? They all seem pretty het up about something?"

"Oh, there's the press-show, you know," Douglas replied, "plenty to drink and a lot of blah. I've worked in galleries before and I must say I like press-shows. Do you?"

"I?" Mr. Carr was even more solemn, "I like anything where there is plenty to drink and where no one questions your right to drink it. Tell you what, old cock, can you get me an extra card for the private view to-morrow, do you think? I'd like to bring my old mother along. I'm bringing Maggie and the kids anyhow, but I thought the old girl herself might like an outing."

"I'll see what I can do," Douglas promised. He looked at his watch and realised that he had quite a lot to do before the press arrived. He made his excuses and left Mr. Carr to his contemplation of beer and the back page of the *Star*.

Inside the Museum there was a tremendous hustle. Men in green baize aprons were running around like automatons, picking up pictures and objects and laying them down again. The learned Doctor had taken up his stance again in the centre of the main gallery.

Douglas sneaked up the stairs successfully. He stood in the middle of the library in an unconscious parody of the Doctor's pose. Looking round he felt fairly satisfied. The place looked pretty good and all the books were on the shelves.

He sat down at the desk and wondered what he should do next. He really did not want to have to go and give Dr. Bellamy any assistance. However, after a few minutes he came to the conclusion that he really should go down and see what he could do to help. It was not that his conscience was worrying him so much as the fact that he knew there was a great deal to be done. He told himself that if he went now, he would be able to take things easily. If, on the other hand, he delayed until they called for him at the last moment, he realised that it would be the most awful rush. In self-protection he went downstairs.

Crab-like, the figure of Julian Ambleside went before him into the gallery and scuttled towards the Doctor. Douglas arrived in time to hear Julian saying something about the other Chiricos in his possession.

Dr. Cornelius Bellamy turned an amused face. "My dear fellow," he said in a bland patronising tone, "you really shouldn't worry yourself about them. I have told you that they are genuine and that should be sufficient. But, if it will help to reassure you, I'll take another look at them after the press have gone. As you see," he swept his hand round the gallery, "I will not have a minute that I can call my own until then, as I want to get everything arranged perfectly. By the way, my dear Ambleside, we, that is, dear Emily and myself, have come to the conclusion that we will keep your great Max Ernst hidden until the private-view, when it will be unveiled as a special treat."

He caught sight of Douglas, hanging around trying to look as though he was busy.

"Oh, Douglas, my dear fellow," he called out, "I wonder whether you would be good enough to move the Arp over there?" He pointed, "Yes, that's right, under the Juan Gris."

Douglas looked at the large white mass. He wondered whether the Doctor thought he was a reincarnation of Hercules. He gave the stand a shove with his shoulder and found that it moved easily. The large white stone was hollow.

Francis Varley came in with Emily. He seemed to be feeling very pleased with himself, but then, as Douglas thought, he usually was pleased. He ran his slender hand through the greying curls, so neatly placed on his head, and smiled cheerfully.

"Everything proceeding according to plan, Bellamy?" he asked and the Doctor nodded his head portentously.

After that, it seemed to Douglas, the fountains of the deep were opened and the deluge began. By the time the first newspaper men arrived, he was feeling as though he had been swimming in a Turkish bath. He did not know what he looked like and he did not care, but, judging from the looks of the others, he knew he must look pretty damp and dirty.

Among the early arrivals he noted an old acquaintance. This was Mr. Alec Dolittle.

"Hullo, Alec," Douglas said, "how did you manage to persuade them that you are an art critic?"

"Hush, Douglas," Alec looked conspiratoral, "I'm anything they like to call me, and I'll go anywhere they like to send me. I am the voice of the great British public. I know nothing about art and I don't know what I like. The trouble with most of the people who go to galleries is that either they know nothing about art but know what they like, or else they know all about art but don't know what they like. I am original. I know nothing. I record my impressions with the fresh eyes of the Polynesian savage. I am the mass-observer's standard rule. I was thinking of offering myself to Tom Harrisson but I doubt if he'd buy me. What do you think?"

Douglas was saved the trouble of thinking by the beaming vision of Mr. Carr who appeared in the gallery waving a newspaper.

"Hullo, old cock," he said, "we're winning. We are nearly rich men. If the horses don't all get glanders before the next race we may be rich men."

He looked at Alec enquiringly. "You know anything about horses?" he asked and Alec shook his head. "Sorry, if you had you might have helped me. I'm working on a system. It's bound to make me a millionaire—the only thing is that I can't quite understand it myself."

Alec cocked an eye at Douglas. The latter understood that he was not doing his duty so he performed the necessary introductions. He said that Mr. Carr was a famous interior decorator.

"Don't you believe it, son," Mr. Carr leered villainously, "I'm just one of old Bellamy's geniuses. He has geniuses as some people have mice. If he can't understand anything he comes to the conclusion that the thing is a work of genius. It makes life very simple for him. Hush, here he comes."

The figure of Dr. Cornelius Bellamy was bearing across the floor with the dignity and determination of a full-rigged ship carrying a load of wheat.

# Chapter 6

# Morning Meditation

THE NEXT day Douglas felt as though he had been living in a factory for turning rabbit-skins into bowler hats, and that somehow the whole production of fur had landed in his mouth. The top of his head was made of very thin cellophane and there were little men dancing on it. He tried to remember what he had been doing. It came back to him gradually.

He had managed to play his part to perfection at the press-show. So it could not be that. Somewhere or other, like a figure of ill-omen he could recall seeing Mr. Carr, a Mr. Carr full of all the joy of life and a good deal of the less-poisonous spirits of the West End. This was a clue.

The whole story unrolled itself before him. About two-thirds of the way through the press-show Mr. Carr had come up to him.

"Here you are, Douglas cock," he had said, withdrawing an immense wad of notes from his pocket, "your winnings." Douglas had looked at the money as if it was not real, and Mr. Carr had become impatient. "Come on," he had said, "take it. It won't bite you. But don't you play dice. They bite."

That was, Douglas realised, all that there was to it. He had thought that the money was unreal and had tried to spend it buying drinks. There seemed to be a conspiracy on his behalf. Almost all the barmen in town had seemed to be only too pleased to accept the bogus money.

He turned over in the bed and felt like an Indian fakir on a mattress of sharp pointed nails. He realised that he had not done more than take his shoes off. Very slowly, in case he broke, he rolled himself off the bed and undressed. He went into the bathroom and greatly daring, lowered himself into a tepid ten inches of water. The noise of the water running sounded like all Niagara in his head. He certainly felt better. He took a look at his watch. As he feared he would be very late indeed. He hoped that no one would have noticed his absence.

Every step he took on the hard pavement seemed to be amplified at least a million times by the time the jarring reached his head.

Much to his surprise he entered the Museum and made his way up to the library unobserved. He sat down at the desk and took up the cards from various booksellers, reporting books which they assumed the library might require. It really was rather fun, Douglas thought, to be able to sit down and order a thirty-guinea book without the least hesitation.

He was about two-thirds of the way through the job when the slim figure of Francis Varley inserted itself through the door. He came over and sat on the edge of the desk, swinging one leg, clad in a perfectly creased grey tweed. Douglas was suddenly aware of the bagginess of his own Harris trousers.

"Good morning, my dear Douglas," Francis's tone was slightly mocking, "how do you feel this morning?"

"Not at all well," Douglas replied, "did I do anything really awful last night?"

"It all depends on what you mean by 'awful'," said Francis; there was a far-away look of amusement on his face, "Emily was buying dinner for the learned Doctor and myself in the Café Royal when you looked in through the back door and spotted us. You wove, rather than walked, towards us and stopped, looking sternly at Bellamy. You fixed him with what I can only describe as an Ancient Mariner glare and announced that you were a genius. That was all right, but to justify your claim I'm damned if you didn't take a piece of paper from your pocket and proceed to read a sort of sonnet on the subject of the judgment of the learned Doctor. I don't think he enjoyed it. My dear Douglas, as you know he has no sense of humour. He was less amused than Queen Victoria ever was."

"My God," said Douglas, clutching at his stomach which had just performed a semi-revolution on its own, "bang goes my job."

"Oh no," Francis sounded positive, "Bellamy was furious and would have done you out of your job if he could have, but you have an ally in the shape of dear Emily, she stood up for you like a hero and I did my best to say what I could for you. You're all right, but I would suggest that the next time you see the Doctor you do a little polite grovelling and that, next time you get lit, you pick on someone else. Now, my dear, if you had picked on me, I would have been, I may say, flattered to think you thought me worth pen and ink."

Douglas felt rather hollow. Every time he got really drunk, it seemed, he managed to do something which he afterwards regretted. He pulled himself together.

"Is the Doctor around?" he asked Francis, who nodded, "oh well, I'd better get it over."

He rose to his feet and it seemed that he was about to hit the roof with his tender scalp. Escorted by Francis he went slowly down the stairs. He would not have dared the lift with his inside the way it felt. The lift would, he was sure, have killed him.

Dr. Bellamy with the look of one who had performed a useful work of creation, was standing in the middle of the large gallery. There was something god-like about him. It was obvious that, so far as he was concerned, he found it good.

Francis left Douglas at the door and he went slowly across the polished floor. Dr. Bellamy did not hear him coming. He was looking with great satisfaction at a piece of cloth which was draped at one end of the gallery, one of the pieces which Ben Nicholson had printed with his blocks. This held the secret of the Ernst until the afternoon, when a large mechanical rat, which could be seen in a corner, half-hidden by the stuff, would be released to drag the veil away.

"Hum," Douglas cleared his throat awkwardly and stood with his weight on one leg. Dr. Bellamy turned his head and looked at him as if he was a particularly bad painting by Millais. There was the cold appraising look which augured no good.

"Oh," said Douglas, "I hear I was very rude to you last night. I just wanted to say I was sorry. I was drunk or I wouldn't have done it."

"My dear boy," the voice was not full of endearment, "I know that you were drunk. It was obvious to everyone in the room. The only question that interested me was why you had to choose me as the subject of your puerile lampoon. Did you like your father?"

This seemed a bit odd to Douglas who had a momentary fleeting vision of the painting of the little boy in blue being asked by Cromwell's soldiery, "When did you last see your father?" Then he realised that the Doctor was being psycho-analytical.

"No," he said hopefully, "I loathed my father. Why?"

Dr. Bellamy did not seem to hear him, but became engrossed in his own ideas. "Ah, that," he murmured, "explains it all. I am the father-imago. It is a simple case of transference."

He suddenly realised that Douglas was waiting to see if he had been forgiven. He looked at him with the benevolence of an Old Testament god, unbending, knowing all and forgiving all.

"My dear Douglas," his voice was patronising, but kindly, "I quite understand your outbreak now. You were substituting me for the figure of your hated father and, uninhibited by drink, you desired to do what you could to hurt, not realising, of course, that I am above such hurts. Naturally, realising that the sickness does not lie in your conscious mind, but in your neurotic personality, I can do nothing but forgive you. You, my dear Douglas, were not to blame."

"Thanks," said Douglas, thinking that it was very odd as he had, in the first place, never known his father, and in the second, he had written the poem when he was sober. It had merely been an expression of his dislike of Dr. Cornelius Bellamy and had had nothing to do with father-imago, whatever that might mean.

Dr. Bellamy was now, having satisfactorily explained things to himself, full of not only the milk but also the cream of human kindness. He beamed at Douglas in a paternal way. It seemed that the words "dear little fellow" were almost clogging his throat.

"I wonder, my dear Douglas," he said, "if these Chirico photographs have ever turned up? I wished to consult them myself, for, as you heard yesterday, Ambleside seems to be anxious about the genuineness of certain paintings in his possession. Of course, he is wrong, but I feel that, should I be able to produce satisfactory documentary evidence, it would put the dear fellow's mind at rest."

"No," said Douglas, "I'm afraid that someone's swiped them. It's really a bit thick that anyone should do that."

"Indeed, I agree with you," the Doctor was affability personified, "it is indeed most provoking. I had hoped that a careful examination of the photographs through a strong glass would shew an unmistakable identity of brush-strokes. This would have eased Ambleside's mind considerably."

"Hullo, Bellamy," it was Francis Varley. "Has this young scoundrel said he's sorry about yesterday evening?"

"Why, yes," the Doctor looked surprised and a little offended, as if it was none of Francis's business, "we have discussed the matter and have come to the conclusion that owing to a neurosis of his personality his uninhibited self performs acts of transference. I was about, when you entered, to suggest that he put himself in my hands. I know a most excellent analyst who would quickly solve his conflicts for him."

Hell no, Douglas kept his thoughts to himself. I'm not going to be psycho-analysed. If I was I might stop being neurotic and then I might stop writing poems. He nursed his neuroses carefully, and thought of it fondly, as a sort of pet kitten. He thought of a beautiful chorus for a comic song: "So we nurse our neuroses around Russell Square." He decided that he would work it up one of these days.

Francis did not pay any attention to the Doctor's statement. "I thought you were talking about Chirico," he said, "and I wondered whether there had been any further information about the outrage?"

"No, my dear fellow," Dr. Cornelius Bellamy looked rather as though he had been assaulted from behind, "I consider that my statement, that it was the act of someone who had become obsessed to a psychopathetic extent, is all that we will ever know."

"Yes," Francis spoke slowly, "*if* that is the reason. I myself feel that there was something about the painting's genuineness which resulted in its destruction."

"Nonsense, my dear fellow," the Doctor was almost genial, "of course, the painting was genuine. Do you not believe that I would not have known at once if it had been spurious, or even a copy by the artist?"

"I suppose so," Francis did not sound convinced. He shook his head gently and wandered off to look at the large cubist Picasso at the far end of the room. To one side of the Picasso hung a painting on glass, one of the studies for *The Bride stripped bare by her own bachelors,* by Marcel Duchamp, and on the other there was a picture of a bicycle suffering the torments of hell, by Oscar Dominguez.

Douglas realised that he had nothing further to say to the Doctor, so he made one or two obscure noises and pushed out of the gallery. On the landing outside he found Alison and Jeremy Flint. They were, as usual, engaged in quarrelling, or rather Alison was telling Jeremy that he had no sense and he was agreeing weakly, in a voice that shewed that he had no hope that his agreement would still her bitter tongue. They did not stop as Douglas approached. This, he told himself, was rather embarrassing; if they had tried to appear pleasant to one another when a third person came near he might have been able to sympathise with one or other of them. He did not like the way that they involved chance passers-by in their domestic or professional troubles.

"Look here, Douglas," it was Alison, "don't you think that the old Countess Moonstone should have been invited?"

The tone was threatening. Douglas looked rather helpless. "I don't really know," he said, "but then, you see, I don't know the old Countess."

Both of them looked at him as if he had declared that he did not know the name of Cézanne. He saw that he had dropped a major social brick. He tried again.

"That's the old bird with the blue hair," he began and was stopped abruptly by Alison, who pounced on the inaccuracy. "Violet," she said, "very pale violet." It seemed to Douglas that he had committed another gaffe. He held his tongue.

"She is of no value whatsoever," Jeremy seemed to draw strength from the presence of a third party. "She never buys pictures nowadays and, as news value, she is completely worked out, and no reputable editor will pay the least attention to her. They all know that she is nothing more than a publicity seeker. She committed social suicide the day she hired that hansom cab outside the Café Royal and proceeded to bite the horse in the beam end. Everyone knew that she was thinking of the 'man bites dog' story and not a paper in the country dared print it. If they had she could have got immense damages for libel. After all, she *might* have fallen forward on the old horse and her old clackers *might* have drawn blood. Don't you agree, Douglas?"

"I wouldn't know," Douglas was intentionally vague. "You see I can't think about things like that. They make me sad. I feel so sorry for the horse."

Neither of them seemed to be able to think of a good come-back to this, so Douglas gave a wave that might have been interpreted as the 'we who are about to die salute thee, O Caesar' gesture and passed on up the stairs.

On the landing outside the library he saw the crouched figure of Mr. Carr. He thought that Mr. Carr was alone for a moment and then he realised that, equally crouched at the far end, there was a bunched figure wrapped in a long black coat. This figure presented a face which looked as though it had been blown upon by half the sand-storms and blizzards in human history. The rheumy eyes seemed to be looking inwards.

Mr. Carr looked up at Douglas. "We're just having a game of marbles," he announced with the satisfaction of one who announces that he has suddenly become convinced of the imminence of life after death. He sighted skilfully and flicked his thumb. The gaily striped glass marble shot along the terrazzo flooring and scattered the collection in front of the black clad bundle.

The bundle produced a cackle. "Ye're going off, Ben," she said, "I don't know what your father would say."

"Ho," said Mr. Carr in a disgusted voice, "who have you decided *was* my father this time?"

"None of your business," the bundle said sharply. By this time Douglas had gathered that this was the fabulous mother, aged a hundred-and-two.

Mr. Carr looked at her in an injured manner. "I'd like to know," he said in a bitter voice, "whose business it is if it isn't mine?"

"Can't you see the gentleman wants to pass?" the mother said, waving a thin blue claw at Douglas. Mr. Carr seemed to be suddenly aware of Douglas.

"Hullo, hullo, hullo, cock," he said in a pleased voice, "meet my mother. The worst mother any man ever had but still my mother. It's funny," his voice became pensive, "a man mayn't know who was his father but he's bound to be damn well certain of his mother."

"I'll thank you, Ben," the bundle was prim, "to keep a clean tongue in your head. By God, sir, if your father was here he'd horsewhip you within an inch of your life."

"If he had a horse," said Mr. Carr darkly. "I don't believe I had a father. I think that I was one of the earliest experiments in artificial insemination. That," he became indignant, "is why I don't like biology. I don't believe in it. As for her, she calls herself my mother, well," he shrugged his shoulders, "she may be my mother for all I know. Sometimes I think I'm a changeling. You know the sort of thing. She gets drunk and leaves me lying around and the Salvation Army come and take me away. Then she starts looking around for me and finds another baby, so I'm no longer me, but someone else."

This involved sentence seemed to exhaust Mr. Carr. He ignored the cackle of protest that came from his mother. He put his hands round his person as if fitting on a life-belt and they came away holding a stone litre bottle of Bols gin.

"Have a drink," he said hospitably, and his tone became threatening, "you'd better have it now, before she gets hold of it. I don't know," he sounded a little bewildered, "why they call it mother's ruin—it ruins me buying the stuff."

Douglas wondered what his stomach would say to the sudden acquisition of a quantity of Hollands gin. He decided that he might as well risk it. He tilted the bottle to his lips. It went down all right and the carnival which various insects were holding inside him shut down abruptly.

Mr. Carr's mother looked at him drinking. Her old face became smooth with emotion as she watched the drink go down.

"Steady, now steady," she said anxiously, "don't take it all. Did your mother never tell you that ladies came first?"

"You don't call yourself a lady, do you?" said Mr. Carr. "It's the last thing I'd call you, you hag, you harridan, you succubus, you witch, you

old hen, you mare, you mule, you bitch, you—bah!" His imagination
ran dry. Mrs. Carr was not put by this. She beamed at him and, reaching out, took the bottle from Douglas. Mr. Carr made an ineffectual
grab for it in mid-air.

Douglas could hear the gin gurgling as it left the bottle. He envied
her her command of a bottle at her mouth. When he drank from the
bottle he took it in short sips and nearly choked. Not so Mrs. Carr, she
poured the stuff back.

When the bottle started to sound hollow she decided that she had
better leave some for another time. Somewhere beneath the black
cloak she secreted it. Mr. Carr looked annoyed and then he smiled.

"Well," he said, "let her have it. I've got another." As if by magic he
produced that and took a drink himself before passing it to Douglas, saying sombrely, "Be careful she doesn't lay her old claws on this one too."

Mrs. Carr was vociferous. "That's not the way to speak of your
mother," she squawled, "where were you brought up?"

"You should know," said Mr. Carr, "I wasn't interested. As a matter
of strict fact I sometimes wonder if I ever was born at all and if I didn't
just appear from nowhere. We geniuses are like that," he said modestly,
by way of explanation.

"You were born all right," said his mother peevishly, "you were a
nice baby—but by God you've gone off since."

Mr. Carr took advantage of this diversion to pick up most of his
mother's marbles and put them in his pocket. She took this action
without a murmur, but Douglas noticed that, with amazing adroitness
for one so aged, she removed the contents of her son's pockets as he
leaned forward.

"Ha," she said, running her fingers through the packet of papers and
removing a five-pound note, "this'll be useful."

"I hope so," Mr. Carr took back his papers, "it's a forgery and they'll
run you in the first time you try to pass it. They are making very good
forgeries these days." His mother was crackling it between her fingers
and listening anxiously to the noise, "Oh, you wouldn't know the difference unless someone told you. Give it here and I'll shew you."

The old lady surrendered the note unsuspectingly and Mr. Carr
folded it up and put it in his trouser pocket.

"That one, I've just remembered," he said happily, "is all right. But
now you know that you should keep your eyes open for bad ones.
There are some about, not that I've ever encountered them myself.
They'd just better try giving me a bad fiver."

He looked at Douglas as though he was a forger who had just tried to palm some of his products off on an unsuspecting genius.

"I don't know why we go on sitting on the floor," complained Mrs. Carr, "hasn't this young man got any chairs that he can offer to an old woman? I am old," she said as if Douglas doubted her word, "a hundred-and-three come four Sundays after Martinmass."

Douglas did not follow this method of calculating one's birthday, but he said, "Good Lord, yes. There are plenty of chairs in the library. Come in and make yourself at home."

He led the way into the library. Mrs. Carr looked at the steel chairs and sniffed. She looked at the books and sniffed even harder.

"Books," she said in a tone of disapproval, "Books, eh? I don't approve of books, young man. They just make mischief. I had one once. Called *Married Love* it was and full of the most extraordinary stuff. Lots of things I didn't know in it, too. Can't say they did me any good." She sniffed again, "Mechanics—that's what it was, and I never could get on with mechanics. You take a telephone, young man, it tells you to press button A or press button B. Do you ever press the right button?" She looked at Douglas as if daring him to say that he did; "No! You always press the wrong button. Well that was me and that book. I pressed the wrong button. Every time. Seventeen I had and glad I was when it finished. If I'd had eighteen I think I might have gone mad."

"Don't you believe her," Mr. Carr sounded exceedingly pessimistic, "she only had three and she killed two of 'em. Drowned 'em like kittens, I say. She would have drowned me but there was a drought at the time, and the only water she had was the drinking water and she didn't like to spoil that."

Douglas was beginning to think that he had wandered into the middle of a Marx Brothers' film. There was a complete but crazy logic about Mr. Carr and his mother which seemed to have no connection with life as he knew it.

Mrs. Carr tried one of the steel and fabric Marcel Breuer chairs. She sat down very gingerly, and then she stood up again. She fingered the steel tubing anxiously.

"It looks awfully thin," she announced, "and I don't like tubes. You ask Ben and he'll tell you. Tubes are the trouble of my life. If it wan't for tubes I'd be a millionairess."

"Yes," said Mr. Carr, but he gave no explanation of the statement, so that Douglas was left in ignorance of what tubes had done to blight the life of his mother.

"What's this?" asked the old lady, pointing to a construction in black plastic and plexiglass by Mogoly-Nagy. Douglas did his best to explain. Even in his own ears the explanation sounded rather thin.

"I don't believe it," said Mrs. Carr. Her son looked at her sternly.

"Don't believe what?" he asked. She waved at the library as a whole.

"Any of this," she said largely, "it's not real. It's all a dream, and I don't believe it. It's all gin."

"Not at this time in the morning, mother," Mr. Carr was insistent, "you haven't had all that gin yet."

"How do you know what I've had?" she demanded sternly. "For all you know I may have been drinking all night. In fact," there was triumph in her tone, "I have been drinking all night."

"Where did you get the drink?" Mr. Carr was persistent. She looked at him shyly. "Oh," she said magnificently, "I've got my sources. You needn't think I have to run to you every time I want a drink. No, indeed, I have plenty of friends who are only too willing to deal out a drink when they see me, and," her voice was threatening, "they don't spend the rest of the time complaining about the cost of it. My friends are not mean, thank you. I wish I could say the same for my son."

She looked wistfully at the bottle of Bols in Mr. Carr's hand. His knuckles whitened as he strengthened his grip on the bottle.

"You needn't think you'll get this," he said, "fair's fair and keep your fingers out of *my* gin. You've had your whack and that's all you'll get. You'd better make it last. Have a drink, Douglas old cock. Let us drink to bigger and better geniuses and faster horses."

Douglas took the drink. He had decided that there was nothing he could do about it. If the Carrs always behaved like this he could not help it. He gave it up.

# Chapter 7

# Enigma of an Afternoon

THE FINAL preparations for the private-view went ahead smoothly. The bottles of drink gathered in a smooth array on the tables and the upturned glasses sparkled on the white cloths. Emily looked as smart and as enamelled as if she had just stepped out of the *Excelsior Beauty Parlours* after challenging them to do their damnedest.

Dr. Bellamy sat in a corner of her office, pulling odd faces as he made notes on a pad of paper laid out before him. It was understood that the Doctor was in the throes of preparation of his speech in which he was to declare the Museum open. No one dared to interrupt him.

Douglas, having escaped from the enervating and crazy company of the Carrs, wandered about aimlessly, flicking a Calder mobile so that the red and black discs moved in their seemingly endless variety of patterns, or looking at the materials which had combined to form a *Merz-bild* by Kurt Schwitters. He looked at the array of drinks and wondered whether anyone would say anything if he went and helped himself to a short one. He pondered this idea lightly in his mind and decided that, perhaps, it would be tactless to take a drink before anyone arrived.

The large Max Ernst was still covered at the far end of the room. Douglas remembered that it was his job to release the expensive mechanical rat which was to draw away the veiling. All he had to do was to bend down and press back a little trigger which would release the brake and start pandemonium. It was a very real-looking rat, he reflected, and he wondered whether Emily would be angry if he introduced a real cat to chase the toy rat. This idea, also, appeared of little value. The cat would be sure to make a mess or to upset one of the constructions or objects which cluttered the place in a carefully arranged abandon.

Francis Varley came into the gallery. He still looked as calm and unperturbed as a summer's day. Not one of his graying hairs was out of place.

"My dear boy," he addressed Douglas, "have you seen Julian Ambleside anywhere about? I want to see him."

"No," said Douglas, "I haven't seen him all day. I wonder what he's up to? You'd have thought he would have been here as so many of the pictures have passed through his hands, wouldn't you?"

"Um, yes," Francis was cautious, "I wanted to see him about the subject of these pictures. I want to see him rather badly, so if you should run across him I wonder if you'd tell him that I was looking for him?"

"Still chasing the Chiricos?" asked Douglas flippantly, and Francis nodded seriously. His nod conveyed his feeling that there was nothing in the world more important than the question of a picture's genuineness. The whole of Francis's world hung on little points as to whether a certain picture was painted before or after a certain date or whether an artist had been familiar with the work of another artist at the time when he painted such-and-such a work.

Douglas looked nervously at his watch. The balloon was due to go up before long. He had a feeling that something was certain to go wrong with the works. Gloomily, he reflected that on such occasions there was always a great deal which could cause trouble, and, it was his experience that there usually was trouble. Trouble meant that he would have to do his best to clear things up. The thought did nothing to cheer him. He scowled at a painting by Dali which, in chromolithographic paint, presented at least a dozen different images hidden in the shapes of others.

The Flints, bickering as usual, were taking up their positions near the door. They were to collect the cards of those who had been invited to the private view. As a general rule they would have delegated this job of stewardship to some underling, but the opening of the Museum of Modern Art was of sufficient importance to demand their personal attention.

"Are you certain," said Alison, "that old Lady Pampole got a card?"

"Yes," said Jeremy wearily, "and Rupert Hollywell and Sir Arthur Carpathian and Edith Entwistle and Lord Lemmon and the Honourable John Figgleswick. They all got cards—every damned one of them. It's no use going over things again and again, Alison, I think that we have done everything. If anyone fails to turn up who should turn up it is not my fault."

His wife looked at him. Her look said as plainly as any words could have that she would certainly blame her husband for any failures. His

look shewed that he knew that she would and that he knew that he
would accept the reproaches, without much protest.

They saw Douglas, and Alison beckoned him across. He went slowly
and unwillingly. He knew that she had thought of something for him
to do, and he did not want to do anything except moon about antici-
pating calamity.

"Do be a dear," said Alison, "and give us a hand by distributing the
catalogues to the people as they come in. We'll have our work cut out
in collecting the invitation cards."

"All right," Douglas was not gracious, "I'll hand out catalogues till
the learned Doctor starts spouting and then I'll need to go. I've got a
job to do then."

He took up a position by the door, beside a large pile of catalogues.
He held half-a-dozen gloomily in his hand, so that the leaves drooped
like the withering leaves of a plant.

People started to arrive, slowly at first, in twos and threes, but then
in a crowd so that Douglas had his time fully occupied in seeing that
everyone had a catalogue. The large gallery started to fill up. No one
seemed to be terribly interested in the pictures and other works of art.
They seemed to have met together to see one another. People greeted
their friends with the fervour of those who had not met for many years,
oblivious of the fact that they had had drinks together that very morning
or had met at the same parties the previous evening.

Only a very few tried to see between the crowd to look at the pictures. Most people held their catalogues listlessly in their hands while
the conversation ranged around their friends' frailties and scandal.

"Hullo, cock," it was Mr. Carr, accompanied by his mother, "you
don't mind if I bring the old girl in, do you?"

"Not the least," said Douglas, ignoring the Flints who were looking
rather askance at Mrs. Carr. Mrs. Carr was quite obviously drunk. She
fixed Douglas with small bright beads and breathed Hollands Gin at
him. Douglas remembered the proverb which declared that the wages
of gin is breath. He thought of repeating it but people were pressing
upon him for catalogues. He handed one to Mr. Carr who rolled it up
and put it in his pocket. Mrs. Carr started to nibble absent-mindedly at
her catalogue. The printer's ink left black smears at the corners of her
mouth. She took a final bite and washed it down with the remains of
the bottle of Bols which she had had secreted somewhere on her person. With the gesture of royalty conferring a favour she handed the
empty bottle to Douglas.

He looked around to see where he could dispose of it. There did not seem to be anywhere to put it.

As bad luck would have it, at that moment Dr. Cornelius Bellamy swept into the gallery, with a swish of invisible academic robes. He looked at the bottle in Douglas's hand and glared. For a moment he seemed to be on the point of making some remark, then, with an expression that shewed that he considered that he had far more important things to do than to try to deal with the dipsomania of a poet, he passed on.

As he went down the room people became silent. He took this silence as his royal right and moved with dignity towards a little table set in front of the veiled Max Ernst. He placed himself behind the table and coughed one or twice, self importantly. Those who had been too engrossed in gossip to notice his arrival became aware of his presence. Emily stood near him.

Douglas began to work his way through the crowd towards the mechanical rat, which was hidden beneath a decent white cloth.

The Doctor cleared his throat once more. If he had had a gavel he would have thumped the table briskly, not that this was required, for there was a deep silence, broken only by the grunting of Mrs. Carr who had found the tables of drink and was, apparently, intent upon reducing their quite ridiculous load as quickly as possible.

"Ah," said the Doctor and even Mrs. Carr became silent, "we are met together this afternoon to—ah—celebrate an occasion unique in the history of these islands, nothing less, in short, than the foundation of a Museum of Modern Art. And when I say 'Modern Art' I mean the art of to-day, the living and vital art which is being created around us, in the world in which we live. To become the home, the centre of this art, is the aim of this Museum with which I consider myself honoured to be connected."

He looked around the room as if asking for contradiction. There was none.

"I suppose," he went on, "that you are all familiar with the controversy which the generosity, the very great generosity, of my friend Miss Emily Wallenstein has occasioned in the columns of the—ah—Press? Yes. Well, as you no doubt know, all movements of intelligence have had their detractors and their opponents whom time has scarified. So let it be in this case. We do not need to worry about the yapping of the gutter-Press, nor do we need to concern ourselves with the no less ignorant mumblings which come from old gentlemen, securely ensconced in their club chairs. Fortunately, I may say, we have no reason to fear their criticism nor to thank them for their tolerance."

Emily had blushed pinkly at the Doctor's references to her generosity. Her generosity had been largely actuated by her love of being in the "centre of things."

"Never before in the history of art in this country has there been an individual sufficiently interested and enthralled to devote not only the money, but the thought and care necessary, to the job, for I may call it a job, of presenting art as art, and not as we see it through the glasses of a Royal Academician, to the peoples of this country." The Doctor, Douglas thought grimly, was gradually getting into his stride. He went on, "Oh how often, how very often, have I been asked by my students and by those who are interested, where they could see works by modern artists, and I have been shamed, yes, shamed, by having to reply that these works, the vital living works expressing the experience of our time, could only be seen in private collections—that the spectator who enjoyed them was privileged indeed. Certainly," his voice was smooth, "there have been galleries in London which presented the works of the artists of to-day. We remember the London Gallery, that noble venture of Monsieur Edouard Mesens—we remember the Guggenheim Jeune, where the interested could see the works of Yves Tanguy for the first time, and we remember the Mayor Gallery, the storehouse of Paul Klee and Picasso drawings. Yes, as I say, we remember these, and we recall, also, the International Surrealist Exhibition of 1936, the shows organised by the Seven and Five. We recall the Redfern Gallery and we recall Messrs. Reid and Lefevre, and Mr. Ernest Brown of the Leicester Gallery. We recall these and we are grateful. We honour those who organised the exhibitions and who risked their reputations by backing the vital artists of our time. These names are the roll of honour of art. They are emblazoned on the sheet of time. Yes. Yes, I say, nothing can ever take the honour from Mr. Anton Zwemmer of his Miró and Picasso exhibitions. Let us think of these honourable men, for they were honourable and brave men. Let us think of them. Let us praise Herbert Read and Mr. Wilenski. Let us sing the praises of the *Listener* and those lesser papers which praised and reproduced the art of to-day. Yes, I repeat, we cannot forget them. But," his voice was sombre, "was this enough? No! Most decidedly no! We needed more than that. We needed more than the transitory show—the pictures round a gallery walls which vanished at the end of the month—into a private collection, perhaps, or—more likely, to adorn the collection of the artist himself, neglected and forgotten. For the artist goes on. He does not stand still. The work which he has finished, is finished so far as he is concerned. It is only the spectator who knows and appreciates the value of what has been finished. Yet these works, incomparable works, were neglected or hidden in the sitting-rooms of those who had the taste and the courage to purchase them. Now, however, no longer is the work of art an object which is left on the artist's hands, or something hidden in a private house—no, indeed, it has become the privilege and, I may say, the right of the man in the street to come and see it when he wishes."

The Doctor paused and Douglas distinctly heard Mr. Carr give way to a low but piercing "Coo, lumme, what's he talking about?" This interpolation might not have existed so far as Dr. Cornelius Bellamy was concerned. He shook himself like a retriever which has just left the water.

"As I was saying," he said, "we can now count ourselves among the really fortunate. We do not need to rely on our friends when we wish to see a painting by, let us say, Réne Magritte or Piet Mondrian. No, Miss Wallenstein has made the sight of these things the common property of us all. We can see them when we want to see them. We do not need to hang expectantly on a telephone receiver for the voice that informs us that its owner will be away this week-end. No, we can come when we like and see what we like, when we want to see it."

Douglas thought that the Doctor had finished. He took out a clean handkerchief and wiped his forehead. He looked slowly around the room. But he started again.

"It is depressing," he said, "to look around a room like this, and to ask oneself how many of the people here are interested in the works which hang around them, and how many, desiring to be as they say in the swim, came to see their friends and not the pictures. Look around you," his startled audience looked around it, "do you not find something that stirs you in these pictures? Can you look at that Picasso," he waved towards one of the paintings of the Guernica period, "and go home quite the same people? Before you you can see fragments of what it takes to make men, pieces wrung by torture from the lives of men. Is it nothing to you? Can you go on living your unimportant lives full of absolutely unimportant things and still have the hearts to look paintings in the face? Can you, however inflated your sad egos may be, face these works unashamed—unashamed of your triviality, your worthlessness?"

Douglas looked at the audience. They seemed to be pleased by the way the Doctor addressed them. Vaguely, Douglas had a memory of a nineteenth-century divine who had condemned his congregations to hell, much to their enjoyment. He realised suddenly that the people in the gallery were, in spite of their mental pictures of themselves, no more sophisticated than the divine's congregations.

"It only remains for me," Dr. Bellamy looked at the crowd with a face that displayed deep disgust, "to thank Miss Wallenstein on behalf of us all for her unprecedented generosity—yes, and enterprise. But for Miss Wallenstein we would still be in an aesthetic dark age."

Mrs. Carr, who had managed somehow to get up close under the Doctor, looked up at him. She let go a loud and rather offensive belch. "That's the stuff, cock," she said noisily but unsteadily, "don't you let 'em tell you otherwise. She's a jolly good fellow, and so say all of us."

She looked pugnaciously round the gallery as if asking for a challenge. From the folds of her garment she took a bottle of Harvey's Bristol Cream sherry. She waved this hopefully. Douglas realised that she had stolen it from the table of drinks.

"Tally ho," said Mrs. Carr, "it gives me much pleasure to propose the health of Miss Wallstone, Miss Wallysteen—oh, cut it. Here's to you, hen."

She pointed ferociously at Emily with the neck of the bottle and then put it in her own mouth in case she lost it.

Emily looked rather startled, as if someone had just stuck a pin into her, but Dr. Cornelius Bellamy was unabashed. One felt that not once or twice in his career as an educator had he encountered worse hecklers than Mrs. Carr. He looked at her severely and dismissed her from his mind.

"Without thought of personal glory," he said, "and at, I may say, more than considerable personal cost, Miss Wallenstein has seen fit to prepare and erect this Museum to teach people to appreciate the art of their own epoch. It is only too easy for a man to say that he likes such-and-such a picture in the National Gallery when all the time he is only repeating judgments adopted from the accepted ideas of others. Here the spectator has to form his own judgments—he is the new man faced with new things and he has no handy—ah—cribs to help him. His aesthetic is entirely his own."

Douglas, standing beside the toy rat was getting restive. He wished the Doctor had learned that brevity was the soul of wit. He fastened his eyes on the back of the speaker and concentrated on wishing that he was telepathic. He might as well have fastened his eyes on the brick wall in the painting by René Magritte beside him.

"In preparing this gallery," Dr. Bellamy went on gracefully, "we have had the assistance of many workers who have not stinted their time nor their energies in the efforts to make everything as perfect as it can possibly be made. At Miss Wallenstein's request I will name these people."

Ha, said Douglas to himself, that'll hurt you, you old windbag. I'll bet you wanted to take all the credit to yourself. Dr. Bellamy looked at a scrap of paper hidden in the palm of his hand.

"Firstly, for the organisation of this very pleasant meeting, we have to thank Mr. and Mrs. Flint whose unflagging enthusiasm overcame all sorts of difficulties. Then there is Mr. Julian Ambleside, who may be known to many of you as a most enlightened dealer and who has collected a great many of the pictures which you see before you."

Douglas wondered where Ambleside was. He had not seen him all day and it did not seem like him to miss the opening of an exhibition, particularly one where he might make promising business contacts.

"Then we have Mr. Francis Varley who, in addition to much else, has compiled the catalogue of the Museum, aided by our librarian, Mr. Newsome, the poet. Miss Wallenstein's assistant, Miss Rampion, should come in for a special meed of praise, for she has been a veritable tower of strength when we felt our hearts grow weary and our limbs grow tired. But for these people the Museum would not be ready. I would like to thank them myself."

There was a polite ripple of half-hearted clapping. Douglas felt rather surprised that the Doctor had mentioned his name, but reflected that, after all, he had done a great deal of work.

"It only remains for me," the suave voice went on, "to unveil our latest purchase."

He turned to Douglas who bent down and under cover of the cloth, pressed the trigger that was to start the mechanism.

The mechanical rat started to scamper across the room. There was a sudden diversion.

"Rats," screamed Mrs. Carr and threw herself full length on the toy rodent. It was a minute or two before order was restored and before people looked up at the Max Ernst.

There, dangling in front of the picture, was the missing Julian Ambleside. He looked very dead indeed.

It was doubtful for a moment or so whether people did not accept the hanging figure as a part of the exhibition, but the fact that it was a dead man gradually filtered through their minds, which had been attuned to accept any absurdity except this.

"Cover it up," the Doctor turned smartly to Douglas, "cover it up."

Douglas rescued the cloth which had been attached to the rat and tried to reach up to hang it over Julian Ambleside. He was not tall enough and had to fetch a chair. He draped it clumsily enough and then climbed down again.

There was a deep silence in the room, deeper even than that which had welcomed the Doctor. Douglas looked around and wondered what he was supposed to do next.

"My dear fellow," it was Francis Varley coming to help him and speaking in a quiet voice, "I suppose we'd better have a policeman, don't you?"

Douglas turned to Emily. "Shall I get a copper?" he asked nervously, and she stopped biting the lipstick off her lips and nodded.

Douglas left the room and went into Emily's office. He rang Whitehall 1212.

"Look here," he said when he was connected, "I'm speaking from the new Museum of Modern Art in Iron Street. We have just been unveiling a picture and there was a dead man, a Mr. Julian Ambleside, hanging in front of it. Would you come along and deal with him. My name? Oh, I'm the librarian. My name's Douglas Newsome. Thank you."

He went back into the gallery and approached Emily who seemed to be on the point of having hysterics. Dr. Cornelius Bellamy, looking surprisingly indecisive, stood beside her.

"I've rung the police," said Douglas, "and they'll be along in a few minutes. Have a drink, Emily?"

"What did you ring the police for?" the Doctor demanded in a tone which shewed that he considered that he should have been consulted first.

"I asked her if I should," said Douglas, gesturing at Emily. He went and collected a drink for her.

Having delivered his drink he thought he could do with one himself. Beside the table of drinks stood Mrs. Carr, holding the mechanical rat in her hands as if it had been the one toy she had spent her hundred-and-two years hoping to find. Mr. Ben Carr stood beside her.

"Hullo, Douglas cock," he said in a cheerful and piercing undertone, "some interior decorating, what? Better than meat, eh?"

Douglas poured back his drink quickly and served himself another. He noticed that people, having got over the initial shock of seeing Julian Ambleside dangling from a picture hook, were now trying to pretend that nothing out of the ordinary had happened. They were moving around the drinks and the attendants were pouring them out, and the conversation ran on everything except the late Mr. Ambleside.

That there was something wrong was filtering through Douglas's brain. It would have been all right if he had found Ambleside hanging. He would have assumed that he had committed suicide, but to find him hanging behind a veil was going a bit far. He could not have put it back in place after killing himself. Therefore it seemed unlikely that Julian had, in fact, committed suicide. Of course, there had been that question as to whether his pictures were genuine, but, Douglas was forced to confess to himself, Julian had seemed as anxious to find out the facts of the matter as anyone else. And there was always the possibility that the whole subject was a sort of hare started by Francis Varley. Francis had a habit of starting such hares. There was nothing he liked half so much as a really acrimonious controversy. The ruder people became the more he seemed to enjoy it. He whetted his pen on the steel of their tongues.

Ho, said Douglas to himself, it looks as if it was murder. I wonder what'll happen next. One murder case is enough in a lifetime, and I've had that. I don't want to bullied about by the coppers. I will take steps to protect myself.

He reached out and grabbed a half-pint glass which he filled with whisky. That, he thought, should support him through the coming ordeal. He left the gallery and made his way up to the library. It looked very deserted after the crush downstairs. He sat down at his desk and pulled the red telephone towards him.

# Part 2—Chapter 1

# The Joy of Return

WHEN I got back from my holiday I found, as I had expected, that the old man had had a series of field-days in the creation of chaos. Anything that I had anticipated or feared was nothing to the reality. There were books all over the place. I don't believe that one book in the house was in its rightful place. It seemed to me that Professor Stubbs had quite deliberately set to work to destroy my systems.

The only good thing was that I had taken the key of the filing cabinet, where I keep the Professor's notes for his *History of Botany,* away with me. Even here I found that he had tried to break in to undo my work, but the good solid steel, bless it, had withstood his assaults with the poker.

I spent at least a month restoring something like order into the house. It was difficult to do this as the old man raised a howl of protest whenever he saw me at it. He claimed that he would never be able to find anything again so long as he lived.

With considerable restraint I pointed out that he employed me, at a very reasonable salary, just to find things for him and to see that he did not live in a kind of regal pig-sty. I might as well have presented myself with a tinsel halo. He paid no attention to my claims for an early beatification.

"Max, dam' 'ee," he said, "I got on very well wi'out ye, an' I know me way around among me own thin's. I'll ask ye to let me ha' just a little muddle so's I can find what I want to find."

In my turn I was adamant. I ignored the pathos he put into his voice and cleaned up sternly.

At last it seemed to me that I was getting on top of the primæval chaos. I copied a piece out of William Whiston's *New Theory of the Earth,* 1696, and left it lying on his desk. It read: "The *Chaos* was a mixed Compound of all sorts of Corpuscles, in a most uncertain confus'd and disorderly

State; heavy and light, dense and rare, fluid and solid Particles were in a great measure, as it were at a venture, mingled and jumbled together."

This got him. He apologised and I accepted his apology. We set to work on several papers which, in my absence, Professor Stubbs had rather rashly undertaken to prepare. When the old man works he works harder than anyone I know. We kept our noses to our work for nearly a fortnight, never going further than to inspect the various plants which rioted in a botanist's dream of plenty in the garden.

This afternoon we seemed to have finished the last of the papers. I had just typed it out and the old man was engaged in reading it and making corrections. Thank God, he has a very neat small handwriting so that I do not need to retype after he does his revision.

He laid down the last page and hoisted himself heavily to his feet. He lumbered over to the barrel of beer in a corner of the room and drew a pint for me and a quart for himself.

He lowered himself into his capacious chair and sucked back about half his mug. Then he dug through his pockets for his beastly little black pipe which he proceeded to fill with appalling brown plug and to light with a petrol lighter the size of a portable typewriter. When the vile fumes were climbing visibly and odorously around his head he sighed.

"We finished then, Max?" he asked and I nodded my head, "ah well, then we got nothin' to do. Let's go out an' find a murder. It's about time I had a bit o' holiday meself, don't you think?"

"Look here," I said, "I do not wish to get mixed up in murder again as long as I live. So far as murder is concerned I've had the matter. I want a quiet life with nothing going faster than the germination of a seed. I want to avoid all disturbances and emotional upsets for the rest of my life. I want peace."

He chortled quietly. "What ye want an' what ye'll get are likely to be two different things," he said.

I agreed rather bitterly, knowing that I had as much chance of standing up to the Professor as a gazelle has of opposing a charging buffalo.

"Well," I said cheerfully, "that being the case, we might as well get on with the *History*. There are no interesting murders in the papers at the moment—only burglaries with violence and such like. Even if there were any good murders, do you for one moment believe that the Bishop would let you in on them. His opinion is that you are as disruptive as a cyclone and rather less predictable."

The Professor winked heavily and drained the rest of his beer. He stamped heavily over to the barrel. I am not allowed to fill mugs at this holy place. Once, by accident, I jerked the barrel and the beer was undrinkable for the rest of the morning. Anything else might have been forgiven me, but not that.

"Max son," he said deeply, "there's always a good murder around if ye know where to look for it. It may be masqueradin' as accidental death or suicide, but once ye start rootin' around ye'll find that it's murder."

"God forbid," I said with all the piousness of which I am capable in my voice. The last case we had, had resulted in my falling heavily for the murderer, who had done her best to poison me off with the rest of the company. And I could not forget that but for the Professor's interference the case would have passed into history as one more accident from mixing up the Death Cap, *amanita phalloides,* with the common field mushroom. I had to admit to myself that Mary, that was the girl's name, might have murdered me if she'd got tired of seeing me around. It might not have been a perfect match. There was a lot of this in my mind, but all the same I could not say that I felt grateful to the old man for saving me from my fate.

I must admit too, that the Professor had been extraordinarily nice about things. He had somehow wangled it so that I was not called at the trial and he had given me a holiday. The holiday was the trouble. It had resulted in the chaos which I have just been describing.

He glowered at me across the room and picked up *The Times* which lay rumpled on the floor beside his chair. He retired behind it and I looked over some notes dealing with a piece of work I was doing on my own.

"Oi, Max," he grumbled suddenly, "did ye realise that that Museum o' Modern Art was openin' to-day? Ye got an invitation, didn't ye, an' now I come to think o' it, so did I, didn't I?"

This was a fact. Douglas Newsome, who had been mixed up in the murder to which I have referred, had sent us both invitations to the private-view. I had done my best to forget all about it, as I felt that, although I liked Douglas, I had better keep away from anyone who had been connected with the Death Cap case. There was no point in scrabbling at my wounds.

Not so Professor Stubbs. He is a great believer in the idea that things that are past are past. He forgets all about them. This enables him to assume an attitude of infallability. He always manages to forget his mistakes as soon as he realises them. The fact that other people do not forget he looks upon as a dirty trick played upon him by fate, and he will protest that it was a very small mistake, rather on the principle of the girl who had the illegitimate baby and told the parson that, after all, it was only a very small baby.

"Why didn't ye remind me?" he demanded, "ye know there's nothin' I like so much as a party. An' this sounds as though it might be quite a good party. Let's get goin'."

I was still unwilling to venture forth, but I knew that I would have to go. The one consolation would be that we would be frightfully late and would miss all the speechifying. I pointed out that, dressed in a pair of dirty flannels and a short-sleeved shirt, I was not sartorially in keeping with a private-view. Besides, I had been working so hard all morning I had not had time to shave.

"All right, all right," he grumbled, "if ye want to be fussy about little things like that, ye can be. Go on now an' change as quickly as ye can. I'll be waitin' for ye."

I wandered up the stairs to my rooms. As usual the chaos which had overflowed from downstairs seemed to have landed there. The trouble was that I had not had time to deal with my rooms, though I had dealt with the rest of the house, and during my absence my rooms seemed to have been used as a repository.

I had to move a pile of calf-bound volumes of Abstracts of the *Philosophical Transactions* of the Royal Society before I could get into the cupboard where I kept my suits. All the same, shaved and with my hair brushed, I was downstairs again in ten minutes.

I went into the large workroom and found the Professor just laying down the telephone. There was a positively fiendish look of glee on his face. I knew that something had happened.

"What's up?" I asked, more in hope than in expectation of receiving a satisfactory reply. He closed one eye in one of his special brand of winks which contorts the whole of his face. He is under the impression that he can wink without anyone noticing it. I have suggested that he does it in front of a mirror sometime, but he never seems to get around to taking that action. "What's up?" I repeated.

"Ye'll see," was all he gave me in reply, "are ye ready to get crackin', as I believe the sayin' goes? Ha' ye got yer winter woollies on an' are ye ready for all eventualities?"

"Yes," I said shortly. It seems to me that sometimes the old man's sense of humour stopped growing when he was in his preparatory school.

As I feared the Professor would not let me ring up for a taxi. He insisted that he would drive me himself. Being driven by Professor Stubbs is no pleasure, no pleasure at all. Men of far greater courage than myself have winced when offered a lift by the old man, and those of really supreme braveness have rejected the offer.

I climbed into the Bentley in fear and considerable trepidation. The old man crashed his gears with a careless abandon and we were off. Every time I travel in the car I think that hell can have no terrors worse than the journey I have just completed, and every time I realise that I have only reached the portal and that there are worse terrors to come.

As jaunts with Professor Stubbs go this one was only medium bad—they are all bad, but there are degrees of badness. I only shut my eyes about half-a-dozen times and each time he extricated himself from an apparently imminent death with a degree of luck which only he enjoys.

Bond Street, as usual, was crowded with traffic which crawled along at two miles an hour. It would have been too optimistic to hope that the old man would take his place in the queue. Not him, he cut in and out like a particularly agile snake. How he avoided the eyes of the traffic policemen I do not know. I never will know how he gets away with so much. He swivelled the car round a turning and we were in Iron Street.

I knew there was something the matter when I saw two long black cars drawn up in front of the glaring white tower of the Museum of Modern Art. The Professor drew up behind one of these cars, missing its back bumper by a distance which could only be measured with a micrometer.

A uniformed policeman stood between the Brancusi and the Moore carvings. There was a small crowd of idlers gathered in the street. The Professor piled out of the Bentley and I followed at a more leisurely pace. He went straight up to the policeman. I thought he would be refused admission, but he only hesitated for a second. I did not hear what he said but from past experience I would not have been surprised to have been told that he had said he was a special envoy from the Home Secretary. Professor Stubbs never lets a little thing like a trivial untruth stick in his way. We sailed through the white hall unencumbered.

At the end of the hall there was a lift. The Professor looked at it doubtfully and sniffed.

"We'll walk," he announced, "I never learned to trust these things. Once got stuck in one for two an' a half hours. Wi' three men bigger than meself an' none of us had room to move. We had to take turns at breathin'. Let's go up the stairs."

There was a little landing half-way up the stairs and the wall facing us looked as though it had been blasted by a rubbish heap. Tins and broken crockery were stuck in cement around Victorian valentines and horrible garish postcards conveying greetings for birthdays and so on.

I wondered what the idea was. The Professor glanced at the wall but made no comment. He puffed on up the stairs. On the landing there seemed to be a convocation in being. There were three or four police-men and several people in ordinary clothes. From these latter a familiar figure detached itself. It was Douglas Newsome.

"Hullo, Professor Stubbs," he said, "and you, Max. Thank God you've come. Come and have a drink."

"That," said the Professor heavily, "sounds like a sensible suggestion. I will have a drink."

We passed the uniformed policemen and went into a large gallery, hung with abstract and surrealist paintings. The place was pretty full. The crowd had gathered in a hard knot at one end of the room and at the other end there was a small collection, standing in front of a piece of drapery on the wall. I could see the plump figure of Chief Inspector Reginald F. Bishop. The Professor, I realised, saw him too, but he paid no attention. He lumbered heavily behind Douglas to a table laden with bottles and glasses. Behind the table there was a worried-looking waiter. Douglas obtained drinks from him.

The three of us walked up the long room towards the hanging drapery.

"My God," said Chief Inspector Bishop, wearily and rudely, "look who's here. Can't you keep away, John, just to oblige a friend? Where there's trouble I seem fated to find you. Who invited you along?"

"As a matter of fact," Douglas was nervous, "I'd invited Professor Stubbs and Max Boyle to the private-view and when this happened I rang up and asked if they were coming. The Professor said he was just starting."

"Umph," the old man grunted, "ye needn't look as though someone'd stolen your sweeties, Reggie. I got as much right here as ye have—more if it comes to that, for I got an invitation an' I'll bet ye didn't. Come on now an' tell us what it's all about."

The Chief Inspector looked exceedingly tired. This I knew meant that he had not yet found out all about the case.

"As a matter of fact, John," he said listlessly, "I've just arrived. It seems that this place," he waved his hand expansively, in such a way as to convey his impression that there was madness and madness and that this was the worst sort, "was being opened this afternoon and that one of the pictures, which had been newly acquired and not publicly shewn in this country was to be specially unveiled. Well, there was some nonsense about having a toy mouse pull the covering off it. That side of the business was worked by your friend there," he looked at Douglas, "and the veil came off all right. The trouble is that behind the veil there was not only the picture they expected to see, but also the body of a Mr. Julian Ambleside. He was, it seems, a well-known dealer in modern pictures and the picture was one which had been acquired from him. He was hanging by his neck and it seems that he had been dead for at least twelve hours. I haven't found out much else, yet. I haven't had time."

"Oy," said the Professor gustily, "was he murdered or did he string himself up?"

"That," the Chief Inspector was portentous, "is something about which we are not yet certain. But one thing is quite obvious and that is that if he hanged himself someone else covered him up with the cloth. He could not have done it himself."

There was a slight stir at the door and three men came in. One of them was carrying a rolled-up canvas stretcher. They came up to the Chief Inspector and waited for orders.

The Bishop looked around him and sighed heavily. "You'd better cut him down," he said.

The men advanced towards the hanging drapery. One of them gave it a twitch and it came down.

Hanging against a surrealist picture was the body of a short, little man with a frog-like face. At least it looked frog-like to me, but I could not say whether that was not to some extent due to the suffusion of his face.

One of the men put his arms round the body while another climbed on a chair, holding a sharp and efficient looking knife. He cut through the cord carefully a few inches from the top and the man below steadied himself to take the strain.

As the rope parted the corpse expelled some air with a horrible sound. I heard various people in the crowd at the far end of the gallery gasp with horror.

The man who held the body of Julian Ambleside lowered it carefully on to the stretcher which had been unrolled and placed in readiness by the third man. The police surgeon came forward and stooped over the body. Carefully, so as to preserve the knots in the rope, he loosened and removed it. He bent over the corpse more closely. He ran his hand over the dead flesh.

"Chief Inspector," he said suddenly, "take a look at this."

The Chief Inspector moved up beside him and Professor Stubbs who was never backward on such occasions came forward too. Seeing there was a general move in that direction I saw no reason why I should not also be a spectator of such mysteries as were to be propounded.

"If you examine the neck carefully," the police surgeon said, "I think you will agree with me that there is bruising which is not consistent with the rope alone. Of course, I cannot be certain, at least until I have performed an autopsy, but I would say that it is probable that this man was strangled before he was hanged. I might even go further and say that I think it is probable that he was manually strangled—that is that someone strangled him with their hands and not with a piece of rope or cloth."

"Careful cove, ain't ye, Joe," the Professor grunted, going down on one knee to have a closer look.

The police-surgeon grinned. "You have to be careful in my profession, John," he said. "It's all very well for you amateurs to jump to conclusions straight away. If I started doing that I'd land myself out of my job in a week."

Professor Stubbs was mumbling to himself as he examined the corpse. "I'd say ye were right though, Joe," he announced finally.

"That's handsome of you," said the police-surgeon, "I'm glad to find that you agree with me for once."

The old man looked up to see if the police-surgeon was laughing at him. That worthy kept a perfectly straight face, and the Professor seemed satisfied.

"How long did ye say he'd bin dead?" he asked, and the police-surgeon shrugged his shoulders.

"Over twelve hours at a rough estimate," he said, "you know how it is, you can't be accurate on these things to within an hour or two. It's only in thrillers that a doctor looking at a body can say that it was killed precisely at four-fifteen in the afternoon."

"Come to think of it," said the old man rudely, "I don't know what the police force employs doctors for. They'd get along just as well wi'out 'em, don't you agree, Joe?"

The little police-surgeon, who seemed to be determined that the Professor, whom he knew of old, should not ruffle him, grinned once more.

"No doubt, John, they would," he said, "but far better would it be if they could have a force made up entirely of Professor John Stubbs's, eh?"

The old man glared at him and straightened up. Down the room there came the most startling vision I think I have ever seen. It was a little woman dressed in a black cloak. She seemed to have been drinking. In one hand she held a large and very real-looking rat and in the other a half-empty bottle of lemon gin. She stopped half-way down the room to refresh herself.

Wavering slightly she went up to Douglas.

"Hullo, Douglas Cock, if that's your name," she said. "My guess is this rat did it. God knows what else it would have done if I hadn't caught it."

Even the Professor looked slightly startled by this intervention. He looked a large question at Douglas.

"This," said Douglas, "is Mrs. Carr. She is a hundred-and-two and she caught the toy rat when I let it go."

"Let's ha' a look," said the Professor reaching out for the rat. Mrs. Carr surrendered it unwillingly and the old man examined it carefully. I could see that it appealed to him. He is an absolute glutton for mechanical toys of all sorts. He insists that he has a mechanical mind. I suppose all great men suffer from some fallacious idea about their capabilities and this is Professor Stubbs's failing. "I must say, ma'am," he addressed Mrs. Carr politely, "that it was dam' plucky o' ye to tackle the thin'. I'd ha' let it go meself, but then I'm frightened o' rats."

"Oh, it's easy enough when ye know the way how," said Mrs. Carr helpfully, "to just swing 'em up and catch 'em by the tail in your teeth. Like this."

She proceeded to give a demonstration of the gentle art of rat-catching. I was so astounded that I could only look on in silence. The Professor seemed to be deeply interested. He took the rat from Mrs. Carr and tried to do as she had done. "Like this?" he asked.

"No," she said and did it again, "like this."

The Professor had another shot. Mrs. Carr looked sadly at her bottle and poured the few remaining dregs down her throat. She looked at the Professor's antics with disgust and shook her head.

"No," she said, "we'll never make a rat-catcher of you. Give me my rat."

The Professor surrendered it. He looked around rather guiltily at the group who, I could see, agreed with my feeling that with a corpse on the ground it was neither the time nor the place for lessons with a toy rat.

"Very interestin'," said the Professor, "well, where do we go from here? Who," he addressed the Bishop, "murdered this feller an' why? D'ye know yet? Come on, tell me?"

The Chief Inspector let his sleepy eyelids fall on his cheeks. He sighed. "My dear John," said said wearily, "if I knew who did this thing I would not be still here."

"I suppose not," said the Professor, "unless o' course ye were stayin' in the hope o' havin' a drink. Come to think o' it, now," his face brightened, "I could do wi' a drink meself. Be a good feller, Max, an' go an' collect one."

Accompanied by Douglas Newsome I went across to the temporary bar.

"What the devil is all this about?" I asked Douglas, "I feel as though I had landed in the middle of a lunatic asylum."

"You have," he replied gloomily, "and you've still got to meet the rest of the lunatics. Mrs. Carr is balmy enough but her son's worse. He did the decor on the stairs—you know the mess of potage and tinnage. I," he was slightly defiant, "like them though. They are the only people here who treat me as if I was a human being and not a repository of the fine arts or a drudge. You wait though till you meet Dr. Cornelius Bellamy. He'll put the fear of God into you. He is a superior person and he does not like me. My trouble is I'm not superior. I'll need to try taking lessons in it. If you'll take my advice we'll knock back a quick one here and take another drink back with us. We'll need it."

As Douglas suggested I had a drink at the table and took another back, along with one for the Professor who stood in the centre of the group, looking, in his baggy grey trousers, rather like an elephant surrounded by pygmies.

The stretcher bearers were pulling a white sheet over the remains of Julian Ambleside. They did not seem to be happy in their work. I handed the Professor his drink. He looked around rather as if wondering whether he should propose a toast. He decided against it and took a pull at the glass.

# Chapter 2

# The Joys of a Strange Hour

DR. CORNELIUS BELLAMY seemed to me to be a frightful ass. His long face only wanted a pair of long ears to complete the transformation. He sat in Emily Wallenstein's office looking pompous and benign. I'd rather he had looked anything else. He was carefully posed behind a desk of ebonite and steel. His finger tips were joined and he looked round us. His look conveyed two things; first that he did not like our company and that there was nothing which could be said in our defence and second that, if we had to ask questions (a point upon which he seemed doubtful) there was no person in the world so fitted to give us the correct and really appropriate answers as Dr. Cornelius Bellamy.

I dare say that I was wrong in feeling this before the man had done more than look at me with visible distaste, but in these accounts of the various exploits of my boss, Professor John Stubbs, I do my best to be pretty honest about my feelings. After all, I am usually around with the old man and so I meet the same people as he does and, as the reader sees him through my eyes, I don't see why he shouldn't have my feelings too. The intolerance which I display or the tolerance, may help him discount or justify my portrait of the Professor.

Anyhow, Dr. Bellamy sat there, looking as if the whole world might be wrong, but he was bound to be right. He examined the tips of his clean fingers and rubbed a slight roughening of one nail with the thumb of the other hand. He looked up at us as if we were a lot of juvenile delinquents waiting for judgment and his roving eye settled on the Chief Inspector.

"Ah, yes, Sergeant," he said and beside me I could feel the Bishop's fur beginning to rise, "Ah, yes, Sergeant," he repeated the offence, "I dare say that the surroundings which your—ah—vocation has brought you are most unfamiliar. After all," he appealed to the rest of the company, "we cannot expect the honest—ah—bobby," he looked at the Bishop as if inviting something in the way of applause for his witticism, "to appreciate the finer manifestations of the finest minds and imaginations of our time. I forget who it was—probably the late D. H. Lawrence—who observed that one of the most ridiculous sights known to mankind was the policeman as art critic. Well, Sergeant," he was interrupted by Professor Stubbs.

"Oi, man," the deep voice growled, "where were ye dragged up? The man's a Chief Inspector an' ye'd better treat him as such."

The Doctor was not crestfallen. He beamed at the Bishop in a friendly fashion.

"I beg your pardon," he said, in a voice that did nothing of the sort, "I am as you no doubt know a man of considerable, I may even say very considerable commitments, and, naturally, I can be expected to be exactly—ah—*au fait* with the ranks of the constabulary. I hope you will forgive my—ah—pardonable error?"

The Chief Inspector nodded briefly. It did not matter to him whether Dr. Bellamy addressed him as constable or as commissioner. He didn't care. All he wanted was the facts of the case and he did not mind where he got them.

"Well," the Doctor's words grated like a hacksaw blade on a piece of tungsten, "well, having got things, as I might say, on a reasonable basis, I feel that we may now make some progress. As I was about to remark, the humble policeman cannot be expected to know anything about the finer manifestations of such minds as he finds himself, thus fortuitously, thrust among. This Museum, a remarkable monument to the work of our time, owes its existence to the generosity and farsightedness of our hostess, Miss Emily Wallenstein," he bowed towards her and she flushed, "and we were met together to-day to declare the place ready for the reception of those enquiring minds and, let me say, eyes which have, for so long, been denied the right to gaze their fill upon the aesthetic productions of their time. In the preparation of the outward and visible essence of this Museum, Miss Wallenstein, I feel she would agree with me, can say that she has not been without her willing helpers. These people who gave of their best and did not count the cost," I felt he was making an appeal for a war-memorial, "included the—ah—late Mr. Ambleside. Mr. Ambleside, I feel I should tell you, was a gentleman of varied attainments. A collector of reputable works in his own right, he also, as a gentleman who lacked private means, chose to deal in such works as a pleasing way of living. Only those of us who knew him well," the Doctor sighed theatrically, "could have any idea of the pangs he suffered in parting with a supreme work of art. Anyone who bought, let us say, a blue period Picasso from Mr. Ambleside immediately became aware that they were buying more than a mere picture—they were buying a part of a man's soul. By the words 'mere picture,' Chief Inspector, I hope you will not consider that I am being insulting to the Landseers and Frank Dicksee's which adorn the walls of your, no doubt charming, suburban villa."

The Chief Inspector said nothing. I chortled quietly to myself, for I had rarely seen a man open his mouth so wide to cram both feet into it. I knew that the Bishop lived in a dignified eighteenth century house in Highgate and that one of the chief joys of his life was his collection of really first-class English water-colours. His dining room was hung with one of the finest selections of the two Cozenses, father and son, and of Francis Towne which I had ever seen, while a magnificent Girtin, above the fire in his study, was flanked by a Turner and a Cotman. On the stairs hung half a dozen sketches by Constable and Gainsborough. Completely unaware of his stupidity, the supreme Doctor blundered on.

"Of course," he said patronisingly, "I cannot expect you to know the names of modern painters, but I will have to inform you about one of these. This is an Italian, by the name of Giorgio de Chirico. So far as I and those who think like me are concerned, this man died in 1918. I believe," his voice carried no conviction, "that the gross body of the man, his let us say earthbound portion, still exists in some part of Italy. But that is of no importance to us. As a painter he died in 1918. But, and it is a large and important BUT, before that date this man Chirico managed to paint a certain number of pictures which are of inestimable importance to the history of the modern movement. No one, least of all myself, can attempt to gauge the importance of this mere handful of paintings. However, I think I can venture to say that no one, not even the great Pablo Picasso himself," his voice took on the hushed quality of one who enters a large and solemn cathedral, "has had greater or more beneficial influence."

I realised then that the Doctor had made up his mind that he was dealing with a parcel of ill-educated children. I thought I would say nothing about the fact that I had hanging on my bedroom wall in the Professor's house a pen drawing of a railway engine in a lonely and quite limitless square and that this drawing was signed, clearly and correctly, "G. de Chirico 1915." To mention that, I decided, would not only be tactless but it would rob me of a lot of fun. It was rather nice being treated as if one was a kindergarten child.

"The importance," the Doctor continued, "of these drawings and paintings cannot be over-estimated. But there have been rumours that all the paintings of the early period which we see cannot be strictly claimed as being genuine. In fact it is said that Chirico, finding during the nineteen twenties that there was something seriously amiss about his artistic vision, accepted the innocent suggestion of certain surrealist friends and painted copies of his works, in the effort to recapture the original innocence of his eye. This, you will no doubt say, seems harmless enough, but when I say that Chirico signed these paintings with the dates of the earlier ones, you will realise that deceit entered into their creation and that, even as copies, they became valueless to those of us who appreciate the true values of these things."

"Why," said the Chief Inspector, sleepily and guilelessly, "they were all painted by the same man, weren't they?"

"That," Dr. Cornelius Bellamy was pompous, "is something which I cannot begin to explain to you now, my dear Ser—I mean, Chief Inspector. The appreciation of the finer points of art is above your comprehension. You will merely have to accept my word for the fact that these copies are inferior to the originals. I cannot do more than tell you that as a fact. I could, of course, suggest that you read a certain number of books on the subject of modern art—my own contributions to the subject are not, I am told, altogether negligible," he coughed with a mock modesty, "but I fear, my dear sir, that you would need to learn more than comes from books before you could appreciate the difference between a real Chirico of the right period and one of the copies. As I was saying, these copies exist and a Mr. Francis Varley, whom you will no doubt encounter, started a ridiculous story that certain of the—ah—pictures in Mr. Ambleside's possession were not consistent with their dates. This idea naturally interested me, and I looked at the pictures, with which I was already familiar, again. I found that Mr. Varley was wrong in his contentions, which were characteristically rash and hasty, and that Mr. Ambleside's Chiricos were certainly all that they professed to be. However, I feel that a man of the, let us say sensitiveness of Mr. Ambleside might have been more deeply wounded by Mr. Varley's suggestion than any of his friends realised, and that this doubt, preying upon his mind, might have urged him to commit the awful deed of *felo de se*."

"Uhhuh," the old man leaned forward, "he hanged himself an' then he covered his corpse up wi' a decent bit o' cloth, eh? Think again, son, think again. It won't hurt yer brains to make 'em do some work, son."

Dr. Bellamy jumped as if he had been stuck with a long and very sharp pin. He looked at the old man as if he was something which had found its way out of a middle-aged cheese.

"Oh, yes," he said and his voice was superior, "I presume, my friend, that you have a right to speak about brains?"

I leaned back in comfort. I had an idea that I had a ringside seat for a really good fight. The old man snorted. He finished the drink in the glass in his hand. He looked at the glass and for one glorious moment I thought he was going to throw it at Dr. Bellamy. He laid it down.

"Yah, you baboon," he howled, at the startled Doctor, "Ye talk a whale o' a lot o' nonsense an' ye expect us to swallow it because we don't know yer jargon. An' then, to finish off yer tall story ye start to spin us a yarn about somethin' that couldn't ha' happened. I may tell ye, son, that I'll believe yer story about Ambleside committing suicide when I ha' a seat to watch ye hangin' yerself an' coverin' yer corpse up after ye're dead."

Unfortunately for my hopes, the Doctor recovered his composure and turned towards the Chief Inspector with a look which enquired whether the presence of the Professor was really necessary. The Bishop ignored this look. If he had thought of throwing the old man out of the room I wonder how he would have proceeded. Professor Stubbs would not have gone too easily.

"Ah, Chief Inspector," the tone was offended, "I hope you do not consider it wise to reject my carefully pondered suggestions with the—ah—light flippancy shewn by your friend here, who appears to me to be a hasty character, who has no ideas of how to work out a logical sequence of events. I will allow that he is correct when he says that it would have been impossible for Mr. Ambleside to—ah—drape the cloth over his body, but he was hasty. He did not wait until I had finished relating my theories. As you know doubt know, among artists we sometimes come across the neurotic personality who is not so well fitted to face the world as, let us say, you and I are. Well, I would like to suggest that one of these characters encountered the body of Mr. Ambleside hanging from the picture-hook, and, with an instinct common to such undeveloped persons, performed a primitive burial of it.

Naturally he could not dig a hole in the polished floor and so, seeing the cloth, he placed it in position. After all, my dear sir, you must agree that the burial instinct is one of the strongest instincts of humanity. You have just to watch a band of children who have found a dead sparrow to realise this. You should always, my dear Chief Inspector, remember these primitive instincts when you are dealing with any case the least out of the ordinary. Now, my dear sir, are you satisfied with my suggestion that the unfortunate Julian Ambleside became obsessed with the idea that his pictures were not genuine and that this obsession, preying on his mind drove him to kill himself?"

"No, sir," the Bishop opened his eyes the fraction of an inch as he spoke, "I can't say I'm satisfied. You see, sir," his voice was very gentle and quiet, "the police surgeon looked at Mr. Ambleside and on removing the ropes he found signs which indicated that Mr. Ambleside had been strangled before he was hanged."

Dr. Cornelius Bellamy looked startled. He pressed the tips of his fingers together so hard that the backs of his hands whitened.

"Nonsense, my dear sir," he said, "I can't believe that. I do not believe it. I refuse to believe it."

"Sorry, sir," said the Bishop, "but it is so, and nothing we can say can make it any different."

The Professor, beside me, was enjoying himself. He looked at the discomforted Dr. Bellamy as if he had been a plant suffering from some fungoid disease.

"Hum," he said, "Ho, so yer idea ain't worth a penny, Doctor Ho-hum. Ye may be a bright boy in yer own line, but ye'd better leave the rest to those who understand it. Ho, ha, you go suck a Dali."

Dr. Cornelius Bellamy glared at him. I myself would have glared if someone had told me to go and eat a Michelangelo. My sympathies were all with the Doctor, ass though he might be.

"My dear sir," the Doctor's tone was so lofty that he lost my little sympathy; it was like a beggar asking alms from a passer-by while he was on top of the Eiffel Tower, "My very dear sir, permit me to correct you. I am doing my duty as a citizen in striving to help the unfortunate police in the execution of their duty. I know these people, and our friend the Chief Inspector does not, therefore I do my best to supply him with reasons for this—ah—regrettable happening, which seem to be in keeping with the characters and personalities of the people involved therein. I do not know, my dear sir, who are you, nor can I say that I am very interested in the question of your identity. My remarks were addressed to this policeman and not to you, so I would ask you to restrain your ill-considered levity and to keep your unbecoming flippancy to yourself."

He might just as well have addressed his remarks to a bulldozer. The old man appeared to be vastly amused and pleased by them.

"That's the stuff, Clarence," he said vulgarly, "You shew 'em where they get off."

The Doctor gave vent to an explosion of irritation, faintly reminiscent of Miss Hotchkiss in ITMA when offered some new absurdity by Tommy Handley.

"Thank you, Doctor," the Chief Inspector was polite, "with regard to your suggestion that some person might have hung Mr. Ambleside after he was dead and covered him with that bit of stuff, I wonder if you could give me any hints as to who, had the circumstances been as you thought, might have done it?"

I noticed that the Doctor's habit of speaking in subordinate clauses seemed to have bitten the Bishop. Dr. Cornelius Bellamy seemed to become suddenly shy.

"Oh, I don't know," he said airily, "I am not in a position to, let us say, point the finger of suspicion at any single person. So many artists are so badly adjusted, and in this ill-adjustment lies their strength. Take," he seemed thoughtful, "young Newsome now. There is a young man of certain gifts, minor gifts one must confess, but still of a certain facile accomplishment. Yet when you look at him from the social angle you immediately realise that he is without any conception of social responsibility. He lives in himself and for himself alone. The world is an unpleasant reality from which he does his best to divorce himself. At a guess, I would say that, finding Ambleside dead he was quite capable of arranging the body beneath the drapery. It is the sort of unpleasant practical joke which would appeal to that young man's totally undeveloped sense of humour. He might even," the long face became even more pensive, "have heard me declare that art should be explosive and dangerous and that people require to be shocked into either appreciation or dislike, and, pondering this in his immature mind, have considered that his action would meet with my approval. You must realise, however, that I am very far from suggesting that Douglas did this thing. I am merely arguing a hypothetical case, to shew that, all circumstances being equal, he might have done it. My approach to life, I am afraid, my dear sir, is very different from your own. I approach all human actions from the point of view of the psychologist, while you have to judge from the actions themselves, without a thought of the conflicts behind them."

"I know Mr. Newsome," the Bishop said thoughtfully, "and I doubt if his character is as involved as you would suggest. He has always appeared to me to be a young man of an essentially simple though melancholic turn of mind."

Dr. Bellamy looked at the Chief Inspector. His long mouth fell open. "You know Newsome?" he asked incredulously, as if doubting the Chief Inspector's right to know any one from his superior world.

The Bishop nodded blandly. "Oh, yes," he said comfortably, "I know him all right, and I think I can say that I know what to expect from him under most circumstances. As you say, Doctor, he is quite capable of playing a macabre joke in the worst of taste—that is the sort of thing which would appeal to him—he is, you know, a great admirer of Beddoes's *Death's Jest Book,* and like Beddoes I fear he wants to reduce Death in rank by laughing at him."

Dr. Bellamy looked rather put out. I could see that he did not like being lectured by the Chief Inspector. If there was any lecturing to be done, it was fore-ordained that Dr. Cornelius Bellamy should do it.

"So," the Bishop was smooth, "having, for the moment, removed Douglas Newsome from the ranks, who else would you consider?"

"Well, now, let me consider," the Doctor looked like an analyst telling a patient to relax, "of course, there are a great many maladjusted people about any concern of this sort. Take Miss Wallenstein, even— the only—if I can put it that way—beggetter of this Museum. She is a spinster who has sublimated her natural desires in other activities, and, as you may know, the repressed character of this sort breaks out at intervals. On the other hand, however, I cannot see Miss Wallenstein murdering Julian Ambleside with her bare hands. Miss Wallenstein might, in a moment of some stress, have, let us say, stabbed Ambleside, but I doubt if, even had she the strength, she would have hidden him in a place like that."

The Doctor looked around us. I could feel the Professor getting rather restive beside me. I placed one of my feet heavily on his toe and he turned to glare at me. Dr. Cornelius Bellamy was not finished.

"Or," he said, "you can consider Mr. Francis Varley, the professional and eternal young man, the Peter Pan of our world. His maladjustment will doubtless grow greater with every grey hair he discovers in his head. I do not know what there was between him and Ambleside, but there was something. Of course it might be some trivial affair such as an agreement on Varley's part to write up Ambleside's pictures in return for some consideration, but they were always conversing and that they had something between them I think you will discover by asking any of the people who have been concerned in the preparation of the Museum. I have no doubt whatsoever, I think I may say, that if sufficiently roused, Varley would have been capable of killing Ambleside and would have carried out the rest of the pantomime."

The Professor lit his pipe with a sudden flare of his gargantuan petrol lighter. Neither the Bishop nor I were startled, as we were conditioned to the performance, but Dr. Bellamy turned his head sharply towards the old man, his expression plainly saying that if anyone did that again while he was lecturing he would ask them to leave the room.

The jerk of his head seemed to suggest something else to Dr. Bellamy. He chewed his lips unhappily for a moment. When he spoke his voice was slow and rather doubtful.

"As you know," he said, "I can make no guess as to who killed poor Julian. That is your province and not mine. But this senseless charade in hanging his body in front of the painting by Max Ernst worries me. It has just occurred to me that there is one more possibility. As you entered the gallery you no doubt noticed a wall decoration on the first landing of the stairs?"

He paused and the Professor puffed a cloud of nauseous smoke into the room before he grunted, "D'ye mean that junk-heap that's somehow defyin' the laws o' gravity an' stickin' on the walls?"

"Well," the Doctor was again benign, "if you care to put it that way you can. I can hardly expect art-criticism or appreciation from a man of your profession," I don't know what he thought the Professor did; I suppose he thought he was a strange sort of policeman. "To one trained in appreciation, like myself, that decoration expresses all the *zeitgeist* of the works in this Museum. It has a freedom from preconceived notions which lifts it into the class of inspired works. But, be that as it may, the decoration is the work of a young artist called Ben Carr whom I was privileged to discover employing his unique gifts on the walls of a deserted chapel in the East End. Being, if I do not flatter myself, a man of some little perspicacity, I immediately drew him to the attention of Miss Wallenstein, suggesting that she might offer him some employment more commensurate with his genius and gifts. I am glad to say that Miss Wallenstein thought highly of my suggestion and offered him the needful encouragement. Now, you must not for a moment think that I am suggesting that Mr. Carr had anything to do with this outrage, but I would suggest that, if he had found Mr. Ambleside lying dead in the gallery, the idea of hanging the body in front of a picture is just the sort of idea which would have made an immediate appeal to a man of his free and untarnished vision. After all, only the other day, he came to me with the suggestion that he should employ raw meat in the decoration of the ladies' lavatory, and I had to use, I may say, considerable tact in dissuading him from this no doubt laudable idea. Finding Ambleside dead, say, I fear that Carr, robbed of his expression through the use of raw meat, might have considered that he had found the ideal chance to, shall I say, get back at me for my interference. And once he had done the deed, I fear that the dear fellow is quite capable of having forgotten all about it. He is eccentric in the way that all the most free and uninhibited characters are called eccentric by the world, but there is not, I may say, any essential evil in his eccentricity. He has no repressions which need release. I, however unintentionally and with the worthiest of motives, may have been responsible for the creation of a repression, which he took the earliest opportunity of releasing."

He looked round at us again. I thought he looked pleased with himself. The Chief Inspector looked puzzled, as well he might. I was pretty puzzled myself, but then I had not encountered either Ben Carr or his work.

"That old woman with the rat," I asked, "would she be any relative?"

Dr. Bellamy shuddered with elaborate distaste. "That old woman," he said tartly, "is his mother. She is a disgraceful old harridan and old enough to know better."

"If she's a hundred and two, as she claims," the old man broke in, "she'd better start learning soon or she never will learn. I thought her a gay old girl an' she taught me how to catch rats. I've always wanted to know how these chaps go about the job. She shewed me, but," ruefully, "she says I'll never make an expert. Most disappointin,' most disappointin'." He relapsed into a series of unintelligible grumbles. I knew he was regretting the loss of the mechanical rat and I knew damn well that I'd have to find another, even if it meant crawling all over London on my hands and knees for it.

# Chapter 3

# Nostalgia of the Infinite

I WOULD hardly have called the interview with Dr. Cornelius Bellamy a piece of gay social intercourse. He was as solemn as an old dog and about as helpful, We were the students and we had to put up with his lecturing. And he certainly did lecture.

Professor Stubbs, rather to my surprise, sat there drinking it in as if he had all his life wished to be instructed in the less well digested parts of psychology. The Doctor invoked the ghost of Freud till that learned Viennese gentleman must have groaned in his grave, and the names of Jung and Horney were bandied about with a nonchalance that would have startled anyone but the old man.

I was glad when it was all over. The Chief Inspector, his heavy lidded eyes opening a slit, looked across at the Doctor, who still sat with his finger-tips pressed together.

"Well, Dr. Bellamy," he said politely, "I must thank you for all the trouble you have taken in telling us about these people. You have been most helpful. I do not think that I will need to detain you further."

"Thank you," the Doctor rose, "but before I go I would like to ask you whether you think that we should open the Museum to the public, as we originally intended, to-morrow morning? Would you, as the spokesman of the police, have any objection to our doing so?"

The Chief Inspector shook his head. "I have no objection at all," he said, "but I think I should warn you that you will probably find that the newspapers have got hold of this story and that fact, combined with the publicity the Museum has already received, will mean that you will be inundated with crowds of people who would not otherwise have come here You will probably find it difficult to control the crowds."

"My dear sir," the Doctor was patronising, "I have already thought of that eventuality. One cannot control the morbidity of the gutter-press, but one can at least control those whose ghoulish instincts prompt them to come and gloat over the scene of any untoward happening. I intend to ring the Corps of Commissionaires and ask for two large and strong— ah—fellows, to assist in controlling these sightseers. On the other hand, sad though I am that this should have befallen the unfortunate Mr. Ambleside, I may say that there is always the possibility that it may result in some converts to the cause which he had so much at heart—the cause of modern art. Some of those who come to gloat may stay to admire."

Coldblooded fish, I thought, but Professor Stubbs beamed.

"Eh, Doctor Ho-hum," he growled, "Ye might say that nothin' in his life became him like the leavin' o' it, eh?"

The Doctor bowed stiffly and left the room. The Chief Inspector waggled his hands like a pair of helpless flippers.

"Well," he said, without cheer in his voice, "here we are in the middle of another muddle. Here's a fine mad-house for you. So far as I can judge from what that chap says anyone here might have done the murder for the most trivial reasons. The reasons he puts forward are not such as would appear logical to a simple man like myself, and I've seen some pretty queer motives for murder in my day. What do you think, John?"

"I'd like a drink," the Professor complained, "I dehydrate so thun- derin' quick. But if ye ask me me opinion on the matter I'd say ye should discount most o' what that windbag blew at ye. He was shewin' off how clever he was. He's read all the blinkin' books an' he can't let ye forget it, not by a long chalk. I'd say that he is a bit worried himself, too. Did ye notice that?"

The Bishop nodded pontifically. "Yes," he said, "but I think that is only natural. After all Dr. Bellamy has dreamed all his life of a place like this," he waved his hand and it got tangled in a small Calder mobile hanging above him. "Damn it. Well here he is with his Museum of Modern Art and just as he thinks the balloon is going up good and proper some small boy sticks a pin in it. I'd have said he was more irritated than worried, myself."

"Perhaps ye're right," the old man grumbled and he stumped towards the door. "I'm goin' to see if I can find somethin' to slake me confounded thirst."

We left the Chief Inspector to his unhappy thoughts and went back into the gallery. It was deserted except for two figures beside the table which still carried an incredible load of drinks. One of these was Douglas Newsome and the other one I did not know. We went towards them.

"Hullo, sir," said Douglas gloomily on seeing the Professor. I noticed that he was drinking whisky out of a half-pint glass. "This is Mr. Carr. He knows all about interior decoration and horses. Mr. Ben Carr— Professor John Stubbs."

Mr. Carr lifted a glass to his lips. "Here's to you," he said, "and plenty of murders, old cock. How is the trade in death—does it flourish and will it bloom this year?"

I thought that Mr. Carr was going a bit far. The inappropriate use of quotations was Douglas's prerogative.

The old man looked pleased, however. He snorted violently. He blew his nose with a noise like the last trump on a brilliant bandanna handkerchief.

"Oh," he said beaming, "it goes fine. It'll ha' plenty of flowers soon. How's interior decoratin'?"

"Ruddy awful," said Mr. Carr gloomily, "all they want is plenty of rubbish spread on their walls and I can't find original rubbish. You'd think that a few old tins and scraps of paper would do, wouldn't you? Well, not a bit of it. They all want bits of rubbish that you can't find. Bits of rubbish that don't lie around every junk-heap. What they want is the junk of a museum and not the junk of a household. Now I tell them that the junk of a household is much more significant. 'Significant'," he repeated the word admiringly, "good word that. I learned it from the Doc himself. But do they want significance? No! Have a drink."

He leaned over and found a bottle of sherry which he practically emptied into a mug. All the glasses on the table were of a reasonable size, but Douglas and Mr. Carr seemed to have gone in for glasses of a more thirst-quenching capacity.

Douglas caught my eye looking at the glasses. "These," he said in a sepulchral tone, picking two of them up, "come from the Department of Industrial Design. Mr. Carr and myself came to the conclusion that it was a pity to let all this drink evaporate on the table, so we're trying to save it from that fate, but we wouldn't have got far with the ordinary glasses that they'd laid out for the guests this afternoon. So we went and raided the Industrial part—the only good thing that can be said for it is that there are plenty of glasses of all sorts. I," he sounded more miserable than usual, "wanted to take one that held a litre. But Carr, here, said that it would be immoderate. What do you think?" He appealed to the old man.

"Moderation in all things is excellent," said Mr. Carr before the Professor had time to answer, "remember that, Douglas cock, and you won't go far wrong."

The Professor shook his head solemnly. "I must say," he grumbled, "that I like a drink that's a drink. I can't do wi' yer fiddlin' little la-de-da glasses. I like a mug meself."

Douglas looked even more miserable and finished his glass. With a complete disregard for his interior he filled the glass with the remains of the sherry.

"Harumph," Professor Stubbs snorted, "I came here to ha' a drink. Ye know I dehydrate hellish quick? Well, I do. But since I'm here I might as well find out a few things about the death o' Julian Ambleside. Mr. Carr, now, would ye mind tellin' me if ye killed Julian Ambleside?"

This direct approach did not seem to embarrass Mr. Carr at all. He looked thoughtful, as if he was trying to remember something. It was at least half a minute before he answered.

"No," he spoke slowly, "so far as I can remember I didn't kill him. I feel sure I'd have remembered if I had. You see, I didn't know him well enough and I feel sure that you've got to know someone very well before you murder them. No. I didn't kill the poor fish."

The Professor nodded his head heavily and the mop of grey hair wagged up and down on top of his scalp.

"I thought ye didn't, son," he said comfortably, "but now 'ud ye mind tellin' me if ye found him dead an' hung him up as a kinda decoration?"

Mr. Carr looked even more thoughtful. He took a short and rough looking cheroot from his waistcoat pocket and stuck it in the corner of his mouth. He lighted this carefully before he replied.

"No," his voice was regretful, "that was an idea I didn't think of. It's a pity, isn't it? He'd have looked tasty stuck to the cement in the ladies' lavatory, wouldn't he? Particularly after the flies began to get at him."

This seemed pretty unpleasant to me and so I helped myself to another drink. A rather more moderate size of drink than those which the others were taking.

"Say, Prof old cock," Mr. Carr suddenly brightened, "do you play cards at all? We could get up a nice game if you do."

"Don't play cards with him," Douglas was sombre, "all his cards are marked and he's bound to win. Not that it does him any good."

"Not half it don't," said Mr. Carr, who apparently did not resent Douglas issuing warnings against his cards, "I win packets. I don't play unless I think I'm going to win packets. I take them home with me. I go into the place with the money dripping from me like dew, and what happens—I ask you?—why, Maggie, she's my concubine—she takes it all off me at dice. I keep on saying that I'll either have to get a new woman or a new set of dice, but I never get round to doing anything about it. I'm lethargic, that's my failing."

So far as I could see the proceedings were about to degenerate into a common boozing party, not that I'm averse to boozing at the right time, but it seemed to me to be a bit early in even the old man's investigations for that. I looked at him disapprovingly. He was completely enthralled by Mr. Carr.

"Um," he said solemnly, "an', if it's not too personal a question, what started ye interior decoratin'. I mean is it a vocation in the same kinda way as goin' into the church, or do ye just suddenly discover ye've got a gift for it?"

Mr. Carr closed one eye. He was as solemn as Professor Stubbs.

"To tell the truth," he said cheerfully, "I just sort of drifted into it. Speaking technically I'm an inventor. I invent the sort of little gadget which makes the housewife's task less of a burden. If I'd come early enough on the scene I'd have invented the safety-pin and possibly even the whistling kettle. I like gadgets and there aren't enough of them in the world, so I have to invent my own ones."

Hell, and likewise damnation, I said to myself, now we've got onto the subject of gadgets nothing on earth will pull the old man away. I made a feeble effort.

"I say," I said with the bright hopelessness of a vacuum cleaner salesman, "have you managed to find out yet when Julian Ambleside was last seen alive? It seems to me that if you could discover that you might be able to get a line on the murderer."

"Eh?" he scowled at me through the gap between the tops of his steel-rimmed glasses and his grey bushy eyebrows, "Eh? Oh, there's plenty o' time for that. No need to hurry. That," his voice took on a complaining tone, "is the trouble about ye, Max. Ye're always in such a thunderin' hurry to get over things. Me, I got the scientific mind, an' so nothin' comes amiss to me. Anythin' may be o' some importance. Ye'll never know. Now, Mr. Carr, ye were tellin' me about yer inventions. What d'ye think is the best o' 'em?"

Mr. Carr looked down at his glass. His face contracted with the bitter agony of intense concentration.

"I'd say," he said it slowly, "that my best idea was a combined shoe-tree and polishing outfit, designed for the traveller. You see, I have always noticed how much waste there is in the body of a shoe tree and I have always found, too, that whenever I go away and pack some stuff to do up my shoes when they get dirty, that there's no end to the mess. You know, you get boot-polish in your toothbrush and you try and clean your teeth or shave with Meltonian cream. So I solved the problem. I just have hollow ends to the shoe trees and all the cleaning materials live inside them. Simple, isn't it? You'd have thought it would have made me a fortune, wouldn't you? Not a bit of it. Nobody is interested. The only maker of shoe-trees with whom I had an interview said that he didn't carry cleaning stuff with him when he went away. His shoes were cleaned by the staff of the hotel where he happened to stay. Disgusting, that's what I call it."

"Eh?" said the Professor, "As for livin' our servants can do that for us, eh?"

"Exactly," said Mr. Carr, still registering the extreme of bitter and unfathomed disgust. "But that's not all. I invent thousands of things, but there's always something wrong with them. Why I spent four years making a typewriter to write in Chinese, and that meant I'd already spent five years getting a smattering of the language. It was a beautiful machine, as big as a house, though. They said it wasn't very portable, but then it wasn't meant to be portable. You can't carry all these characters in a pint-pot. You could, though, have moved it about in an average railway van, and then all you had to do was to plug it in to the nearest electric light plug and there you were. You just picked your character and pressed the key and it came out clear. As you can imagine, Prof, it was no easy job making a typewriter which not only had all these characters, but which also began on the right hand side of the page and went, so's to speak, backwards."

I had a momentary and pleasing vision of Mr. Carr astride a typewriter the size of a newspaper printing machine, vainly hunting for character number 1700.

"I also," Mr. Carr was modest, "invented a new language. It was a peach. A winner. I could speak it perfectly and I taught my boy, Hurley, to speak it too. We got along top-hole. There again though, there was something wrong. Nobody else seemed to be able to learn it. It really was so much better than Volapuk or Esperanto and Basic English and all the rest. It sounded so nice."

So far as detection was going it seemed to me that I might as well just call it a day. I beckoned to Douglas and he drifted away from Mr. Carr. We made a great shew of looking at the pictures on the walls. While we looked I did my best to get some information out of him, but it really seemed that he did not know very much. He did, however, tell me that a painting by Chirico had been destroyed and that it was a picture which was of doubtful authenticity. I stored this bit of information up in my mind and wondered why nobody had thought of telling us about it earlier. It seemed to me that perhaps it might have some bearing on the murder.

The Professor was laughing heartily. He shook like a gargantuan jelly and the noise of his bellowing was most unseemly. I walked back to see what the joke was. Mr. Carr had just been telling him about a friend of his who had undertaken to dress a flea as a clown. He had got the pants and cap on beautifully and had generally painted up the flea, but when he put on the coat, which had taken him a week to make, the flea died—the coat was too tight—and he couldn't find another flea the right size, let alone one that was trained.

"Who d'ye think murdered Julian Ambleside?" the old man said suddenly. Mr. Carr looked preternaturally solemn.

"Oh, Dr. Cornelius Bellamy," he said, "perhaps, or any one of the rest of us. It might have been me, but I don't think so. It might have been Douglas here, but I don't think so. It might have been dear Emily, but I don't think so. No. I pick Dr. Bellamy."

"Why do you pick Dr. Bellamy," the old man was interested. Mr. Carr did not hesitate.

"Hell," he said, "he's an outsider. There'd be no money in backing a favourite would there? Always go for a strong outsider, that's what I say, and you can't go wrong. All you can do is lose your money, but you'll do that anyhow, so what's it matter?"

This struck me as good a way of finding murderers as most which I had seen Professor Stubbs try. I said as much. He glared at me as if I had insulted him horribly.

"All right, Max, all right," he growled, "you just wait till ye're murdered an' yer dry blood is cryin' out for vengeance on the dusty earth. (Nice that, ain't it? I got it out o' Kiplin.') Then we'll see if I bother meself to try an' find out who killed ye. Bah!"

This was not an impressive come-back, but I let it ride. There seemed to be no point in starting arguing with the old man when he was so very obviously enjoying himself in the company of the eccentric Ben Carr.

Miss Emily Wallenstein, escorted by Francis Varley, came into the gallery. Miss Wallenstein looked tired and worried. She came towards us. Douglas seemed to try to pull himself together. It was clear that he was more than a little drunk.

"Good afternoon," Miss Wallenstein looked at us vaguely, not recognising us. Douglas hastened to perform introductions. There is nothing, I think, that he likes so much as introducing people to one another.

"Oh yes," she said, and her voice still sounded far away, "you are Douglas's friends who are going to try and help clear up this dreadful affair, aren't you?"

Professor Stubbs bowed in a courtly manner. "Ye're quite correct, ma'am," he said heavily, "I hope ye don't mind us samplin' yer hospitality at a time like this. The trouble wi' me is I got a kinda kiln inside me which drys me up thunderin' fast."

"Not at all," she said listlessly, "not at all. Do have another drink if you want one. Just help yourself."

Francis Varley helped himself to a drink. He was a very smartly, or perhaps that is the wrong word, well dressed man of about forty-five. His clothes somehow managed to look expensive without seeming to fit him too well. His carefully dressed hair was greying and he gestured rather nervously with long white hands, which fluttered to and from his tie like pigeons on Nelson's Column.

"Douglas, my dear fellow," he said and his voice was cultured and soft, "The learned Doctor has decided that the gallery will open as arranged to-morrow morning."

"My God," said Douglas blankly, putting his hand to his head, "the blessed Assyrians will come down like wolves on this fold. God help us all, said Tiny Tim."

"Etcetera," said Mr. Carr, "Etcetera, and in case you missed my meaning, etcetera again."

"How the devil," Douglas ignored the interruption, "are we going to control the crowds."

"My dear fellow," Varley was smooth, "you can trust the Doctor to see to that. We are to have a couple of stalwart commissionaires."

"Yes," replied Douglas, "I suppose they'll help, but God knows how I'll manage up in the library by myself if they start swarming in on me."

"To shew you that I also was at school," it was Mr. Carr, "I suggest that I and my mother come as supporters to your Horatius act."

The idea that he was to have the company of Mr. Carr and his mother did not seem very attractive to Douglas. He poured himself a very large drink. Miss Wallenstein noticed the glasses we were drinking out of.

"Oh, Douglas," she said, "you are naughty. I believe you've been raiding the industrial section?"

"My fault entirely," Mr. Carr spoke up, "I got the glasses. I don't think Douglas knew where I got them. I certainly did not tell him."

After this there was nothing Douglas could do but accept Mr. Carr's offer of support upon the following day. I had to admit that he did not look overjoyed at the prospect, but then I have rarely seen Douglas looking overjoyed at the prospect of anything at all.

"I trust, Professor," Miss Wallenstein turned to the old man, "that you will again visit us in happier times, when you will have a better chance to appreciate the works on the walls. Oh, I wouldn't have had this happen for the world. The newspapers have been so horrible about the Museum already. They said that this beautiful building was a shameful desecration of the eighteenth century dignity of Iron Street. Just," she sounded indignant, "as if the writers had never walked down the street and seen the horrible vulgarity of some of the shops and the Victorian public house at the corner." I noticed that the Professor's face cheered up as he thought of the public house; though he will drink anything that is offered to him he is a beer-drinker by nature and by inclination.

"I cannot bear to think," her voice was a trifle shrill, "what they will say to-morrow. They will seize upon this unfortunate man's death as a sort of proof that there is something wrong with modern art. Oh, I do wish that this hadn't happened."

"Tell, me, ma'am," the Professor was polite, "can ye think why any-one would ha' wanted to kill Ambleside. He seems to ha' bin a harmless enough fellow an' an honest enough dealer. That's right, isn't it?"

"Certainly," Miss Wallenstein was positive, "Julian Ambleside had his peculiarities and difficulties, but as a dealer he was absolutely honest. Why, if he had the slightest doubt about a picture he was quite unwilling to sell it. He used to take a great pride in the fact that his reputation was absolutely untarnished, and that any picture which he sold was certain to be absolutely correct. I do not know why anyone should have wanted to kill him. In fact I cannot believe that anyone did kill him. Do you think that he could have had a heart-attack and that some spiteful person could have hanged him up like that just to damage the Museum?"

"I'm afraid not, ma'am," the Professor was firm, "there seems to be no doubt that he was manually strangled by some person, and I'm afraid that we'll have to find out who that person was."

I noticed that Francis Varley seemed about to say something, but that he also seemed to change his mind. I made a mental note of this for future reference if needed. Douglas also looked as if he wanted to speak. The Professor saw that Douglas was pregnant with some thought. He made no sign of this.

"Do you think," he addressed Miss Wallenstein, "that any unauthorised person could have got into the gallery?"

"No," Miss Wallenstein was positive, "we had a most unfortunate occurrence here which resulted in the destruction of one of the pictures and, after that, I made certain that no one would be allowed in who was not fully connected with the Museum. For the last two days no person could have got in unnoticed and unchallenged."

"Um," the Professor looked thoughtful. Rather to my surprise he did not ask what was the occurrence to which Miss Wallenstein had referred. "Um. Can ye think o' any person who had any grudge against Mr. Ambleside who also had any opportunity to enter the Museum, eh?"

Miss Wallenstein looked puzzled. "No. That is what I can't understand. I cannot think of any one who would wish to kill Julian. Of course there were people who had disagreements with him about pictures, but they weren't serious, were they, Francis?"

Directly appealed to like this Francis Varley seemed startled. He fingered his white, blue-spotted, bow tie before he answered.

"No," he said absently, "they weren't serious. I have disagreed with him myself but I didn't murder him. No, they weren't serious. I liked the old frog."

Emily Wallenstein looked slightly shocked by Varley's description of the dead man, and then she smiled for the first time.

"You are terrible, Francis," she said with something approaching a giggle, "You never mind what you say."

Varley smiled in a friendly way. "All the same," he said, "I can think of reasons why someone might have murdered Ambleside."

Mrs. Carr, weaving like a top, came into the room. She spied her son and sailed towards him, her black cloak billowing out on either side of him.

"You're a fine one," she said, "leaving your mother to die of thirst while you drink your bellyful. There was I having a little snooze and you push off and leave. I'm sometimes sorry I ever had you."

Mr. Carr was unabashed. I noticed that his mother still clutched the mechanical rat to her bosom. It would obviously take a lot to separate her from it.

# Chapter 4

# Uncertainty of the Poet

I DO not know how it happened but when we left the Museum of Modern Art I found that we were escorted by Douglas. I gathered that the old man had invited him to come home to dinner. It was none of my business, but I had not seen the Professor issue the invitation.

As I had expected, as soon as we got out of the door the Professor made a bee-line for the pub on the corner, called the *Ely Arms*. Douglas made towards the lounge, but the Professor was already ensconced at the saloon bar before he got started.

It is doubtful whether any doctor would have given an opinion upon the probable effects of large quantities of beer on top of the mixture we had already taken. No doctor was asked for his opinion. We just had the beer. I must confess that I did not want beer, but I might as well have addressed my murmured refusals to the porcelain beer-pump as to the Professor. The beer appeared and I had to drink it.

Douglas opened his mouth to say something but the old man fixed him with a basilisk glare which turned him solid. "If ye're goin' to speak about murder," he roared, "don't." Everyone in the pub looked round. "It'll keep. Tell me this though. Are ye happy in yer work?"

This sounded rather like the beginning of one of these "let me be your father" advertisements. Douglas grinned uncomfortably.

"Oh," he said mournfully, "it's all right, you know. Better than most jobs. The trouble," he was confidential, "is I don't really like jobs at all. I'd much rather just wander around and think, and write when I want to, but, unfortunately, I've got no money at all of my own and I do need to earn whatever I need. I expect this Museum will be pretty average hell for the next day or two—perhaps," he did not sound hopeful, "even for a couple of weeks, but—if the learned Doctor doesn't get me sacked—it should settle down eventually and then I'll be able to do some of my own work in the library, particularly if Emily gets me an assistant as she has promised to do. I will say that for her, she spares no expense. I asked if I could have a typewriter and she got me a silent one so I could use it without interfering with people who are trying to read. I want to retype all my poems—if I can find them— as I've got a publisher who'd like to do all my poems in one book. I don't know why."

When we had engulfed what the Professor considered to be a suitable amount of beer, we climbed into the Bentley and made our perilous way back to Hampstead. The Professor, as usual, frightened me into fits. I think Douglas must have been some sort of fatalist as he seemed to enjoy the ride without a thought of its dangers.

In the hall the Professor met Mrs. Farley, his housekeeper. She was obviously waiting for us.

"Chief Inspector Bishop rang up," she said rather breathlessly, "he says he'll come round after dinner to see you, unless he hears to the contrary."

"Family gatherin', eh?" said the old man, looking pleased with himself. There is nothing he likes so much as getting a small collection of people together and letting himself go.

"Dinner will be ready in about half an hour," Mrs. Farley said and went through the door that separated her part of the house, which is as clean and tidy as you could wish, from the part where the Professor's love of chaos runs riot.

The big room, despite its appalling untidiness, looked comfortable. Mrs. Farley had kept a cheerful log fire burning in the big open fireplace. The Professor, having discarded his outdoor clothes, poured out drinks and placed himself carefully in his large chair. Douglas and I took up our positions in other chairs, after removing piles of learned periodicals and books ranging from thrillers to the works of seventeenth century scientific divines.

From his pocket the old man took his little pipe. The ritual of preparing this for action always fascinates me.

He first of all scrapes out the bowl with a small pearl-handled knife he keeps for the purpose and then, satisfied that it is all clean within and without, he fishes in his waistcoat pocket for a piece of brown plug tobacco, which he carefully shreds into the palm of his hand. He rubs this tobacco between his hands and then tilts it into the bowl of the pipe, cleaning out the fragments that have stuck between his fingers. The bowl of the pipe full he then tamps the vile stuff down with his thumb and inserts the stem between his teeth. To light the thing he employs an immense petrol-lighter which looks as though it was the father of all petrol-lighters. Until the war he used to use old-fashioned fusees of the sort which fizzled violently for nearly half a minute, but somewhere or other he picked up this lighter and discarded the hard to obtain fusees.

Once the pipe is giving forth its volcanic fumes and the eruption is taking place around his head, he seems comfortable.

"Tell me, Douglas," he boomed suddenly, his voice appearing even larger than usual in the silence of the large room, "Who d'ye think did the murder? Can ye think o' anyone who might ha' done it for any reason at all?"

Douglas looked thoughtful. He creased his forehead and then shook his head. "I wouldn't know," he said, "but there's been a lot of funny stuff going on in the Museum. Photographs have been disappearing and then there was that Chirico."

"What Chirico, and what photographs?" the old man demanded, and Douglas gave him an outline of the story which he had already told me. The Professor ran his fingers through his grey hair, making it look more like a much-used floor-mop than before.

"Hmm," he said slowly, "that's interestin'. Ye say that Varley was kinda positive that the picture which was destroyed was not all that it seemed to be? That there was somethin' phoney about it, eh?"

"Yes," said Douglas, but he wavered and then went on, "but you see the trouble about Francis is that he is always thinking up ideas like that. He gets an idea into his head and he will keep on at that idea till nearly everyone, except himself, is fed to the teeth with it. Francis is one of those people to whom a painting is more important than a human being. He says that you can tell whether a painting is genuine by just looking at it. Roughly his idea is that a picture provides a sort of photograph of the mind of the painter at the time when he painted it, and that, if you know enough about the painter at that time—which means reading his letters and all the rest of it—you can date that picture to within a few weeks. A forgery, no matter how carefully and well it is done, gives a kind of picture of a different man—usually a dishonest one. Well, you take the case of the Chirico, Francis says that everything about it indicated that it was painted nearly ten years later than it claimed to have been painted. He said it was painted by a man who was almost a completely different man from the chap who painted the pictures in 1916 and 1917. I wouldn't know myself, for you see I'm not an art expert. In fact I don't quite know how I got the job of librarian in an Art Museum. I suppose it was just that I was around, doing nothing, at the time when Emily wanted someone, so I got the job."

"Well, then, I suppose," the old man rumbled, "there was a fair chance that Varley was kinda right in his supposition that the Chirico mightn't ha' bin as genuine as it was supposed to be?"

"Yes," said Douglas, "there's always that chance, but, you see, a good many of Francis's mare's nests have proved to contain nothing but mares, after all. The trouble about that picture, though, was that Emily had bought it from Julian Ambleside and Francis succeeded in getting Julian pretty well muddled up about it. He started to worry very badly about it. I know, because he spent hours in the library poring over all the repros of Chirico which he could find. That was how I discovered the loss of the photos. Dr. Bellamy insisted that the picture was all right, but then he would have to, as he had advised Emily to buy it. You know that he has been her adviser in chief? And you have also probably found out by this time that it doesn't matter who is wrong, for Dr. Cornelius Bellamy is bound to be right. If he was to be proved wrong he would go flat like a badly baked cake, all soft sticky dough inside. I don't like the Doctor," he was frank, "but I must say that he really does know his stuff. He is not very often wrong. When he says a picture is a good one he is usually right. My trouble is that I find his books are quite unreadable. I only look at the pictures in them. But I'd never pretend that I knew enough to contradict the Doctor about anything."

"Um," the old man bent over his beer mug, "but you know, Douglas, there must ha' bin someone who had reason for killin' Ambleside. Take yerself, f'r instance, did ye like him?"

"Oh, I don't know. He was all right. A bit of a nuisance, of course, when I was trying to get the library going, but polite and willing to understand that I could not do everything to help him, as I had not got all the books arranged and catalogued. He was much easier to get on with than the Doctor was. I forgot to include the Doctor's books in the little bibliographies I made in the catalogue of the Museum and you'd have thought I had done it intentionally. No, I can't say that I'd ever have had any reason to bump Julian off. I nearly batted him one when he got out of the lift and left me to carry a lot of books into the library by myself, but that was just a passing irritation."

"Uhhuh," the old man nodded, "that's fine. Now will ye tell me what ye know o' the Carr's, mother an' son?"

"Sweet damn all," said Douglas, "he's a pet of the Doctor's and she's his mother. She claims to be a hundred and two, but I don't believe it.

I'm not sure that I believe anything that either of them says. Ben Carr has told me stories which are quite impossible and his mother is as bad. I think that they live in a sort of mad dream world where everything is topsy-turvy, and that they cannot appreciate the ordinary life around them. Ben Carr is very amusing, in small doses, and he certainly seems to know about horses, for he took five bob off me and then gave me pounds and pounds as my winnings. He always seemed to be able to get money when he wanted it, but he complains that the woman he lives with uses crooked dice and wins all his money off him. I don't know if it's true."

"Ho," the old man seemed to have an idea, "you don't think that he could be blackmailing anyone, do you? I never yet heard o' a man who could consistently make money out o' backin' horses, did ye, Max?"

Addressed thus suddenly I thought hard. No, I was forced to admit, I had never known anyone who had managed to make money regularly out of horses. My own experience had been that I lost every time I tried to back a horse. My only lucky bets had been when I had picked a horse for the sake of its name, and it seemed to me that that was about as good a system as any, except picking them with a pin.

"I doubt if Carr would blackmail anyone," Douglas said, "you see, as I've said, he lives in a sort of dream world where things like money don't matter. He's just as happy when he has to borrow half a crown as he is when he is dripping with pound notes. I don't think that he'd bother to descend to blackmail. It would be too much like hard work. He likes the job of doing interior decorating because it gives him a chance to get along nicely while he is amusing himself. He is quite frank about the decorations he does. He just can't understand how or why people like his work. I can't say that I like it much myself. He told me that the idea was the property of one of his daughters who was amusing herself in a deserted chapel with stolen cement and a lot of rubble. He's got a simple mind and so he joined in. If the Doctor had not stumbled on him while he was making his lunatic grotto, he'd have forgotten all about it and would have been occupied the next day in inventing a new method of tying shoe-laces, or something of the sort."

"All right, then," the old man growled, "say we put the Carrs aside for the moment. How about Emily Wallenstein?"

"Good God," Douglas was shocked, "you don't mean that you think that she would have murdered Julian. I mean you just can't see her strangling him and then lifting him up and hanging him on that hook. I doubt if she's strong enough."

"You don't think she could have done it, eh?" the old man was thoughtful, "because ye doubt whether she'd ha' had the necessary strength. Well, I'd say that ye wouldn't need to be very strong to lift him up, an' that if ye came up behind him ye'd strangle him easy enough. He wasn't what ye'd call a big man an' he suffered from some kinda physical disability, didn't he?"

"Well," said Douglas, "I'd hardly call it that, but he did incline to move sideways, rather like a crab. I suppose that he must have had something the matter with him, for he never seemed to lift his feet very high, and his walk was peculiar. All the same I doubt whether Emily could have killed him, and if she had whether she'd have put him up like that. You see, the Museum is the realisation of all Emily's dreams, and I must say that I don't think that she'd have done anything which would have brought it into disrepute. You must have noticed how distressed she was at the very thought of what the papers will say, and, believe me, they'll say plenty." He looked slightly ashamed of himself and made a face. "As a matter of fact," he went on, "I really shouldn't have done it, perhaps, but I'm afraid that as soon as I had rung you up I thought of Alec Dolittle and got hold of him. I owe him one, anyhow, and I thought he might as well get in on the ground floor of what appeared to be a juicy murder as anyone else. After all, he is a friend of mine, and even in a case like this I felt I should help him. I told myself that it wouldn't make any difference, as the journalists were sure to get hold of the case anyhow, and I didn't see why Alec shouldn't get in first with the news. He deserves a break anyway."

The Professor nodded his head solemnly. I knew that he was thinking of the case of the Death Cap mushrooms when we had all suspected Alec Dolittle unjustly and, I am afraid, had let our suspicion shew in our treatment of him. I didn't mind Alec having a break at all, but I found that I still could not think of the case without pain.

Mrs. Farley announced that dinner was ready. We went in. During dinner the old man did not refer to the death of Julian Ambleside, and instead told stories which seemed just as improbable as those of Mr. Carr.

After dinner we again retired to the large room, and had not had time to do more than settle down before Chief Inspector Bishop was announced.

"Hullo, John," he said sleepily, but I knew that these weary eyes had noted with satisfaction the bottle of brandy laid out for him, as he is not a beer drinker. "It's quite like old times isn't it? Gathered round the fire with a case to crack. Have you made up your mind who did it and why?"

The Professor growled and snorted. "Gi'mme time," he said, "I just started this afternoon an' here ye are askin' me to gi' ye the murderer already. No, I don't know who done it," his voice was angry, "but I got me ideas, lots o' ideas."

"I've never known you without them," the Bishop said comfortably, "ideas are your stock in trade. It doesn't matter if they are good ideas or if they are rotten ones, you've always got plenty of them. Mostly, I must say, crazy."

"Hoo," the Professor hooted, "me have crazy ideas? Ye're shewin' yer thunderin' ignorance o' the way me mind works. I ha' nothin' but good ideas. That they don't always work out," he complaining, "is not me fault. It's just what me friend Merrivale 'ud call the innate perversity o' things. I got the scientific mind, I have," he was as proud as a gorilla just about to beat its chest, "an' I like to see things clear all the way round. I do like to approach things impartial like."

"Yes, yes," said the Chief Inspector soothingly, "by assuming that perhaps the murder was committed by all the people in the case working together, or else by the people who could not have done it. The trouble with this case seems to be that every single person in that damned Museum could have done it. Even you," he turned to Douglas who looked slightly surprised, "could have done it. I don't believe that anyone there could produce a decent alibi, even," his voice was slightly bitter, "if that damned surgeon could give us some idea of the time of the murder, which he can't. He just says that the body had been hanging there for over twelve hours and that it was hanged very shortly after death, or even preceding it. He's a fine lot of help."

"Uhhuh," the old man grunted, "that's the trouble wi' doctors. They'll bet their boots on some things, but when it comes to anythin' ye really want to know they'll shilly an' shally, but all the same there's somethin' in what Joe says. Ye see it?"

"What?" asked the Chief Inspector in a voice that shewed that he expected no enlightenment from anything Professor Stubbs said.

"It means," the old man spoke heavily, "that I got to discard me nice idea that maybe one person did the murder an' another hanged the body up like a bit o' meat in a butcher's shop. I was rather hopin' that I could prove this as it would ha' simplified the case a bit. Ye see, the hangin' o' the body was an act o' fantasy an' not of concealment. There were plenty of other places where the body could ha' bin better concealed, but no, whoever hung it up there had a kinda idea that it would be unveiled along wi' the Max Ernst paintin'. The hangin' o' the body is the kinda joke that might ha' suggested itself to Mr. Carr. He's got a kinda likin' for puttin' things on walls an' I thought he might ha' found the body lyin' on the gallery floor an' played a joke wi' it. He is not one o' these people who'd be squeamish about dealin' wi' a dead body. What d'ye think o' that?"

The Chief Inspector helped himself to a long and expensive cigar and lighted it carefully before he replied.

"Naturally," he said, "we had realised that the surgeon's report meant that it was probable that the person who killed Ambleside and the person who hung him up were one and the same, but I would hardly have thought of describing the hanging of the body as a joke."

"O' course it was a joke," the old man was indignant, "can't ye see that whoever hung it up also knew that the picture was to be unveiled durin' the course o' the afternoon, an' they assumed that it would be a shock. It was, in a way, a kinda clever idea. There was obviously no point in hidin' the body o' Julian Ambleside somewhere in the Museum. It would be sure to come to light before long, so the murderer hung it in a place where he knew it would be secure for a certain number o' hours an' would not be discovered before it suited him."

"Oh, I don't know," Douglas broke in, "if I hadn't been kept so damned busy all morning I'd probably have tried out the veiling and the toy rat. You see I was to let the thing go at the right moment and it would have been a pretty average farce if the rat had dashed across the room and had not pulled the covering off the picture. I'm sure I'd have given it a trial, but I really was too busy to think about it. And, apart from myself, I think that someone else might have done the same, but we were all in the same boat and none of us had time to think about it until it was too late to start worrying."

"There, ye see," Professor Stubbs was triumphant, "whoever hung the body knew dam' well that, no matter what they intended, it was a safe bet that no one would ha' time to start fiddlin' wi' the drapery until the openin' an' the unveilin'. The body was, I think we can take it, discovered at the time when it was meant to be discovered an' not a moment before."

"All the same, John," the Bishop glanced along the brown cylinder of his cigar, "things may be as you suggest and the body may have been meant to be discovered when, in fact, it was discovered, but I don't see where that gets us. What exactly are you driving at?"

"Bah!" the Professor was exasperated, "Bah! What I'm drivin' at is that for some reason which we don't yet know, it was important for the murderer that the body must be discovered in that way an' at that time. Naturally, I don't yet pretend to know why this was so, but I got no doubts that once I start thinkin' about it, I'll find some reason."

The Chief Inspector looked amused. "No doubt you will, John," he said, "and if you can't find a reason you'll invent one and in some way known only to yourself, you'll persuade yourself that that is the only possible reason. Then, of course, you'll set to work to build up a case, a very fine case, no doubt, with only one trouble about it—the fact that it is completely wrong."

The Professor hoisted himself out of his chair. For a brief moment I thought and hoped that he was about to throw himself upon the Chief Inspector in a deathly grapple. I've been waiting for him to do this all along, but somehow, irritating though the Bishop may be, Professor Stubbs has not yet arrived at the violent stage. He lumbered heavily across to the beer-barrel in the corner and replenished our glasses.

"There's no teachin' you anythin', Reggie," he complained plaintively, "Here I am, solvin' yer cases for ye an' ye tell me I'm a dunderhead. How d'ye think I get me answers right? Guess 'em, eh?"

"No," the Chief Inspector was slow, "I'd hardly say that, but I would say that you build up cases upon the flimsiest grounds and that you are right by a process of elimination rather than by one of deduction. You quite solemnly build up a case against every single person connected with a murder and you forget how often these cases have been wrong, because eventually you proved to be right. You only remember that you were right in the end and forget the awful errors you make in arriving at your right conclusions."

"Bah!" the old man was scornful, "how often to-night ha' I got to tell'ee that I got the scientific mind. I look at things all the way round an' I got to work that way. I got to think it out by sayin' that if A did this then B did that, an' I gradually discard the solutions which I've shewn to be wrong."

"Yes," said the Chief Inspector, "but so many of your solutions look exactly right until they are carefully examined. Now I'll admit that your way of working does get you somewhere, but the trouble is that, before you arrive at the correct solution, you are apt to find a solution that works, or seems to work, and you announce that that is the correct solution."

The old man was hopping mad. He had just been accused of publishing results too early, before he had proved that they were right beyond all possibility of a doubt. I must say that my sympathies were with him. He is often wrong, but his wrongness is understandable. After all, in murder one is dealing with human beings who are infinitely variable and unpredictable, while in his scientific work the Professor is dealing with plants with more or less predictable mutations and consequently results which are more capable of being worked out logically.

He sunk the whole of his quart of beer in one ferocious swallow and stumped over to the barrel to replenish the mug. The face which he turned to the Chief Inspector, who sat innocently enjoying his cigar and brandy, was a mixture of injured martyrdom and fury.

"Bah!" he said, "an' Bah again. Ye got no conception o' how ye think I work. Just because ye can track down a murderer who leaves his signature on the case, ye think ye're a mighty fine feller an' can do everythin' by yerself. Yet, when ye get a difficult case ye come crawlin' to me an' askin' me to gi' ye a hand out. Bah!"

He had voiced his favourite fallacy which is that the police keep on asking him for advice. This is quite untrue, and I think he derives the idea from his reading of thrillers, but there is no doubt that where there is an interesting case it would take more than the whole of the Metropolitan Police to keep him out of it. One might as well try to keep a thirsty elephant away from a watering-hole with a bamboo rod, as try to prevent the Professor getting his fingers into the pie-crust of an odd murder.

# Chapter 5

# Soothsayer's Recompense

BY THE morning the Professor's irritation had vanished. When I crawled from my bed and started shaving I could hear him singing downstairs. It is a horrifying sound as he has no sense of the way a tune goes, but what he lacks in tunefulness he makes up in volume. The noise is sufficient to waken the dead in Highgate Cemetery. I knew that I was in for a bad day.

I was right. When I got downstairs the old man was fully dressed. This is a bad sign, too. He usually breakfasts wrapped in a tartan dressing-gown of uncertain clan and age, but violent enough in its colourings to burst a chameleon. He had done all the chores, such as watering the various plants which have marched in from the garden and taken up their quarters in the house. I won't be surprised in the least the day I find a prickly-pear sprouting in my shaving-cream. The plants are only a little less rampant than the books.

"Hullo, Max," he greeted me with such vigour that I felt ashamed of my suspicions, which, however, did not lessen. We sat down to breakfast and he buried himself in *The Times*. I had the *Daily Express* and the *Mirror*. Anything that Emily Wallenstein had feared from the papers was small in comparison with the reality. The reporters really had laid themselves out.

From the noise they made one might have thought that modern art was a kind of Upas Tree which killed anything that came within miles of it. I was, frankly, astonished that reporters who treated it as if it was such a dangerous thing had dared to approach the Museum of Modern Art to get their stories. I discarded the papers and found the *News Chronicle*. As I had expected the *Chronicle* was rather more reasonable, though still sensational. At least they had not delegated the job of art critic to a man who did not know when a painting by Paul Klee was the right way up.

The Professor laid down *The Times* and helped himself to a large slice of toast upon which he spread masses of Oxford marmalade. He washed this down with about two-thirds of a pint of coffee. He always takes in liquid in such quantities that a normal person like myself would be unable to contain.

"Ho," he said cheerfully and noisily, "Hum. We're goin' out. We're goin' a-huntin'. Yoicks! Tally-ho!"

I did my best to remind him that we had, really, intended to settle down to work on his *History of Botany*. This is a book upon which he has been working for many years and which looks as though it would take a great many more. At the present rate of growth it will occupy at least ten volumes by the time it is finished. It will be a most remarkable book, but I am not sanguine about its appearance during my lifetime.

I might just as well have suggested that we stayed at home and learned to knit. The Professor dismissed my suggestion with a wave of his hand and trundled towards the front door, picking up an absurd broad-trimmed black sombrero which he sometimes wears. The trouble with this hat is that, having been left behind by an American botanist with a narrow head, it is much too small for the old man and all it does is give his face the impression that it is topped by a black hell-begotten halo.

He must have been up earlier than I thought, for the Bentley was standing in front of the gate. With fear and trepidation I climbed in. As I fear I say too much about the old man's driving, I will merely state that it was as bad as usual, but that we reached Iron Street safe in wind and limb, if not in mind.

The Museum could not have been long open, but already there were large crowds of people gathered before it, trying to get in. I thought it would take hours before we did get in, but the Professor just shouldered his way through the crowds. When people complained too audibly he growled, in a most unofficial tone, "Police," and we went through.

We did not hesitate at the gallery, which was crammed like the floor of a night club, but went on up the stairs to the library. There was quite a large collection of people there too. Douglas, looking the picture of gloom, sat behind a large black desk. He was flanked by the figures of Mr. Carr and his mother, who were seated in steel and fabric chairs.

"Hullo," said Douglas miserably, "I've got the hell of a hangover. Did I drink the hell of a lot last night, Max? I thought I was rather moderate."

I answered him truthfully. I had to admit that he had drunk rather a lot the previous evening, and I had had my doubts about the wisdom of trying to liven up bitter with large brandies. Douglas nodded his head, and then looked as if the action hurt him seriously. He put his hand on the top of his head as if to find whether it was still there.

"Hullo, hullo, hullo," said Mr. Carr. I was to learn that this was his usual form of greeting. "How's detection going this morning, cock? Come to arrest me?"

"Hardly," said the Professor kindly, "I don't think things have come to that yet. Though they may, they may."

The thought of the possibility in store for him did not much perturb Mr. Carr. Mrs. Carr withdrew a bottle. Her son turned to her sternly.

"Not at this time of day," he said, "It's a bit early. You just wait till I tell you that it's time for a drink. She," he turned towards us, "has a hangover like nobody's business and the only cure she knows for it is a hair of the dog. I told her that lemon gin was not the same as lime, but she would insist on diluting ordinary gin with it. When I was at Rugby," he looked sternly at Douglas, who was too engrossed in his own troubles to pay any attention, "I used to think there was nothing like a good cold bath for a hangover. But she won't take a bath. I think she's like the old woman in Ireland who attributed her great age to the fact that she had a bath once a year—whether she needed it or not."

"Water," said Mrs. Carr suddenly, "terrible stuff. I once drank some by mistake and I was in my bed for three weeks. Chill on the stomach it was. Take my advice and I'm old enough to know—never you touch water. There's too much of it about in my opinion. If there was less water and more alcohol it would be a better world to live in."

"Ma'am," said the Professor deeply, "I cannot say how profoundly I am in agreement with you."

"I was brought up on water," the old lady went on inconsequently, "but I haven't touched it since I was eleven, excepting that time I took it by mistake. I thought it was gin. That's the only trouble about gin. It looks like water and I don't like being reminded about the stuff. Ugh."

She shuddered violently. I began to wonder whether I was to stand a whole morning's discussion on the faults of water. Douglas groaned quietly. He looked paler and more miserable than usual.

"But," said the old man, "with all due respect to ye, ma'am, I didn't come here this mornin' to lament the abundance o' water in the world.

I came here to try an' find out a bit more about the murder o' Mr. Julian Ambleside."

He fished out his pipe and lit it. The one quality which I think Professor Stubbs shares with Sherlock Holmes is an ability to enjoy really strong tobacco early in the morning. Holmes smoked the pipe-dottles of the previous day, while the old man merely goes in for the strongest and vilest tobacco he can find.

"Now, Douglas," he boomed and various people who had looked in at the door of the library vanished, "if it's not shakin' you too much in yer present state, I wonder if ye'd mind shewin' me the place where ye kept the photographs which were stolen."

Douglas got up delicately. He moved across the floor as if he was an unskilful skater on very slippery ice. He opened the drawer of a sort of filing cabinet and took out a brown cardboard folder. He brought this back to the desk and laid it down. He reseated himself carefully and opened the folder.

"My God," he said blankly, "here are the photographs that were missing. Someone has put them back."

He took out a fat wad of photographs and laid them on the desk. He turned them over slowly. Then he turned them over again. He looked up.

"So far as I can see," he said, "they are all here. Though I must say I don't see how they got back. I was looking at the files yesterday and I'm sure that the photographs were not there then. I was thinking that I would have to get down to the job of writing catalogues of the photos on the front of each folder and I decided that as I had so much to do, I would let it ride for a day or two. I meant to get started this morning, but I haven't felt well enough and, anyhow, there have been too many people popping in and out to let me really get settled. But, I am sure I looked at the Chirico folder for I remember thinking that there was not much point in doing it if all the best photographs were missing. Someone must have replaced them sometime during the day yesterday when I was busy downstairs. But I can't see why. I suppose, though, that whoever borrowed them was ashamed to admit they'd not asked for them, after I kicked up that row about them not being here."

"Uhhuh," the Professor grunted, "an' is there a photo of the picture that was destroyed among 'em?"

"Yes," said Douglas, rooting through the photographs and holding one of them out, "here it is. It's a photo that was taken in Paris in 1917.

If you want a more modern one you can get it from Cooper's, in Hendon."

The Professor took the photograph and looked curiously at the long arcades and the rose tower and the lonely statue in the foreground.

"D'ye mind," he said, "if I borrow this for a little. I'll give it back to you when I've finished with it and I promise that I'll take great care of it."

Douglas looked doubtful, but then his face cleared. "I don't see why you shouldn't borrow it," he said, "after all we'd more or less written the Chirico photos off as lost. But I would like to have it back when you have finished with it. You know, I really was worried about these photos going astray. You see, I'm in charge of this damned library and I feel a bit responsible for the things in it. I don't like losing things that don't belong to me. When they belong to me it's another matter. I'm always losing things. Perhaps it's because I'm always losing my own things that I loathe the thought of losing things that belong to other people."

While he was speaking he was putting the photograph in an envelope with a cardboard back. The envelope, designed by Jan Tschihold, shewed that it came from the Museum of Modern Art, Iron Street, London, W.1. It looked very pleasant. As Douglas had said, Emily had spared no expense in getting up things about the Museum.

The Professor took the envelope and slipped it into an immense poacher's pocket inside his jacket. Mrs. Carr watched him closely, and gave a friendly cackle.

"Useful thing that pocket," she observed to the world at large, "if I had that pocket I could carry several bottles instead of only one measily bottle which doesn't hold enough for two."

As the bottle which she withdrew contained Drambuie, I was rather reminded of the Oxford character who remarked that a goose was a silly bird, too much for one, but not enough for two. Mrs. Carr looked at Mr. Carr with a sort of dumb appeal. He nodded and she uncorked her bottle and let some of the contents trickle down her throat. I listened to the gurgle. She replaced the cork.

"Sorry," she said conversationally, replacing the bottle in its hiding place in her robes, "as I was saying, that's the trouble with a bottle. Not enough in it."

"Thy need," said Douglas solemnly, "is greater than theirs."

"Exactly," said Mrs. Carr in a pleased voice. Her expression added that, no matter how hard she had tried, she couldn't have put it better herself.

We were just about to leave Douglas to his fate among the ravening and bibulous Carrs when we heard the faint whine of the lift. The door of the library opened and the figure of Dr. Cornelius Bellamy presented itself in the opening.

"Hullo, hullo, hullo, Doc," said Mr. Carr in a friendly come-hither voice, "Nobody murdered you in the night, what?"

"Good morning, my dear Carr," said the Doctor in a voice that killed all flippancy and rebuked Carr for his lack of taste.

The old man chewed reflectively at the stem of his pipe. He emitted some of the most noxious fumes I have ever encountered. I stood there and said nothing. I could not think of anything I wanted to say.

"It's very odd, Dr. Bellamy," said Douglas, "you know the photos that were missing?" The Doctor nodded his head portentously. "Well, they've all turned up again. When I looked in the file this morning, there they were."

Dr. Bellamy looked irritated. "My dear Douglas," he said loftily, "we are surely not concerned with the vagaries of a packet of photographs, are we? I came up to see whether you were busy, as we could do with an extra assistant downstairs. The crowds are, I may say, quite unbelievable. Some of those who have come to mock will, I hope, stay to stare and admire." His voice sounded rather as though he was not propounding a statement in the truth of which he had any faith or conviction. He continued rather nervously, after a gentle cough, "The trouble at the moment seems to be that a certain rowdy element has entered with the enquirers after aesthetic qualities, and this—ah—element shews an inclination to disport itself in ways that are not in keeping with the traditions of a Museum. I have already had to rescue the large Calder and one of dear Moholy's constructions from their, if I might say so, none too tender clutches. I fear, in addition, that the soluble saucepan and the decanter of green ink have suffered beyond all hope of repair." His voice took on a savage tone, "All I can hope is that the ruffian who drank the green ink under the impression that it was green Chartreuse will suffer the severest pangs of arsenic poisoning. I may say that I have great hopes that he will—for the ink was of French manufacture and not of English and, I believe that on the Continent, they are less particular about such qualities than we are here."

"But," said Douglas unhappily, "I can't leave the library. Just imagine, Dr. Bellamy, what would happen if these fellows got in among the books. They would destroy them completely. I can't leave this place to its fate as you suggest."

"My dear boy," said the Doctor airily, "surely you can lock it up?"

"How?" said Douglas in a rude voice, "There isn't any lock on the door."

This seemed to be something the Doctor had not expected. He looked very astonished.

"If there was a lock," Douglas went on, "I'd have locked up every night and then we wouldn't have had that trouble over the photographs. Nobody would be able to get in when the place was deserted."

Dr. Cornelius Bellamy seemed to be a bit distressed by this. Suddenly I realised that the old man was trying to say something to me. I edged a bit closer to him.

"Try yer hand at controllin' the crowds, Max," he urged in an undertone, "Offer him a hand."

I did not particularly wish to become a sort of policeman, but it occurred to me that I would be as usefully employed doing that as standing around listening to the Carrs and their nonsense. I do not know whether there was some telepathic connection between my thoughts and the questing subconscious of Mrs. Carr, but whatever it was she spoke before I had time to open my mouth.

"Ah, the Doctor himself, dear man," she observed and took out her bottle of Drambuie. She wiped the mouth of the bottle on her cloak and held it out to the Doctor, "Won't you have a drink, dear man? It's a damnable good drink and it will put the fire of the Lord into your veins. Come on now, take a swig."

The Doctor backed away from the bottle which she presented at his middle with the determination of a gangster with a Thompson submachine gun. He looked nervously at Ben Carr, who came to his aid.

"Put your bottle away, mother," he said, "Perhaps the Doc don't want a drink at this time of day, what with the sun not over the foremast and all the rest of it."

Mrs. Carr looked at the bottle lovingly. I could see that she thought it would be a great shame to put the bottle away untasted, so she sampled it herself.

"You don't know what you're missing," she observed darkly, with the air of a Sibyl issuing an ultimatum, "You'll never find a better whisky in a thousand years."

I thought it was time I pushed in what I had by way of an oar, so I said, "Dr. Bellamy, couldn't I give you a hand downstairs with the crowd? I don't think the Professor wants me for anything at the moment, do you, sir?"

The old man shook his head, scowling. He loathes being addressed as "sir."

Dr. Cornelius Bellamy looked at me. I could see that his sharp and all-observant eyes were taking in the fact that my jacket had patches of dark leather on the sleeves and cuffs. He hesitated for a moment before he replied.

"Well, that would be very nice of you," he said, and smiled the condescending smile of an archangel, "but I'm not sure that you could manage the crowds satisfactorily."

"He'll manage them better than I could," said Douglas suddenly, "He has been a Regimental Sergeant-Major."

It was nice of Douglas, but quite inaccurate. The highest I got was being a flight-sergeant in the Glider Pilot Regiment. However, the Doctor did not ask for details but turned again to me, "In that case I think that I can say that I am grateful for your offer of help and am pleased to accept it."

We went towards the door. I did not want to go, because I wanted to see what Professor Stubbs was up to, for I felt sure that he had some plot which was boiling up. The old man, however, made no effort to detain me, so I went after the Doctor.

Anything which I had imagined downstairs was beside the truth. There were people everywhere, like flies on a piece of carrion under a hot sun except that the flies have a reason for being there and these people had no reason for their existence, let alone for being in the Museum of Modern Art. On the way down, Dr. Bellamy had explained that he wanted me to walk around with the crowd, and, when I saw anyone touching anything, to put it to them gently that the thing was fragile and valuable.

I certainly had a job. It seemed to me that the one aim in life of about ninety-six per cent. of the people there was to destroy something. I managed to rescue the fur-covered teapot from the hands of a small girl who had decided that she wanted to take it home. She was, I think, without doubt the most horrible small girl I have ever met. She had a round face which looked as though it had been parboiled and stringy yellow hair hung in a fringe over her forehead. She kicked up such a row when I took the thing away from her that I would quite gladly have stuffed it down her throat and choked her. I had not, I think, ever felt a genuinely homicidal impulse before, but now I understood all about it. I regret to have to confess that, as she started her bawling when I tried to seduce the damned thing from her by niceness, I was quite unnecessarily rough in wresting it from her. Her mother looked at me as if I had really hurt the child. I was rude to her too.

So, it can well be imagined that I was in anything but a quiet frame of mind when the old man came for me at lunch-time. I could have kicked him for letting me in for the job.

"Hullo, Max," he said cheerfully, "How'd ye get on?"

"Hellishly," I said going into the sulks. "I never want to do a job like that again as long as I live. If the gallery had not been crowded I'd have murdered the most terrible, horrible, beastly little girl I've ever met. I never realised before that so much beastliness could be crammed into a child of five. God help her mother. And I mean that, for no one else will."

"Ah, well," the old man was soothing, "you'll get over it. Let's go an' have a drink, for I'm sure you're needin' one."

That was a sensible suggestion, so I went and had a drink with him.

"I got to go to Hendon this afternoon," he announced, "I want to get a photograph."

"What the hell for?" I asked irritably, "You got a photograph this morning and it'll be just the same."

"Uhhuh," he nodded, "but I want a more modern photo. Some of these old ones aren't clear enough for me purpose. For what I want to do I need one of Copper's photos. They have the negative an' I have the number of it."

I didn't know what he meant to do with photographs. I didn't much care, for I was still haunted by the vision of that most horrible of all female children, with her sulky, down-turned mouth and her nasty little spiteful nose. (I think I have forgotten to mention that she bit my thumb to the bone when I took the teapot from her—this may help to justify my anger and obsession with her. My thumb was sore.)

"All right," I said, "and have you heard any more from the Bishop about the case? You said you'd ring him early to-day, didn't you?"

"Uhhuh," the old man nodded, "he's been looking into Ambleside's affairs in the hope of finding some sort of clue, but there's not much help there. He had at various times paid large sums to a great number of people, including both Francis Varley and Dr. Cornelius Bellamy, but as the Bishop says that they both dabble in dealing to help out their incomes, the payments were probably made for pictures which they sold him. It is improbable that any dealings which were not strictly above board would have been so obviously entered in his accounts."

"Did you say," I asked, "that Dr. Bellamy dealt in pictures? I would not have believed that he would have sunk to sully his hands with the dirt of commercial gold?"

"Why not?" the old man was obviously bewildered, "If I was broke I'd probably start a business as a nursery man. Bellamy and Varley both know about pictures an' they are neither of them rich men, an' they are both in a position to purchase pictures from private owners who would not think of goin' direct to a dealer like Ambleside."

I could see that the Professor was right, but I could still not manage to visualise Dr. Bellamy getting down to the point of speaking about pounds, shillings and pence. I ordered another round of beers.

"Anything else?" I asked, more automatically than with the hope of there being an answer.

"Yes," he said deeply, "there's one new point an' I'm thinkin' it's probably o' some importance once we get things straight in our minds. There was a plain-clothes man on duty in Iron Street all that afternoon when the picture was destroyed,—there's some business about a club three doors away,—and he was curious enough about the Museum— he'd read a lot about it in the paper—to be watchin' that too. He says that he'd ha' noticed if anyone out o' the ordinary had gone in durin' the afternoon, an', as he's a good man, I think we can take his word for it."

"Does that mean anything to you?" I asked blankly. All it seemed to mean to me was that the Chirico had been destroyed by one of those who was working in the Museum and not by a stranger from outside.

"Plenty," said Professor Stubbs and went towards the door.

# Chapter 6

# Revolt of the Sage

I HAD thought that I was to be taken to Hendon to help get the photograph, but not a bit of it. I was condemned to return to the gallery to control morons and mischievous apes. For a good way of spending an afternoon I cannot recommend this. By half-past-three I would gladly have filled the whole gallery with carbon monoxide, not, judging from their faces, that it would have done anything to alter the colours of the complexions of the dowagers who sailed round the place like celluloid swans in a bath-tub.

Certainly I saw one or two people I knew, but I had about as much chance of anything in the way of conversation with them as I would have had if I had been sitting on top of a steam-organ in a merry-go-round.

The Professor did not arrive back until nearly four-thirty. By this time I felt as though I had been pushed into a Turkish bath with all my clothes on. He blundered through the crowd towards me with the determination of a tank going through a forest of saplings. Owing to my abnormal height I was able to see him coming, but I was in such a vile temper that I made no effort to go towards him, and I refused to listen to the sound of my name which he shouted once or twice, with the violence and unexpectedness of a hunter calling on a moose. He had to come right up to me before I deigned to notice his existence.

"It's all right now, Max," he said, "You can come along. Had a good afternoon?"

Rather pointedly I looked round the crowd without saying anything. I let my eyes rest momentarily on the more moronic members of it. The old man followed my eyes and nodded his head.

"I'm sorry about that, Max," he said. The trouble with Professor Stubbs is that he is always only too willing to apologise. It doesn't mean a thing, but it sometimes results in his way of life being easier than it would otherwise have been.

As we went towards the door we encountered my bugbear, the appallingly horrible child. It seemed as though she had not had enough in the morning but had come back for more. I made the most horrible face I could think of and the child burst into tears.

I was so intent on my revenge, for my thumb throbbed beneath the bit of Elastoplast, that I bumped into Francis Varley. "Sorry," I said automatically. Then I thought I should give him a warning. I pointed to the awful child.

"You see that child, Varley?" I asked, "Well, keep an eye on her. She tried to steal the fur teapot this morning and I think she has come back to have another shot at it."

Francis Varley followed my finger. He looked a little surprised.

"Don't you know who that is?" he asked and I shook my head, "That is Miss Zulieka Bellamy, the learned Doctor's daughter. She is being brought up as a genius. I may tell you, my dear fellow," his voice dropped so that no one else could hear it, "that to spend an evening with the Bellamys is a sore trial. They put that child at the piano and sing praises of the discords she manages to create. To be perfectly honest, when my Siamese kitten gets on the keys she makes a better noise. But steer clear of her, old man, she's poison."

"I know," I said grimly as I went on my way, wondering whether the poison extended to her fangs. I hoped not but I would not have been the least surprised if I had developed tetanus. I worked myself into a state when I was almost certain that I was bound to develop some vile disease from the child's bite.

In the hall of the Museum we came face to face with the Doctor himself. He stopped us with a gesture. "I must thank you, Mr. Boyle," he said, "for your very kind assistance this afternoon. Oh, I see you have hurt your hand. I hope it isn't serious?"

"No," I said bitterly, "I was merely bitten by a dangerous and poisonous wild animal. My thumb will probably mortify and fall off."

He looked at me in surprise. Then he laughed. "Oh you scientists," he said, "You must have your little joke, mustn't you?" He laughed again and went on his way, leaving me looking after him. The only consolation I could think of was that, with that child about the place, he must have been bitten himself—her bite shewed considerable dexterity of the sort which is not acquired without much practise—and certainly he appeared to have lost no limbs nor to suffer from many scars.

The Bentley was purring outside. We shot away from the white façade of the Museum of Modern Art, narrowly missing a postman who was crossing the street, and snaked through into Piccadilly.

Our destination, I realised, was undoubtedly Scotland Yard. I wondered what we were going to do there. Sometimes the old man uses the place as somewhere to cash a cheque after the banks are closed. One of the high ups was at school with him and I think he is frightened of the Professor; at any rate he'll always cash cheques for him.

When we entered the place I realised that we were not looking for money but were about to pay an unsocial visit to the Chief Inspector.

I must say that he did not look overjoyed to see us. He looked up from the papers which were spread before him on his desk and groaned very theatrically.

"My God, John," he said, "isn't it enough that I see you during my few hours of leisure without your needing to come and haunt me when I'm at work?"

"Ho," snorted the old man, "Just listen to him. Ho, I do all his blasted work for him and that's all the thanks I get. Anyhow, Reggie, I'm not going to worry you for long. I'm just goin' to leave Max here in yer charge while I kinda wander along to yer ballistics department."

"My dear man," the Chief Inspector was amused, "what *do* you want with the ballistics department? I don't surely have to remind you that Julian Ambleside was strangled and hanged and not shot. You haven't discovered some new way of committing a murder by firing a noose or a pair of imitation hands at your victim, have you?"

Professor Stubbs looked mysterious. He closed his left eye in one of his face-contorting winks.

"Just ye wait an' see, me boy, just ye wait an' see," he said very amiably, "Now can ye put me in touch wi' a chap in yer ballistics department who'll let me fiddle around wi' his instruments for a few minutes?"

The Chief Inspector looked thoughtful, but he picked up the telephone beside him and spoke briefly into it.

"I suppose it will be all right," he said, "so long as you don't break anything, John. Remember some of these instruments are very expensive and are not easily replaced even if you have the money to buy them."

"I know," said the old man, "I won't break anything. I just want to use an instrument which I haven't got lyin' around my own house an' so I'll have to borrow yours. Not," he was slightly nettled, "that I'm in the habit o' breakin' things. I can't remember breakin' anythin' recently."

I thought it all depended upon what he meant by the word "recently." If it was a matter of hours he was being truthful, otherwise he was certainly not telling the truth, for I had seen the remains of a flower-pot in his waste-paper basket only that morning. I felt slightly annoyed at the way in which he was dumping me in the Chief Inspector's office like so much luggage to be left till called for, but I could not think of any reasonable excuse for coming with him, beyond my natural curiosity, so with a look to see if the Bishop minded I made myself at home in a chair, and started to read a book which I had in my pocket, William Derham's *Astro-Theology,* which set out to prove the existence of God from the positions of the stars.

This habit of carrying books about with me is one I have picked up from the old man, whose pockets are large enough to hold a small 17th century folio. No doubt it is a bad habit, but it has its compensations, as on occasions like this, when I am left alone with nothing to do.

Professor Stubbs was gone about three quarters of an hour. When he returned he was looking very pleased with himself. I tried to draw him on the question of what he had been doing, but I might as well have tried to draw the teeth of a hippopotamus with a pair of stamp-tweezers. It was, as they say, no go.

I must admit also that I could make little sense of the questions which the old man put to the Chief Inspector. Mostly they seemed to deal with the question of Julian Ambleside's stock—the pictures and so on in his possession at the time of his death. I remembered that Douglas had told me, talking about the question of the genuineness of the Chiricos, that Ambleside had four more besides the one he had sold to Emily Wallenstein and which had been destroyed.

"Are there any paintings by Chirico?" I asked and the Chief Inspector shrugged his shoulders. I tried to explain the sort of thing which Chirico had painted, but the Bishop said that he had only spent a short time at Ambleside's house in the Chelsea square and that he had not had time to take a proper look.

"D'ye mind if we go down an' take a look?" the Professor asked suddenly, "I'll gi' ye me word that I won't break or destroy anythin' at all. Is there anyone there who'll let us in?"

"I doubt it," said the Chief Inspector, "the house is really large enough to need a full-time maid, but they are in such short supply these days that Ambleside made do with a woman who used to come in every day.

She arrived in time to make his breakfast and went away about fivish, leaving some cold food ready for his supper. From what we know of him it would seem that he was not given to eating in in the evenings, but usually went out to a restaurant or dined at his club. The woman will be gone by this time, but if you'll bring the keys back here as soon as you've done with them, I don't see that there's any reason why you should not go there. You will find that he kept his stock-in-trade in two large rooms in the basement and in two bedrooms on the second floor. Of course it seems, from the look of the house, that a lot of the things which he used to have around him were also saleable. Here, Max," he handed me a Yale key, "you take charge of that and see that he doesn't start breaking things up. If he can't get into anything and he wants to get into it, he'll just need to wait until to-morrow."

We left with the Professor's voice raised in a wail of protest about the ungrateful treatment which he received at the hands of public servants. From the way he spoke one might have supposed him to be a veritable paragon who was being unjustly accused. Having been with him for some time I knew just how justified and necessary the Chief Inspector's warning was. I have seen the Professor break open desks with a poker, and get through doors by the simple expedient of throwing his bulk against them.

I did not enjoy the ride to Chelsea any more than I enjoy any ride with the old man driving. All that could be said for it was that it was no worse than the average.

The house where Julian Ambleside had lived was one of these tall, narrow eighteenth century houses which manage to persist in parts of Chelsea and Bloomsbury in spite of the encroachment of the block of flats, which provides dwellings for fifty where five had lived before.

I opened the door and we went in. The house was well and very expensively furnished. The pictures on the walls were superb. They were not all paintings of the twentieth century. I noticed a good early Corot and a Courbet. In addition there were a great many pictures in the hall and on the staircases which were obviously the work of untrained English artists of the 18th and 19th centuries.

Stiff cricketers bowled an everlasting slow underhand to batsmen who were forever poised to hit the stationary ball into the willow trees by the common, or crinolined ladies were frozen in conversation with top-hatted gentlemen in the market-squares of country towns.

We solemnly set to work to look for any paintings by Chirico. I found three drawings by him, and was pleased to notice that none of them was as good as the one I had. But of the four large paintings which Douglas had mentioned there was no sign.

I would have given up the search when we had looked through the rooms of the house, but the old man was exceedingly pertinacious this evening. He insisted in going up into the attics and on making me crawl, to the sad detriment of my clothes, among between the rafters. We looked in the lavatories and under the bath, we looked in the kitchen, behind the Aga cooker and under the sink. I began to get fed up. The old man went over to the large Ideal boiler. We had already examined this, but he seemed to be determined to take another look.

Of course there was nothing there. I'm afraid that I shewed a slight inclination to crow over him.

"Come on, Sherlock," I said mockingly, "where's your magnifying glass? Why don't you get that out?"

He looked at me gravely, his steel rimmed glasses perched precariously on the tip of his blunt nose and the black sombrero, which he had neglected to remove, shoved back on his head.

"D'ye know, Max," he said solemnly, "I think you got somethin' there. If I had a glass I'd use it." He took out his pipe and started to fill it, glaring vindictively at the Ideal boiler. Suddenly he put the pipe back in his pocket and slapped his hands on his thighs. "By cripes," he bellowed, "I am a thunderin' ass. To think that I was expectin' to find anythin' here in the boiler. O' course there wouldn't be anythin' here, would there now, Max?"

He appealed to me, and I shook my head wisely. I had to confess to myself that I could see no especial reason why there would not be anything in the boiler, except that I had not expected to find anything there.

"An' why," he rumbled, "would there be nothin' in the ash-pan o' the boiler? Well, it's kinda simple once ye think o' the answer. What time o' day was it when Julian Ambleside was found hangin'? Why, by God, it was in the afternoon, an' ye don't think that his woman would come in here an' clear up an' still neglect to make up the blinkin' boiler. She'd want it made up to give her hot water for the washin' up, wouldn't she?"

"Yes," I said, "Your grasp of domestic detail astonishes me, but I still don't see what you're driving at?"

"Ha' ye ever filled one of these boilers?" he demanded, and I nodded my head, "Well, one o' the first things ye do is to rattle the cinders that are in the bottom an' take the ash-pan out an' empty it, ain't I right?"

"Yes," I said, "I think you are right, more or less, but I still don't see where you hope it's going to get you."

"Max, son," he said in a voice which I call his more in pity than in anger voice, "Max, son, will ye for the love of thunderin' Mike try thinkin'. Ye were given good brains an' it's a pity not to use 'em, but just to let 'em lie rottin' in yer head."

I got his meaning that time. I had, I admit, been pretty slow in the uptake. I made for the door into the area and got there ahead of the old man.

By pure good luck the ash-bucket had not been emptied. Lying on top of it was a little pile of grey and brown ash. The old man pushed past me and started to riddle this with his fingers. He soon found several tacks, large-headed strong tacks. By the time he had finished riddling the ash we had quite a sizeable pile of these tacks lying beside us.

We took the pile back into the house and laid them out on the monel metal sink. The old man looked at them thoughtfully. I thought he was trying to conjure them up so that they could tell him a story.

"Umhum," he mumbled to himself, "Umhum. Ye know what these are, Max?" He didn't give me time to answer him, "These, son, are the sort o' tack which is used by a man stretching a canvas on a wooden stretcher. Look at the size o' their heads and the strength o' the shanks. They would not pull out easy, would they?"

I shook my head. I was fingering one of the tacks. It was certainly a very strong one.

"Do you think it would be possible to trace these to their maker?" I asked hopefully. "Scotland Yard are pretty good at that sort of thing these days. Perhaps they might be able to say which shop they were bought at."

The old man shook his head heavily. "I doubt whether there'd be much point in tryin' to track 'em down," he said, "even if they are o' English manufacture, which I doubt. I'm thinkin' that these tacks were the ones which were used to hold the canvas o' the stretcher o' the four missin' pictures by Chirico."

He stopped and held up one of the tacks between a blunt finger and thumb.

"I think we can take it that the murderer was someone who wanted to destroy the Chiricos an' his only way o' gettin' at 'em was to kill Ambleside. I don't think that the blessed Doctor's theory that the picture was destroyed at the Museum 'ull hold water for a moment, even if it could be proved that the plain clothes man watchin' that club had missed seein' someone goin' in. Someone had to get rid o' the pictures, an' the reason that he had to get rid o' them was that they were not genuine, that, in fact they were spurious. I think that we'll need to get hold o' Mr. Francis Varley an' start askin' him a few questions. I got a kinda feelin' that he knows altogether too much. I'll get on to him in the mornin' an' see what he can do by way o' explanation."

It seemed to me that Professor Stubbs was going just a little bit fast in building up a story from a few fire-rusted tintacks. I said as much. He snorted at me.

"Humph," his glare was really fierce, "I got a good story an' I'm goin' to try it out. There's no reason why I should not try it out before I discard it. It's the only story I can think o' which 'ud seem to hang together at all. I got to ha' somethin' to start from an' this idea o' mine gives me a flyin' start. After all, if ye work things out ye'll see that these tacks couldn't ha' bin put in the fire longer ago than the day that Ambleside was murdered. If they had bin put there on the day before that, we'd ha' found two lots o' ash on 'em, whereas there they were, stickin' out on the top deck. No, Max, someone was burnin' somethin' wi' tacks in it on the day or night o' Ambleside's murder an' that's enough to make me wonder in itself. But when ye take these tacks an' the fact that four paintin's are missin' an' put these facts alongside one another, I think that even the dullest bobby on the beat would say that ye were holdin' the remains o' the pictures. It must," his voice was heavily thoughtful, "have bin a kinda long job burnin' these pictures even in an Ideal boiler the size o' this. Ye'd need to chop 'em up an' burn 'em in pieces an' ye couldn't feed the fire too quickly in case ye put it out. At a guess I'd say it 'ud take two or three hours o' hard concentration an' I can't say I'd ha' liked the job." He shuddered like an immense mastiff shaking itself. "No, Max. Can ye imagine the feelings o' the chap, sittin' down here feedin' scraps o' canvas an' wood into the boiler an' wonderin' all the time if the body o' Ambleside has bin found an' if the police will be rollin' round to look at his house."

"No," I reminded him, "the murderer ran no such risks. The gallery was shut up by the last person to leave it, and the door works on an automatic lock which shuts from the outside but which can be opened by a handle on the inside. The murderer knew that, unless the body was found by someone connected with the gallery, and, as Douglas told you, they were all so busy that that was improbable, no one could come in from outside and take a peep behind the drapery over the Max Ernst. You must remember that all the gallery people knew, or thought they knew, what was behind the cloth, and so they had no curiosity. The only person who might have been curious was an outsider, and no outsider could get in to let his curiosity run riot."

He nodded like a large and benevolent owl. "Ye're quite, right, Max," he said, "I was forgettin' that. Did ye also find out how many o' the people connected wi' the Museum could get in, havin' keys?"

"Yes," I said, "and that's no good either. Every single person, even Miss Rampion and Douglas, has a key. They've all been working very late, trying to get things finished in time and they all had keys to let them go out to get a meal in the evening and then go back if they wanted to, without bringing someone else away from their work to open the door."

The old man looked at the pile of tin tacks. They looked rather sordid, oxidised by being in the fire, lying on the shining metal of the draining board.

"Hell," he said gloomily, "I don't suppose there's much more we can do here this evenin'. Ye'd better put up these tacks in a match-box, if ye can find one, an' we'll take them wi' us. They may," he sounded rather doubtful, "ha' some value as evidence."

I looked around till I found an empty bottle which had once held mixed spices. I put the tacks into that and put the bottle into my pocket. The old man took out his immense old-fashioned turnip watch.

"As I thought," he said gloomily, "we're missin' good drinkin' time. I'm gettin' hellish thirsty an' I don't know about you, but I think it's gettin' on for time for a *very* large drink."

He said this with great determination and made off up the stairs. We went to the *Six Bells*. I hoped that the drink would clear my head. It didn't. I was still trying to sort things out in my mind when we finished our fourth pint and went out into the King's Road.

The Professor proceeded to make me more dazed. He started to look for Douglas Newsome. Finding Douglas entailed something pretty heroic in the way of pub-crawls. I pointed out when the old man started for Douglas's home address that we would not find him there, at that time in the evening. From every point of view except that of drinking rather more than plenty, we were unlucky. We tried the back bar of the *Café Royal*, the *Swiss*, the *Intrepid Fox*, the *Salisbury*, the *Highlander* and the *George*. In all of these pubs, which I knew Douglas used, we drew blank. We were thinking of going back on our steps and trying the pubs in between the *Crown and Angel*, the *Helvetia*, the *Two Chairmen*, the *Dog and Duck* and so on, when I thought of the *Wheatsheaf*. We found him there. By that time I guess I was as drunk as Douglas usually was. It would have been all right if the Professor had been content to let me open the door of a pub and just look in, but not him. He said it was an insult to a publican to look into his pub and not have a drink. So it meant that we had two or three in each.

We managed to disentangle Douglas from a heated argument he was having with a young man who had more hair under his chin than on top of his head. I still don't know what they were arguing about and I don't think either of them knew, but they were plenty heated about it.

The *Wheatsheaf* was pretty crowded. Maclaren Ross in a teddy-bear coat and carrying a long black cane was talking to Ruthven Todd who was wearing a shirt which I recognised as belonging to Dylan Thomas. The Professor took up the devil of a lot of room. He put back quite a quantity of Scotch ale and then we pulled Douglas out into the night. The cold air seemed to hit him hard, but we made him understand that we wanted him to take us back to the Museum. He grumbled a bit and said that he thought he had finished with the place for the day, but I pointed out that the *Wheatsheaf* would be closing in a few minutes, and he agreed to come.

Inside the Museum it was rather extraordinary. The place felt rather like the inside of a pyramid. We went up the stairs, because the old man mistrusts lifts so much, and entered the library. There the old man sat down at the desk and started to read every single thing he could find about Giorgio de Chirico. I must say I didn't see where he hoped it was going to get him, but I suppose he justified it to himself on the grounds that all knowledge is valuable.

# Chapter 7

# Serenity of the Scholar

I MUST say that I didn't feel any too good as the Bentley roared through the London streets towards Francis Varley's flat near Gordon Square. It had taken the old man till after three to read all that he could find on the subject of Chirico, and all the time Douglas and I had felt the drink dying in us like the mercury in a thermometer on a frosty day. Douglas had had a half bottle of whisky and a couple of quarts of Tolly hidden in his desk, but these had not lasted very long.

The only consolation I had was that I was not alone in my misery. If I knew anything about Douglas he would be ten times worse than I was.

Francis Varley's flat was the top one of about three in a converted eighteenth century house. We went up the stairs slowly, with the old man grumbling at the number of stairs he had had to climb in recent days. I pointed out that it was his own fault as he would not travel in lifts if he could avoid it. He just growled at me.

Francis Varley, dressed in a light grey suit and with a dark grey bow tie with tiny white dots, opened the door to us and we went in. The place was beautifully furnished with bookshelves to a height of about four feet round all the walls of the sitting room. Before the window there was a large desk, covered with papers and with pots of ink. On the walls there hung a few carefully chosen drawings, shewing the catholicity of Varley's taste. There was a Tiepolo and a drawing which looked as though it probably was a Gainsborough, as well as a water-colour of Bloomsbury by Rowlandson and, coming up to more modern days there was a first-rate early drawing by Millais, and a sketch by Seurat. Then there was a drawing, of the Blue period, by Picasso, a Klee of a little pin-head man walking a tightrope and a very fine cubist pencil drawing by Juan Gris.

I always look at people's books. They interest me. The *Burlington Magazine* and the *Journal of the Warburg Institute* stood shoulder to shoulder with bound volumes of *Cahiers d'Art, Verve* and *Minotaurem* along the large bottom shelves. The other shelves were neatly ranged with the multicoloured paper-backs of French books and the expensive buckram of English and German books on art.

Varley offered us seats and then coffee. I took it, as I thought it would either kill or cure me, and I didn't much mind which it did. He offered a china box of Balkan Sobranie, but that I turned down, as I did not think I could stand Turkish tobacco at that hour of the morning in my wretched condition.

He pulled up the knees of his trousers and sat down himself. I thought he looked mildly amused at the elephantine figure of the old man in his rather delicate surroundings.

"Harumph," the Professor snorted, "I hope ye don't mind me rousin' ye at this hour o' the mornin'?"

"Not the least," said Varley, looking at his watch. It was after ten, but the old man had obviously made up his mind that a man who lived in surroundings like these, was a man who would sleep late.

"Ye see," the old man rumbled on, "I got to find out one or two things about the late Mr. Julian Ambleside, an' I think ye're the one man who can gi'mme a proper lead. Ye see we know that ye some-times received money from him—the coppers ha' bin lookin' into his affairs an' I got the information from 'em. So, if ye don't think I'm horrid pryin' I wonder if ye'd mind tellin' me what he paid ye for?"

"Not the least," Varley was imperturbable, "As you may, or may not know, I am by way of being an art expert, though, unfortunately, I have not the personal means to permit of my also being a collector. Naturally in the course of my work I sometimes come across works which, while they are beyond my personal means, are worth consider-ably more than I am asked for them. On these occasions I have usually purchased such works and have either resold them, or have arranged for a dealer to sell them for me. So far as I can remember, Julian Ambleside did both for me. It all depended upon the work whether he bought it from me, or sold it for me on a commission basis."

"Uhhuh," the Professor nodded, "I can understand that. Now, among the paintin's which ye ha' handled, there wouldn't be any by that Italian feller, Chirico, would there?"

For a moment I thought that Varley looked slightly startled, but he recovered his composure and placed the Balkan Sobranie between his lips before he answered.

"No," he said, "no paintings by Chirico. I did once sell Ambleside a pencil drawing which I was not enamoured of myself, but I have never had the good fortune to stumble upon a really good Chirico." He sounded rather regretful. "I wonder, though, my dear sir, why you asked me that question. What do you know about Chirico?"

This last question might have sounded insulting, as though he was suggesting that a botanist who was also an amateur detective, had no right to presume to a knowledge of modern painting, but he said it so disarmingly, with a charming smile, that nobody could have been offended.

"Um," the Professor mumbled, "Um. That's just it. I'm not sure what I know about Chirico. I just kinda got an idea that there was somethin' wrong wi' the Chiricos which Ambleside was handlin'. Am I right?"

"Well," Varley was cautious, "I would not go so far as to say that. I would only say that I, as a purely personal feeling, was not quite happy about them. You see, the problem with Chirico lies in his extraordinary collapse, from aesthetic standards, from about 1918 on. Before that date he painted pictures which have, probably, had as great an influence, direct and indirect, as the works of any artist of our time, not excluding Picasso. Well, at some period in the early twenties, at the suggestion of his friends among the Surrealists, Chirico set to work and copied many of his early paintings. The Surrealists hoped that by doing this he would recapture the elusive something which he had lost. In copying these pictures Chirico copied every single detail of them, down to the dates upon which the original was painted. Now I enter upon a more difficult subject, upon which I cannot pretend to know the rights or the wrongs. When Chirico quarrelled with the Surrealists they replied by accusing him of selling these copies, some of them magnificent works in their way, as the originals. I do not know whether there is any truth in this story, and if there is it is a difficult matter to decide upon the moral values implicit in it. For the man would be selling, as his work, works which he had done. The only falsity would lie in the matter of the dates, and as the pictures were avowedly copies they would be genuine in everything but the date. Now, there is the question of the Chiricos which belonged to Julian Ambleside—the one he sold to Emily and the four he still had in his possession. My private opinion of these pictures was that they were not the genuine work of Chirico at all, but were supremely good copies, or if you'd rather, forgeries. But as the pictures had been passed by experts like the learned Doctor I did not feel at liberty to announce my private opinion, but, instead, I resurrected the story of Chirico's own copies, as I felt that that would be less hurtful to Julian as a dealer and to Cornelius Bellamy as an expert. You may have realised that if the dear Doctor decided that the world was spinning backwards—the world *would be* spinning backwards. Dr. Bellamy has one serious fault and that is that he is never at fault."

He paused and lit another cigarette. The sight of the plump white Balkan Sobranie reminded me of the crank, collected by D. H. Lawrence, who referred to the cigarette as "this tubular white ant which is sapping our civilisation."

"Now I come to think of it," he went on, "I would like to take another look at the Chiricos which were still in Julian's possession when he was murdered. Unfortunately the picture which Emily bought was so badly damaged by some person unknown," he smiled wryly, "that I could form no further conclusions from the fragments, which, I believe, are now a part of one of Mr. Carr's rubbish decorations at the Museum. Do you think, my dear sir, that the constabulary would permit me to view the pictures?"

"I got no doubt they would," the old man rumbled, "if they were there to view, but they ain't. Yer person unknown got into Ambleside's house an' kinda incinerated the thunderin' lot. All that Max, here, an' I could find when we took a look last night was a lot o' blinkin' tacks in the ashes from the boiler."

"Oh," said Varley a trifle blankly, "Oh, I see. I wonder what that means?"

"If I was sure o' what it meant," Professor Stubbs grumbled, "I wouldn't be here tryin' to pick yer brains, like a man eatin' winkles wi' a pin."

"I wonder now," Varley looked very thoughtful, "I suppose that this means that whoever murdered Julian was also the person who destroyed the pictures. That puts the lid on the learned Doctor's theory that the Chirico at the Museum was destroyed by an obsessional character. You know the line of talk of the amateur psychologist? Yes. Well, the Doctor is an expert at it and he trolled out the most beautiful line about the picture being a portrait of some man's soul or psyche—he invented a new name for it—the Dorian Gray complex. There was a lot of stuff about the vandal's courage in destroying the picture when he might be destroying himself."

He looked vastly amused as he thought of the theory propounded by Dr. Bellamy.

"I wonder now," he spoke very slowly, "have you been able to trace where Julian got the pictures?"

"Haven't got round to that yet," the Professor was cheerful, "but no doubt we'll find out. Then, I can take it that yer opinion is that the five pictures by Chirico were, in fact, not genuine at all, but just simple forgeries, eh?"

"Yes," said Varley, "but for heaven's sake don't quote me. If the dear Doctor knew that I had doubted his opinion as an expert to that extent, he would never speak to me again. For publication you can say that I thought they were Chirico's own copies. Everyone knows that I had that opinion—I had quite a tiff with dear Emily about it, but we made it up. Naturally, dear Emily did not like to think that her pet Museum might be housing pictures which were not all that they claimed to be."

"Could you," the Professor leaned forward heavily, "ha' got into the Museum whenever ye wanted to?"

"Good Lord, yes," said Varley, "I've got a key. We've all got keys as we were apt to be working late. Even that amiable lunatic Carr has one. You know," he leaned forward, "when the body of Julian was unveiled in that manner my first thought was that Carr had got up to mischief. Judging from his wall decorations, I would say that the idea of a dead man on the wall would have appealed to him. I must say that I thought of Carr as the murderer. I suppose you've looked into that?"

"Uhhuh," the Professor grunted, "I looked into it, an' my own idea is that we were all meant to think o' the irresponsible Carr as a likely person to ha' done the murder. The trouble is that I can never believe in the likely person as the murderer. It's too dam' obvious, an' no one in their senses would do a murder which pointed directly at them."

"I dare say not," said Varley gravely, "but if I was to do a murder I think I would leave it so that it did point to me rather strongly, in the hope that you would think it couldn't be me after all."

"That 'ud be dam' dangerous," said the old man, "for I'm not as green as I'm cabbage-lookin', an' I'd probably find ye out an' ha' ye hanged. But in this case we got the spurious pictures kinda mixed wi' the murder an' while Carr might ha' done the murder, I ha' me doubts as to whether he'd anythin' to do wi' the pictures. He's a more direct kinda character. If he wanted money badly he'd steal it, an' wouldn't go the round about way o' forgin' paintin's to get it. Don't you agree?"

Varley nodded his head wisely. He looked towards the papers on his desk. I could see that he was anxious to return to his work. The old man realised this too. He rose slowly to his feet. I felt that he looked very out of place in Varley's exquisite room, where everything was as tidy as it was untidy at home.

"I wonder," he said to Varley, "if ye'd mind if I used yer telephone for a few minutes. I want to find out if the Chief Inspector knows where the Chiricos came from."

"Certainly," Varley pointed to the ivory phone on the corner of his desk. The Professor looked at me with beseeching eyes and I went forward and dialed the number for him. He is quite incapable when it comes to dealing with a telephone and this in spite of his continually reiterated claim to have a mechanical mind.

He took the phone from me and growled into it. He got hold of the Chief Inspector but the conversation was short and brief. He put the receiver down with a crash and turned a gloomy face towards me.

"No," he said, "they have not found anything about Chiricos. It seems that Ambleside did not bother to note down what it was that he had bought, but just entered a sum of money in his books, which were not, strictly speaking, books at all, but merely memoranda for his own use. I suppose that he knew what each entry stood for and that was enough for him."

Varley seemed to be about to say something. He opened his lips and then shut them again. The Professor noticed this but made no comment. He took a last look round the room and lumbered towards the door.

I followed him down the stairs. He climbed into the Bentley and I followed him even there. I did not know where he intended to go next and I doubt if he had any real idea himself. However, we landed up at Scotland Yard.

The Chief Inspector could hardly have been described as looking very delighted to see us. He looked at us through eyes which seemed half asleep and sighed bitterly.

"What have I done," he demanded from the cornice, "to deserve this unholy visitation?"

Professor Stubbs looked at him with vigorous distaste.

"Here am I," he yowled, "doin' me best to help out, an' all ye can do is to blinkin' well insult me. I got an idea in me head an' I want to find out if it's right."

"It won't be," the Chief Inspector said without hesitation, "your ideas so seldom are."

"All right, all right," Professor Stubbs grumbled, "I'll let ye insult me if ye want to. I have a hard life, doin' things to help yer dunderheads

out an' what do I get in the way o' thanks? Nothin'. Sweet Fanny
Adams. But I'll let that pass, for there's no point in me losin' me temper. I'm a man o' the most equable temperament, as ye know," the
Bishop opened his eyes in frank astonishment, "an' I'll take almost
anythin' in the way o' insult wi'out complaint. Ye should thank yer
gods that I ain't given to bein' explosive. If I was, why by God, I'd
gralloch ye, ye stew-eyed spalpeen. Now, havin' said me little say, what
I want to see is the memorandum book in which ye say that Julian
Ambleside kept his accounts. Can I see that?"

He glared fiercely and the Chief Inspector slid a green morocco note
book across the table towards him.

The Professor lowered himself into a chair. It was an old chair, which
I think, Chief Inspector Bishop had resurrected from somewhere in the
depths or heights of the Yard. It had been designed in the days when
policemen were of more ample proportions than they are to-day. It just
fitted Professor Stubbs with a slight squeeze. He opened the little book,
and, settling his steel rimmed glasses more firmly on his nose, started to
study it. On the back of an envelope he made several notes as he went
through the pages slowly. Unfortunately his handwriting was too small
for me to be able to see what he had written, but even if I had been able
to read it, I doubt if it would have been very illuminating.

It must have taken him nearly half an hour to read through the book.
As he read he grunted and puffed away like an aged steam-engine.
Finally, however, he closed the green covers and pushed the book to
the Chief Inspector, who had been trying to fill in the time by dealing
with the mass of papers on his desk.

Professor Stubbs lay back in the chair, which creaked ominously
beneath this attack. He took out his pipe and went through the ritual
of scraping it and filling it. I noticed that the Chief Inspector did not
much like the way in which the old man emptied the scrapings onto
the rather worn carpet, but I think he has learned from painful experience that it is easier to let these things pass.

He sighed again, and laid down his fountain-pen, well out of reach
of the Professor's curious fingers. The Professor had once picked up a
fountain-pen on his desk and after he had toyed with it for about three
minutes it was no longer of any value as a writing instrument.

"Well, John," he said, "and what did you find there? Anything of
any interest to anyone except yourself."

"No," grunted the old man, "it's of no interest to any one but
meself. All I found was who did the murder. But ye see," he stopped

the Chief Inspector who had opened the book and was poring over the pages, "you got to know a bit more than ye do. Ye got to do some real detectin' before ye'll see what that book means. Ye got to be clever, like me."

He beamed immodestly at the Chief Inspector. If he had been able to, I think he would have crowed like a barnyard rooster.

"Dammit man," the Chief Inspector leaned forward, "if you know who was the murderer, you'd better tell me. You realise that it is your duty as a citizen to give every help within your power to the police."

The laugh which the Professor gave was both vulgar and noisy. The room shook for a second after he finished.

"Now then, Reggie," he said admonishingly, "ye know me well enough to know that I wouldn't hold out on ye, if there was anythin' which could be used as proof. That's where ye're handicapped. I can get to work on me suspicions an' I can do things ye can't do in me efforts to find out whether I'm right in me suspicions. As soon as I know where I stand I'll let ye know. In the meantime ye'd better leave me to me own devices an' trust that I'll do me best to get you in for the last act."

The Chief Inspector looked at him with grave doubt.

"I hope, John," he said solemnly, "that you are not proposing to take the law into your own hands? You know I have noticed that you have a slight tendency to do that—all, of course, in the interests of justice and what you would probably call a neatly finished case. But I hope you realise that because you are working on the side of the law you are not automatically outside its control. If you break the law, you know, I will have to deal with you, in spite of our friendship, like any other criminal."

This warning was so much water off the Professor's duck's back. He chuckled to himself.

"Ye're a good soul, Reggie," he said, "but ye needn't fear that I'll do anythin' which'll bring me within yer jurisdiction. I keep on tellin' ye that I'm clever, an' the day that I start breakin' the law in earnest, ye'll find that I don't leave anythin' which ye'll be able to get hold o'. All I'd like to ask ye is that, if I gi'ye a ring an' ask for it, ye'll put a couple o' men at me disposal to catch the murderer."

"I'll come myself," said the Chief Inspector. He still did not look as though he was convinced that the Professor really had got anything which might lead to the solution of the case. As we left the room I looked back and realised that he had opened the green morocco book and was deep in the study of its contents.

In the *Ely Arms,* at the corner of Iron Street, we found Mr. Carr. He was drinking a pint of bitter and was relating a story to an admiring crowd of fellow-drinkers.

"And so," he said gesturing largely, "here was I with a camel standing in the middle of Piccadilly at two o'clock in the morning. The thing was I didn't know anything about camels and I didn't know where the hell I was going to garage this one. It's the hell of a way to Tooting, too, and that's where I was living at that time. I thought of taking it home with me. It would have amused the kids all right, but I was damned if I was going to walk all that way. I tried to get on the camel's back—have any of you tried to mount an unwilling camel?— no, well it just can't be done. The only thing to do was to get rid of the thing. Now a camel's not the kind of thing you can leave in a left luggage office and forget. It bites and it's got the devil of a big slobbery mouth to bite with. It was then I had my bright idea. I would let it loose in St. James's Park and after that finders could be keepers. The camel may be the ship of the desert all right, I tell you, but it's not so hot on a staircase. I still don't know how I managed to get it down the Duke of York's steps, but I did it somehow. Anyhow, as I was saying, the moral of that story is don't play cards with the owner of a menagerie, particularly when you feel you're bound to win."

He turned from the recitation of this particularly tall story to look with surprise at his pint glass, which was nearly empty. His eye fell on us.

"Oh, hullo, hullo, hullo, Prof," he said cheerfully, "How's trade? Have a drink? Three pints of bitter, please Miss."

It was fortunate that both the Professor and I were going to drink bitter for there was no space between Mr. Carr's offer of a drink and his ordering of it.

There was something very festive about Mr. Carr's appearance and it took me a minute or two to work out what it was; then I realised that he was wearing a bright batik by Len Lye as a muffler. I assumed and rightly that he had "borrowed" this from the Museum. It certainly looked very gay.

"Are you still interested in inventions, Prof?" he asked anxiously and I gave a hearty mental groan, "For if you are I've just thought of a winner. Have you ever had to clean out a frying pan? Well, if you had you'd have known how difficult it is to get all the fat out. So I wondered, cleaning out a pan this morning, whether we couldn't make cheap frying pans that you threw away after using. But it seemed to me that that would be kind of extravagant and expensive and it was then that it came to me. Why not have frying-pans with greased paper linings which could be thrown away after use? And that's only the beginning of the great idea. You see the greased paper would be impregnated with cooking fat so that you wouldn't need to bother to put any into the pan when you started to fry. You'd just have your cooking-fat and your paper-lining in one, so as to speak. Don't you think that's a hot one?"

"Very," said the old man, but I could see that he was disappointed that the idea was not mechanical. He is only interested in things that go by clockwork or upon some obscure mechanical principle. I remember watching him erecting a most elaborate Archimedean screw to carry the water up from the tank at the bottom of the garden to a quite unnecessary tap. By the time one had cranked away at the screw to get enough water to fill one pail, one could have filled five by dipping them in the tank. But because it was a mechanical device the old man had been convinced that it must be better.

"Have you discovered your murderer?" said Mr. Carr and did not wait for an answer. "My old mother thinks that Mr. Ambleside just got tired of being alive—she says some people do get that way—and he throttled himself. She's got one thing though. She says that someone hung him up there to make people think that I had done it. Just because I had wanted to put some steak on the walls of the ladies' lavatory. Did you ever hear the like?"

He laughed heartily at the very idea that anyone could have, for one moment, thought that he had placed the body of Julian Ambleside dangling in front of the painting by Max Ernst. The Professor said nothing. There was nothing that he could say. He ordered another round of drinks.

# Chapter 8

# The Blinding Light

THE MUSEUM of Modern Art was not quite so crowded as it had been on the previous day. Going in we met Francis Varley who smiled to us politely.

"You're not thinking of taking on that job again to-day, are you, Boyle?" he asked me, "For if you are I think you'd better borrow a pair of iron-gloves. That child is here again. You know, don't you, that she failed to get away with the fur-teapot again yesterday afternoon, but she dashed it on the ground and broke it. I think that even her father was a bit put out by this. To tell you the truth," he was a bit confidential, "I don't think that marriage is going to last much longer. I've seen it coming for some time. How's your chief getting on with his detection? I hope he doesn't pick on me as the culprit, for I assure you that I didn't do it. All I did was to stir up some mud."

I could not tell whether he was joking or not. I went on into the gallery looking for the Professor. He seemed to be studying the large Max Ernst with great attention. A green amoebic figure was engaged in a deathly struggle with a paler embryonic one, before a background of mechanical cicadas which looked as though they were of doubtful ancestry, with an airplane somewhere in the family tree.

He looked at this picture in silence for a few minutes and then he wandered slowly round the rest of the pictures. It seemed to me that he was wasting time. We spent about half an hour in the gallery and then the old man led the way towards the stairs. We climbed up until we reached the library.

I had been quite right in my assumption that anything I had felt in the way of a hangover that morning would be nothing to what Douglas felt. The one thing that seemed certain was that he could not have felt as bad as he looked. If he had there would have been a bevy, or whatever the collective noun is, of undertakers round him.

He greeted us without joy. I noticed that he was engaged on the job of writing a list of the contents on the front of each folder of photographs. The Professor felt in his pocket and produced the Museum envelope. He handed it over to Douglas.

"Here's your photograph back," he said, "an' you might as well have the one from Cooper's too. Can you tell me, by the way, why there was no copy of that photo in the folder?"

Douglas looked as though thinking hurt him badly, but he managed to produce the answer.

"Oh," he said, "the photograph is at the printer's. You see I rooted out the photos of all the pictures which were in the Museum and sent them along to the printer, who passed them on to the block-maker. Every picture in the gallery is, as you know, reproduced in the catalogue, and we had the Chirico done too, before it was destroyed when Emily thought that it had better be taken out." He creased his brow in thought before he went on. "But, now I come to think of it, I've had the photos back from the block-makers and that one wasn't among them. I wonder why not." Then his face cleared. "Oh well, I suppose that Emily or Dr. Bellamy knew that there was a print in the folder and so they didn't bother to send it back to me. There was no point in cluttering the place up with duplicates."

"Uhhuh," the old man grunted, "d'ye mind if I use yer phone."

He picked up the red receiver and, rather to my surprise, managed to get through to Scotland Yard without much trouble or profanity. "These two men," he growled, "I want 'em. Standin' at the front door o' the place. Yes. That place. An' if they see anyone tryin' to leave in a hurry they'd better stop that person. No. If ye come in ye'll probably spoil it."

He rang off and wiped his face with his brightly coloured handkerchief. Every time he manages to make a successful telephone call one would think that he had succeeded in climbing Everest.

"What's up?" said Douglas, "Is there anything I can do?"

"Nothin'," replied the Professor, "except stay where ye are and get on wi' yer work. I'm just kinda goin' to try an experiment."

He went out of the library and went slowly and heavily down the stairs. I knew that he was working out a plan of action in his mind as he went and I did not dare to speak. It would have been no good if I had spoken. All I would have got would have been growls and mutters. I followed him in silence.

We arrived at the door of Emily's office and he tapped heavily. Her voice told us to enter. Inside there were three people. Emily herself, Dr. Cornelius Bellamy and Francis Varley.

The old man looked round in a pleased way. "D'ye mind if I take up some o' yer space an' time for a bit," he said cheerfully, with the air of an Einstein approaching God with a request for a portion of the heavens.

"Not the least, my dear sir." It was Dr. Bellamy. "Do take a seat."

"Thanks," said the old man, looking doubtfully at the steel and fabric chair which the Doctor indicated. I sat down and he apparently decided that what I would risk he would, too. He sat down and the steel bowed slightly beneath his weight.

Dr. Cornelius Bellamy was correcting proofs. His pencil moved over the page all the time in spite of the interruption. Emily Wallenstein had apparently been speaking to Varley who was perched on the edge of her desk, swinging one leg and smoking a cigarette. They looked at us with a curiosity that was in sharp contrast to the Doctor's off-hand business.

The old man looked round the room again. He seemed to be in no hurry to start anything. He gazed with pleasure at the Calder mobile turning slowly as the warm air reached it. He looked at the pictures on the wall and then he looked once more at the people in the room.

"Umph," he snorted suddenly, "I suppose there's no point in me keepin' you waitin'. I just kinda came along to say I'd solved the problem o' the murder o' Julian Ambleside. I know who done it an' I know why he done it."

Dr. Bellamy's pencil continued to mark the proofs before him. Emily and Varley sat as if frozen. I noticed that Varley's leg had stopped swinging.

"Uhhuh," the old man grunted, seemingly very pleased with himself. "I know the murderer's name and I know why he did it. Trouble wi' him was largely vanity. If he hadn't bin so goddam vain he'd not ha' needed to murder Ambleside."

Automatically Varley's long well manicured fingers pulled out a cigarette case. He extracted a cigarette and placed it between his lips and lit it without seeming to realise what he was doing. Emily picked up a slim pencil and fiddled with it nervously.

"Ye see," the Professor was amiable, "if the murderer had bin able to admit that he'd made a mistake, everythin' would ah' bin all right. He'd ha' bin able to get away wi' the rest o' it."

"Who are you speaking about, Professor Stubbs?" Emily's voice was very brittle as she spoke. Varley was still smoking automatically. I thought I knew what was coming.

"Why," said the old man in a surprised voice, "who is there amongst the people in this Museum who is quite incapable of making a mistake? Who is always right, no matter who else is wrong? Why the answer stands out a mile. Dr. Bellamy, of course."

Dr. Cornelius Bellamy, whose pencil had not hesitated in its course across the pages of proofs, looked up.

"If that is a joke," he said coldly, "I may say that I consider it is in the worst of taste and I demand an immediate apology. If on the other hand you are serious I must say that you are a bigger fool than I took you for. You have just made a statement which is designed to damage me, and you have made it in the presence of witnesses. I will ring up my lawyer as soon as it is convenient to me and I will take legal advice, sir, upon my position with regard to your slander."

"No," said Professor Stubbs shaking his head slowly, "I'm not jokin' an' you know I'm not, Doctor. You know that you murdered Ambleside because he had become worried about the forged Chiricos which you sold him. If ye'd bin a bigger man ye'd ha' gone to him an' ha' admitted that ye'd bin taken in by the pictures an' ha' offered to repay him as the opportunity arose. But ye weren't. Ye couldn't admit that ye'd bin wrong. If ye'd once admitted it yer whole world wi' the figure o' Dr. Cornelius Bellamy sittin' on a pinnacle would ha' crashed around ye. Ye had to kill him."

Dr. Bellamy looked round at us. He frowned and rose slowly to his feet.

"I don't know about you, my dear Emily, or you, Francis," he said, "but I really am too busy to stay and waste time listening to the ravings of this lunatic. I will go and continue my work elsewhere."

He picked up the proofs and moved towards the door. I was about to get up to stop him, but the Professor clamped a heavy hand on my knee and whispered fiercely. "Let him go, son, he won't get far."

The door closed firmly behind the Doctor. I could hear his firm unhurried steps going along the corridor. The Professor roused himself.

"Can I use yer internal phone?" he demanded of Emily and she passed it over to him. He pressed the button labelled HALL and spoke to one of the Commissionaires. He told him to tell the men at the door to stop Dr. Bellamy. I heard the voice of the Commissionaire answering.

"Very good, sir," it said, "but there's no signs of the Doctor, yet."

I noticed that Francis Varley's leg was again swinging negligently and that he seemed to have become aware of the fact that he was smoking a cigarette.

"You know," he addressed the old man frankly, "you gave me the hell of a fright then. I thought you were going to accuse me, and I was trying to think of how I could clear myself."

"Ha," the old man was pleased with himself, "I *was* cunnin', wasn't I? But ye see, I knew that ye hadn't done the murder. Ye told me so yerself. Yes, ye did."

This was because Francis Varley had suddenly interjected a "No."

"Oh yes, ye did, son. Ye told me that ye thought the pictures by Chirico were out an' out forgeries an that ye'd tried to save people's feelings by sayin' that they were copies done by the artist himself at a later date. Well, ye see that the Doctor'd never ha' done that. He had no feelin' about other people. He was always right an' so he had to be the murderer."

"That's all very well," I said suddenly. Emily was still twiddling the pencil between her fingers and looking bewildered. "That's all very well, but where has the Doctor gone to?"

The old man shrugged his shoulders. "Oh," he said airily, "he's somewhere around an' we'll find him when we want him. He'll turn up. I guess he's thinkin' over his sins an' tryin' to make up his mind that he'll ha' to confess."

Emily shook herself. "Professor," she said briskly, "I must thank you for your work, but I must also say that I am very sorry that you ever came into the case. What *am* I to do without the services of Dr. Bellamy? The Museum will not seem the same place."

The Professor smiled. I think that like myself he was amused by the way in which Emily Wallenstein's first thoughts had been of her beloved Museum of Modern Art.

"Oh," he boomed cheerfully, "you got a first-class feller here," he pointed to Varley who looked surprised at this unsolicited testimonial, "who's not the last bit afraid o' people discoverin' that he can be wrong sometimes. He's got his vanity too, but it's not so goddam awful overpowerin' as the vanity o' Cornelius Bellamy. An'," he appeared to think of it suddenly, "young Douglas in the library's a pretty good fellow. He don't like regular hours, but give him an assistant an' ye'll find he'll do all ye could ask o' him. He'll get drunk when he feels like it, an' no doubt he'll disappear occasionally, but ye'll find that in between his bursts the work gets done somehow."

This eulogy of Douglas was interrupted. The door of the room opened and the bland face of Chief Inspector Bishop looked in. "What the something or other hell—I beg your pardon, ma'am—what the blazes are you up to, John?" it enquired bitterly. "Here we are standing in the hall, waiting for Dr. Bellamy to come along to be grabbed, though God alone knows why, and nothing happens. Where *is* Dr. Bellamy?"

The Professor was not perturbed. "Oh," he sounded rather off-hand, "I expect you'll find him somewhere about. Ye'll find that he's yer murderer all right. It was his vanity that was his trouble."

"I'll discuss that with you later," said the Chief Inspector, cutting across the Professor's words. It was obvious that the old man was itching to start a discussion on the subject of his cleverness. "What I want to know is, where is Dr. Cornelius Bellamy at the moment?"

The Professor hoisted himself out of the chair. "Um," he said, the gloom in his face clear, "Um. If ye won't stop to listen to me story, first, I suppose I'd better help ye find the Doctor. He'll be around. He's probably in one o' the lavatories."

We looked in all the lavatories, including the ladies', where the decoration by Mr. Ben Carr with sweets which were already melting in streaks down the wall seemed to fascinate the Professor and infuriate the already irritated Bishop, but there was no sign of the Doctor anywhere. I felt that I was acting rather as a member of the crew in the *Hunting of the Snark.* There was no sign of Dr. Cornelius Bellamy anywhere in the building.

We stood in the library and glared at Douglas. Our last hope had been that he had taken refuge there. We wanted to find him, but he seemed to have vanished completely. Even the old man looked a trifle bewildered.

"Of course," said Douglas with the air of one who was making a rather trite suggestion, "there's always the chance that the Doctor is on the roof. Now I come to think of it I believe I did hear the noise of the lift going up there."

We piled out into the corridor and the Chief Inspector pressed the phosphor bronze button that should have brought it whining towards us. Nothing happened.

"Where are the stairs?" the Bishop demanded of Douglas, who stood sunk in thought and hangover.

"Oh," Douglas was willing to be helpful, "you'd better come back into the library. I'll shew you there."

He led the way back into the library and fiddled with a catch at the end of one of the bookcases. He withdrew a long slender steel rod with a hook at the end of it. He fixed the hook into a tiny notch in the ceiling of the library and gave a pull.

The ceiling opened up and a staircase, rather like the companionway of a ship, slid down towards us. The Professor planted his bulk firmly in the entrance.

"I'm goin' up," he announced, "anyone comin'?"

He was pushed forward by the efforts of those who wanted to get on to the staircase. There was a low loft-like place above the library, and the pulling down of the staircase had apparently lit a light in this. Above our heads there dangled a rope. The old man caught hold of this and pulled heartily. Another staircase, shorter than the first slid down before us, so easily that the Professor nearly fell over backwards with the excess of energy he had expended.

When I arrived in the pale lemon sunlight of an autumn day, the old man was looking across at the far end of the room. There, on a low parapet, sat Dr. Cornelius Bellamy. Spread on his knees were the last few pages of proofs.

He looked up as he heard us arriving. He did not seem to be either disturbed or pleased.

"I have got one more page to do," he announced smoothly, "and I may say that if anyone advances towards me I will throw myself over the edge."

He looked down at his page and the pencil travelled with regularity along the lines and then back. It seemed to me a period of hours before he reached the bottom of the page. From where I was standing I noticed that the proof was initialed, "O.K. for Press. C.B." The hand that made these initials was as steady as if the Doctor had been sitting in Miss Wallenstein's office, instead of perched on a narrow parapet so high above the hard street.

He laid the proofs carefully on the ground and placed his pencil carefully on top of them to act as a paper-weight, so that the slight breeze would not scatter them.

"My dear Douglas," he said smoothly, "I wonder whether you would be good enough to see that these proofs are returned to my publishers?"

"Certainly," said Douglas in an automatic voice, "I'll send them off myself, this evening."

"Thank you, my dear boy, that'll be very kind of you." The Doctor's reply was unhurried.

Chief Inspector Bishop beside me was growing impatient. He stepped forward, looking a trifle self-important.

"Doctor Cornelius Bellamy," he sounded rather pompous, "I am an officer of the law. I arrest you on a charge of having murdered Julian Ambleside. It is my duty to warn you that anything which you say will be taken down and may be used in evidence at your trial."

"At my trial?" said Dr. Bellamy, "At my trial? I thank you, my friend, but I do not desire to stand trial."

I was pretty quick off the mark, beating the Chief Inspector by a clear two feet, but I missed the Doctor by further than that. He just stepped up on to the low parapet. He looked back at us, and without a glance below him, stepped over the edge.

How he missed the crowds on the pavement I do not know, but he hit no one. We went across to the lift which had previously refused to work because the Doctor had left the door open, and all crowded into it, even the Professor.

The crowd, hushed as if in a cathedral, was gathered round all that was left of Dr. Cornelius Bellamy. It was not a pretty sight. Among the faces of the crowd I noticed that of Mr. Carr. He edged towards us.

"Hullo, Prof," he said sombrely, "so you found him out, did you?"

"Yes," said the Professor mildly amazed. "Why? Did you know he had killed Julian Ambleside?"

"Lord bless you, yes," said Mr. Carr, "of course I knew. I saw him trying to hang the body up. A poor job he made of it too. He was all thumbs and the body slipped around a good deal. I expect he was nervous. Why didn't I tell you, eh? Well, I didn't know all the ins and outs of the story and I never did like the law," he glared at the Chief Inspector, "the police are always complaining about something. I told you, tho', Prof, because I knew that if it wasn't a matter for the letter of the law you'd be likely to let it ride. If Ambleside, say, had been doing a bit of blackmail on the Doc, why, I'd have said he deserved what was coming to him."

"No," said the Professor heavily, "it wasn't that at all. The trouble with Dr. Cornelius Bellamy was his godawful vanity."

"Yes," said Mr. Carr nodding his head, "he was sure of himself, wasn't he. He was the great panjandrum himself and he made damn certain that there was no gunpowder running out of the heels of *his* boots. No, not him."

The ambulance arrived and cleaned up the mess. We went slowly back into the building. I met Douglas coming down the stairs. He had gone back quicker than the rest of us. I had assumed that he had wanted to be sick. The sight of the Doctor on top of a hangover like Douglas had would have been enough to make anyone sick. However, I realised that he had not been being sick. I made a wild guess and hit the bull's eye.

"Have you given Alec a ring?" I asked, "and told him the rest of the story?"

Douglas nodded rather guiltily. "How did you know?" he asked. I just looked wise. After all the Professor steals all the thunder so I thought I might as well have a little summer lightning to myself.

We gathered in Emily Wallenstein's office. I could see that the Chief Inspector, who sometimes seems to make a profession of being angry, was very angry at the moment. His eyelids drooped so low on his cheeks that if they had drooped any lower he would have been sound asleep.

"Why, John," he asked in a listless and weary voice, "did you have to do that? Why couldn't you have given me the information you had and have let me deal with the matter? Why did you have to let him kill himself?"

"I'll tell'ee all about it," said the Professor fishing in his pockets, "once I've got me pipe goin'."

# Chapter 9

# Conquest of the Philosopher

"AS I'VE already said," said the old man, repeating it, "the trouble with the late Dr. Bellamy was his vanity. He was a crammed full of vanity as an egg is o' meat. Everyone else in the blinkin' world might be wrong, but he was bound to be right. His trouble was that he'd bin right too often. One or two good hard failures might ha' done him some good an' let him think o' himself as a man. As it was he kinda persuaded himself that he was a god an' that men were inferior kinds of bein's to people like himself. I don't know where he got the forged pictures from, an' I doubt if I ever will know, but I think that he probably bought 'em as copies quite cheaply an' then, despisin' those about him, started to make money by the sale o' 'em. You remember, Reggie, don't you, that I wanted some help from ballistics department an' that you twitted me about it somethin' horrid, eh?"

The Chief Inspector nodded sleepily. I could tell that he was still in a furious temper.

"Well, what d'ye think I'd want in a ballistics department? There is one instrument that I knew they'd have an' that was a comparison microscope. I had got a photograph of the picture that Miss Wallenstein bought from Julian Ambleside an' I also had an old photo from Paris, which I assumed would be the original. So I shoved the two of 'em under a comparison microscope and, by jiminy, they were different pictures. It was as simple as that. If the photograph from Paris was of the genuine paintin' then the one that Cooper's photographed was not genuine, tho' it was a dam' close an' careful copy."

He looked up. I leaned forward and asked Emily Wallenstein if she had a drink. She produced a bottle of sherry and the necessary number of glasses. I think she found that being asked to do something was a bit of a relief. The old man took the sherry gratefully. He sipped at it and the contents of the glass disappeared as if they had been subjected to a blast from an oxygen-acetylene burner. I guess it was the dehydration which he's always complaining about.

"Ho, hum," he went on, sucking in the last drips, "well, supposin' that someone was forgin' pictures an' passin' them off as genuine on to Julian Ambleside and Ambleside suddenly started gettin' worried about them, what was he goin' to do about it. Now if it had bin any o' us here an' we'd bin in the position o' expert, like Bellamy, we'd ha' gone along to Ambleside an' agreed that there were perhaps doubts about the pictures, but all the time we'd ha' praised them up, an' finally we ha' said somethin' to this effect. 'O course, old feller, I may ha' bin taken in, for I can't claim to be infallible any more than the next man, but all the same they're damn fine pictures. Tell you what, I'll buy them back from you for what you gave me, but you'll need to let me have six months to pick up the money again, for you realise I bin had just the same as you, an' I spent some money I couldn't afford on these pic-tures. All the same I think they're good.' The chances are that approached in this manner Ambleside would ha' gone on bein' willin' to take the risk o' the pictures not bein' genuine an' ye'd ha' bin sittin' pretty. But not so Dr. Bellamy. He had to be right an' so he had not only to kill Ambleside but to destroy the blinkin' pictures. So he did it, an' I tracked him down."

He caught the dark slots of the Chief Inspector's eyes fixed on him.

"How was I to know," he complained, "that this blighter here," he shook his thumb towards Mr. Carr, "knew all about it. I was just goin' on what I could discover an' it looked to me as though I'd got no chance o' provin' anythin' on the Doctor unless I could sting it out a him. How was I to know there was a roof to this place an' that he'd go an' sit on it?"

He looked as injured as if someone had just kicked him in the middle of the stomach. Even the Chief Inspector had to grin.

"All right, John, all right," he said passively, "I'll let you get away with it, but I'd just like to know what made you suspect that Dr. Bel-lamy was the culprit in the first place?"

"I didn't like him," said the Professor magnificently and simply. He realised that he had given the Chief Inspector a rod with which to beat him, so he hurried on, "I didn't like him an' he made a shockin' howler the first time we spoke to him. He referred to Julian Ambleside havin' bin strangled by *hand*—well how was he to know that?"

"I don't think you have anything there, John," the Chief Inspector was slowly critical. "We had just announced that Ambleside had been stran-gled, though as you say we had not made it clear that he was strangled by hand. I noticed that and wondered for a moment but then I realised that the first thing that the word 'strangle' does is to produce a mental picture of a pair of hands throttling their victim. It would not matter who you were speaking to, if you said that someone was strangled, they'd think of hands before they thought of a scarf or something like that."

"Um," the old man did not appear to be the least convinced, but I had to confess myself that I agreed with the Chief Inspector. It looked to me very much as though the Professor had been arguing from false premises.

"Ahum," he grunted, "but that don't matter. It just kinda made me think, same as it made ye think, Reggie, but it made me think to more purpose than you. Ye see," he was fiercely honest, "the Doctor's dam' psychology kept on getting me down an' I thought I'd try applyin' his own treatment to himself an' once I'd done that I was able to see how well he fitted the part o' the murderer. In fact, I must say that once I'd seen him in the part, I could not see anyone else in it. I must say though," he looked across at Mr. Carr who was helping himself to Emily's sherry, "that the idea o' this poor fish just standin' there watchin' the Doctor hangin' up a body an' not realisin' that the whole performance was designed to cast suspicion on himself, kinda tickles me."

"What," said Mr. Carr, genuinely surprised, "me hang Mr. Ambleside up like that. Why?"

"I think," said the old man gravely, "that it was supposed to have some reference to your idea of putting meat on the walls."

"But, holy mother," Mr. Carr was excited, "you don't think I'd stick a whole man, all in one piece, on a wall. Good Lord no. Just think what it would do to the composition."

This was too much for the Chief Inspector. He turned his head away and snorted violently.

"I might," Mr. Carr went on, "have used a hand here or a foot there, to sort of help things out. Good rubbish is getting very hard to get. But a whole man, nonsense. It wouldn't work."

He seemed to be genuinely upset that anyone could have thought that he would have spoiled his decoration of a wall in this fashion. He retired into his glass of sherry, still mumbling at the lack of proper feeling in people who could suspect him of such errors.

"Don't you worry, son," Professor Stubbs was kindly, "I didn't suspect you for a moment. I knew ye hadn't done it. Ye wouldn't bother to deal in forged pictures would ye, now? An' so I knew it couldn't be you."

"Oh," said Mr. Carr corning to the surface for air, "I don't mind people suspecting me, but what I'm shocked at is the Doctor's thinking that people might think I was guilty of hanging up a *whole* man as a kind of decoration. I thought he knew more about my work than that. It's a bitter disappointment. I think I'll give up the job of decorating interiors. There's more freedom and more money in horses, and I've got a first-rate treble for to-morrow. I'll let you all in on it, too."

This startlingly generous offer stung a reply from the melancholy Douglas who seemed to be sunk in contemplation of the emptiness of his sherry glass. He looked up absently.

"Thanks, cock," he said and Mr. Carr beamed at him approvingly, as one might beam at a savage who had learned to wish one good day.

"By the way," the Professor coughed nervously, "Mr. Carr, do you think that your mother would consider parting from that toy rat? I'd like to have it as a kinda souvenir of the case. As ye probably know I got a mechanical mind an' I like mechanical toys."

Mr. Carr weighed this question heavily in his mind. Finally he spoke. "Well," he said, "I think you might find that the old girl was willing to part from it for some sort of consideration. If, say, you offered her a bottle of gin when she was feeling thirsty."

"But," said the bewildered Professor Stubbs, "how will I know when she's feelin' thirsty?"

"That," Mr. Carr replied with decision, "will be simple. She is *always* thirsty. Ninety years, girl and woman, no less she's been thirsty, and it looks to me as though she'd go thirsty to her grave. You know, by the way, that she's forgiven you. She heard you were a biologist and, like me, she doesn't believe in biology. Maybe," he was preternaturally solemn, "there was a biologist hidden in the wood pile at the bottom of *her* garden. I wouldn't know. I was just brought up not to believe in biology. But, as I was saying, she's forgiven you for she's found out that you are a botanist. As she said to me, 'Grasses and plants I'll stand for, though, mark you, it's the thin end of the wedge, but fiddling around with ordinary life—no'."

The Chief Inspector was wearing a look on his face that shewed that he thought that he had wandered into a lunatic asylum. He stood up and teetered gently backwards and forwards on his feet. He coughed.

"Well," he said blandly, "I think I have finished with this case. I feel however that I should warn you, Mr. Carr, that had the case come to trial and your suppression of vital evidence been discovered, you would have run the risk of very severe penalties indeed. I would like to warn you, further, that you should not repeat your behaviour."

"All right, cock," said Mr. Carr unabashed and turning an injured face towards me, "there you are, Maxie boy. That's the police for you. If they can't run you in they have to warn you. A man can't call his mind his own these days."

I was watching the Bishop's face and I saw that, for a moment, he let himself toy with the idea of shewing Mr. Carr whether or not the police could run him in for the offence which he had just committed. Then his expression cleared and the usual blandness crept over his features like the mist over an Essex landscape. He went slowly towards the door like a giant Persian cat. I noticed that the similarity struck Francis Varley, and impelled him to get up and open the door.

The Chief Inspector went out. So far as he was concerned his underlings could clear up the remnants of the case. The Professor took out his pipe and looked enquiringly at Emily Wallenstein. She graciously gave him permission to smoke it. I'd be willing to bet that she did not know what she was in for.

"You know," said Douglas suddenly, "I wondered sometimes about the two Flints. They had some connection with Julian Ambleside and I don't know what it was."

Francis Varley laughed gently. "My dear Douglas," he said quietly, "you know what the Flints are? They are people who make a profession of building up other people into respectable social characters. Alison advises them about the people they should know, and Jeremy tells them who should be employed to decorate their houses and what pictures they should hang on their walls. Naturally, if he sent a man to Ambleside to buy a Picasso, he expected a small rake-off from Julian, and he made it his business to see that he got it. That is why they seemed to be connected with Ambleside. I, myself, have done business with them, in the way of putting them in touch with small libraries of art books, from which, naturally, I took the pick first, but in my case they give me a commission for my services."

The Professor was standing up now. He was flicking the Calder mobile gently and watching it go round with the satisfied smile of a child watching a windmill. Emily sat at the desk watching him. He looked down and realised that she had her eyes on him.

"Nice thing this," he said, "can you tell me where I can get one exactly like it?"

"My dear Professor," Francis Varley was slightly shocked, "I'm afraid you won't as you say be able to get one exactly like it. Alexander Calder is an artist and so no two mobiles of his are exactly alike."

"Oh," said the old man, putting on what I call his begging voice. "That's a pity. I'd rather fallen for it, an' I'd ha' liked one just like it!"

After that there was nothing left for Emily Wallenstein to do but to give it to him. I must say she did it very gracefully and the old man's thanks were genuine and effusive. He climbed up on the steel chair, which I did my best to steady, and unhooked the mobile. It folded up nicely and he tucked it happily under his arm. He stumped heavily towards the door.

"Harumph," he said noisily, "It's bin nice meetin' all you people, tho' I can hardly say that the occasion was o' the most auspicious. I hope that ye won't mind if I come back again sometime an' ha' a look at the Museum o' Modern Art when there ain't so many thunderin' nosey people around or blinkin' corpses hangin' on the pictures. What I always say, is that if people would only mind their own business the world 'ud be a much better place."

With this outrageous statement we left the room. I might have thought of some crack that would have come back at the Professor but I was so flabbergasted by the barefaced effrontery of his remark that I failed to think of one of the same standard.

Half way down the stair, standing looking at her son's wall decoration, we encountered Mrs. Carr. She was looking at the wall with real distaste. She recognised Professor Stubbs and immediately fell into conversation with him.

"Can't say I like it," she declared, "it wouldn't have passed when I was a girl. It's all this biology and books has done it. Rough-cast is rough-cast, I say, and it's got its place on the outside of a house. Who wants gravel in a drawing-room? I had an aunt who had the gravel very bad but she carried it about with her. She still didn't want gravel in her drawing-room. I wonder what young Ben will be up to next. Horrible child he was, to be sure. I say so, and I should know as I'm his mother. He's got a bit better as he's grown up but he's got a long way to go yet. Breeding, that's his trouble and always has been. First, it was mice and then it was rabbits and after that it was greyhounds. He'd have taken to breeding elephants if he hadn't thought of breeding children. They take up too much space and too much time. You can't put them in a hutch and forget them. If you do, along comes a nosey-parker and before you know where you are you're doing six weeks in Holloway. Oh yes, things have changed for the worse since I was a girl."

She paused for breath and Professor Stubbs, who had been trying to slip a word or two into her stream of verbiage got a start.

"Ma'am," he said bowing politely, "it's about that rat."

"Oh yes," she said, "I forgot. There was rats too, after the mice, I think. There's one thing to be said for rats—they don't smell. Mice do—something awful. Drown 'em all, I say."

She paused again and the Professor made yet another effort to intrude himself upon her notice. She already held a world's record as being the only person on earth who had ever been able to talk him down.

"That toy rat," he said, "the one you got in the gallery. Will you sell it to me?"

"Toy rat," she said looking puzzled, "Toy rat. I know nothing about toy rats. There are no such creatures. Ben's father used to keep rats, too, but he kept them in his head and they only worried him once a month. He got paid monthly. Then when they worried him he had to wait till pay day before he could stand them a round of drinks. Most obliging they were, to be sure, one drink for each of them and away they went. It wasn't so expensive in these days either. Ah, things have changed since I was a girl."

"The mechanical rat that ran across the floor o' the gallery," boomed the Professor desperately.

"Oh, Bimbo, you mean?" she asked.

"Yes," said the Professor firmly. She shook her head sadly and made a face which expressed her disappointment in the race of people which had grown up since she was a girl.

"Oh, Bimbo," she said again, "no. You can't have him. I'm going to put him out to stud and retire on his earnings."

Even the Professor was defeated. He made on down the stairs, in deathly silence, and mounted the car, swathed in black gloom. It wasn't till we got home, after one of the worst drives of my life, that he remembered the pleasure he would get from his Calder mobile. I spent most of the remainder of the day perched on the top of a ladder while he tried to decide exactly where it would look best in his work-room. I could have given him rats and ladders.

**Finis**

# About the Author

RUTHVEN CAMPBELL TODD (1914–1978) was a Scottish-born poet, scholar, art critic, and fantasy novelist who wrote a series of detective novels under the name R. T. Campbell.